John Nichols, George Steevens, George Whetstone

Six old Plays

Vol. I

John Nichols, George Steevens, George Whetstone

Six old Plays
Vol. I

ISBN/EAN: 9783337147907

Printed in Europe, USA, Canada, Australia, Japan

Cover: Foto ©Andreas Hilbeck / pixelio.de

More available books at **www.hansebooks.com**

SIX
OLD PLAYS,

ON WHICH

SHAKSPEARE

FOUNDED HIS

MEASURE FOR MEASURE.
COMEDY OF ERRORS.
TAMING THE SHREW.
KING JOHN.
K. HENRY IV. AND K. HENRY V.
KING LEAR.

IN TWO VOLUMES.

VOLUME I.

LONDON,

Printed for S. LEACROFT, Charing-Cross:
And fold by J. NICHOLS, Red-Lion Paffage, Fleet-ftreet;
T. EVANS, in the Strand; and H. PAYNE, Pall Mall.

MDCCLXXIX.

OLD PLAYS.

VOLUME THE FIRST.

CONTAINING

PROMOS AND CASSANDRA.

MENÆCHMI.

THE TAMING OF A SHREW.

THE TROUBLESOME REIGN OF K. JOHN. PART I.

* a 3

ADVERTISEMENT.

M R. STEEVENS being of opinion that
thefe fix dramatic pieces, which have been
occafionally quoted in the notes to the laft edi-
tion of Shakfpeare, are requifite in an entire ftate
to his illuftration ; I have undertaken to publifh
them without departure from the original copies.
Their claim to be preferved is built on their
having fuggefted fuch plans as his fuperior genius
and judgment enabled him to improve.—A bafket
placed by accident over a weed, and covered
with a tile, is recorded by Vitruvius as the origin
of the Corinthian capital.

Thefe Plays are here given in a fize correfpond-
ing with that of the three Volumes of Antient
Englifh Dramas re-publifhed by the late Mr.
Hawkins, and may be confidered as fupplemental

to

to his work. The plays of K. John and K. Lear had indeed been feparately re-printed, but were thought neceffary to complete the prefent collection.

March 22, 1779.

J. NICHOLS.

THE

RIGHT EXCELLENT AND FAMOUS

H I S T O R Y E

OF

PROMOS and CASSANDRA:

Divided into Commical DISCOURSES.

In the Fyrſte Parte is ſhowne,

The unſufferable Abuſe of a lewde MAGISTRATE
The vertuous Behaviours of a chaſte LADYE:
The uncontrowled Leawdenes of a favoured CURTISAN:
And the undeſerved Eſtimation of a pernicious PARASYTE.

In the Second Parte is diſcourſed,

The perfect Magnanimitye of a noble KINGE,
In checking Vice and favouringe Vertue:

Wherein is ſhowne,

The Ruyne and Overthrowe of diſhoneſt Practiſes:
with the Advauncement of upright Dealing.

The WORKE of

GEORGE WHETSTONES GENT.

Formæ nulla Fides.

A

To his worſhipfull FRIENDE, and KINSEMAN,

WILLIAM FLEETEWOODE Esquier,

RECORDER of LONDON.

SYR, (deſirous, to acquite your tryed frendſhips, with ſome
token of good will :) of late I peruſed divers ot my unperfect workes, fully minded to beſtowe on you, the travell of
ſome of my forepaſſed time. But (reſolved to accompanye
the adventurous Captaine Syr *Humfrey Gylbert*, in his honorable
voiadge,) I found my leyſure too littel to correct the errors in
my ſayd workes. So that (inforced) I lefte them diſparſed,
among my learned freendes, at theyr leaſure, to poliſh, if I
faild to returne: ſpoyling (by this meanes) my ſtuddy of his
neceſſarye furnyture. Amonge other unregarded papers, I
fownde this diſcourſe of *Promos* and *Caſſandra:* which, for the
rareneſſe (and the needeful knowledge) of the neceſſary matter
contained therein (to make the actions appeare more lively),
I devided the whole Hiſtory into two Commedies : for that,
decorum uſed, it would not be convayde in one. The effects
of both, are good and bad: vertue intermyxt with vice, unlawfull deſyres (yf it were poſible) queanchr with chaſte de-
nyals : al needeful actions (I thinke) for publike vewe. For
by the rewarde of the good, the good are encowraged in wel
doinge: and with the ſcowrge of the lewde, the lewde are
feared from evill attempts : maintaining this my oppinion with
Platoes auctority. *Nawghtineſſe, commes of the corruption of
nature, and not by readinge or bearinge the lives of the good or lewde
(for ſuch publication is neceſſarye), but goodneſſe (ſayth he) is beawti-
fyed by either action.* And to theſe endes : *Menander, Plautus,*
and *Terence* themſelves many yeares ſince intombed (by their
Commedies) in honour, live at this daye. The auncient
Romans, held their ſhowes of ſuche priſe, that they not onely
allowde the publike exerciſe of them, but the grave Senators
themſelves countenaunced the Actors with their preſence:
who from theſe trifles wonne morallytye, as the Bee ſickes
honny from weedes. But the adviſed deviſes of auncient Poets,
diſcredited, with the tryfels of yonge, unadviſed, and raſhe

A 2   witted

witted wryters, hath brought this commendable exercife in miflike. For at this daye, the *Italian* is fo lafcivious in his Commedies, that honeft hearers are grceved at his actions: the *Frenchman* and *Spaniarde* folows the *Italians* humor: the *Germaine* is too holye: for he prefentes on every common Stage, what Preachers fhould pronounce in Pulpets. The *Englifhman* in this quallitie, is moft vaine, indifcreete, and out of order: he firft grounces his worke, on impoffibilities: then in three howers ronnes ne throwe the worlde: marryes, gets children, makes children men, men to conquer kingdomes, murder monfters, and bringeth Gods from Heaven, and fetcheth divels from Hel. And (that which is worft) their ground is not fo unperfect, as their workinge indifcreete: not waying, fo the people laugh, though they laugh them (for theyr follyes) to fcorne: Manye tynes (to make myrthe) they make a clowne companion with a Kinge: in theyr grave Counfels, they allow the advife of fools: yea they ufe one order of fpeach for all perfons: a grofe *Indecorum*, for a Crowe, wyll yll counterfet the Nightingales fweete voice: even fo, affected Speeche doth mifbecome a Clowne. For to worke a Commedie kindly, grave olde men, fhould inftruct: yonge men, fhould fhowe the imperfections of youth: ftrumpets fhould be lafcivious: Boyes unhappy: and Clownes, fhould be diforderlye: entermingling all thefe actions, in fuch forte, as the grave matter may inftruct, and the pleafant delight: for without this chaunge, the attention, woulde be fmall: and the likinge, leffe.

But leave I this rehearfall, of the ufe, and abufe of Commedies: leaft that, I checke that in others, which I cannot amend in myfelf. But this I am affured, what actions fo ever paffeth in this Hiftory, either merry, or morneful: grave, or lafcivious: the conclufion fhowes, the confufion of vice, and the cherifhing of Vertue. And fythe the end tends to this good, although the worke (becaufe of evel handiinge) be unworthy your learned Cenfure, allowe (I befeeche you) of my good wyll, untyl leafure ferves me, to perfect, fome labour of more worthe. No more, but that, almightye God be your protector, and preferve me from dainger, in this voiadge, the xxix. of July, 1578.

Your Kinfman to ufe,

GEORGE WHETSTONE.

The

The PRINTER to the READER.

GENTLE Reader, this labour of Maifter *Whetftons*, came into my handes, in his fyrft coppy, whofe leafure was fo lyttle (being then readie to depart his Country) that he had no time to worke it anew, nor to geve apt inftructions, to prynte fo difficult a worke, beyng full of variety, both matter, fpeache, and verfe: for that every fundry Actor, hath in all thefe a fundry grace; fo that, if I commit an error, without blaming the Auctor, amend my amiffe: and if by chaunce thou light of fome fpeache that feemeth dark, confider of it with judgment, before thou condemne the worke: for in many places he is driven, both to praife, and blame, with one breath, which in readinge wil feeme hard, and in action appeare plaine. Ufing this courtefy, I hould my paynes wel fatisfyed, and Maifter *Whetfton* uninjured: and for my owne part, I wil not faile to procure fuch bookes as may profit thee with delight.

Thy Friend R. I.

Richarde Jhones
See Colophon, p. 10

A 3

THE

THE

A R G U M E N T

OF THE

WHOLE HISTORYE.

IN the Cytie of *Julio* (fometimes under the dominion of *Corvinus* King of *Hungarie*, and *Boemia*) there was a law, that what man fo ever commited Adultery, fhould lofe his head, and the woman offender, fhould weare fome difguifed apparell, during her life, to make her infamouflye noted. This fevere lawe, by the favour of fome mercifull magiftrate, became little regarded, untill the time of Lord *Promos* auctority: who convicting a yong Gentleman named *Andrugio* of incontinency, condemned, both him, and his minion, to the execution of this ftatute. *Andrugio* had a very vertuous and beawtiful Gentlewoman to his Sifter, named *Caffandra: Caffandra* to enlarge her brothers life, fubmitted an humble petition to the Lord *Promos: Promos* regarding her good behavours, and fantafying her great beawtie, was much delighted with the fweete order of her talke: and doying good, that evill might come thereof: for a time, he repryved her brother: but wicked man, tourning his liking unto unlawfull luft, he fet downe the fpoile of her honour, raunfome for her Brothers life: chafte *Caffandra*, abhorring both him and his fute, by no perfuafion would yeald to this raunfome. But in fine, wonne with the importunitye of hir Brother (pleading for life) upon thefe conditions, fhe agreede to *Promos*. Firft that he fhould pardon her brother, and after marry her. *Promos* as feareles in promiffe, as careleffe in performance, with follemne vowe, fygned her conditions: but worfe then any Infydel, his will fatisfyed, he performed neither the one nor the other: for to

keepe

keepe his aucthoritye, unfpotted with favour, and to prevent *Caffandrae's* clamors, he commaunded the Gayler fecretly, to prefent *Caffandra* with her brother's head. The Gayler, with the outcryes of *Andrugio*, abhorryng *Promos* lewdenes, by the providence of God, provyded thus for his fafety. He prevented *Caffandra* with a fe'ons head newlie executed, who (being margled, knew it not from her brother's, by the Gaylor, who was fet at libertie) was fo agreeved at this trecherye, that at the pointe to kyl her felfe, fhe fpared that ftroke to be avenged of *Promos*. And devifyng a way, fhe concluded, to make her fortunes knowne unto the kinge. She (executinge this refolution) was fo highly favoured of the king, that forthwith he hafted to do juftice on *Promos:* whofe judgment was, to marrye *Caffandra*, to repaire her crafed honour: which donne, for his hainous offence he fhould lofe his head. This maryage folempnifed, *Caffandra* tyed in the greateft bondes of affcction to her hufband, became an earneft futer for his life: the kinge (tendringe the generall benefit of the common weale, before her fpecial cafe, although he favoured her much) would not graunt her fute. *Andrugio* (difguifed amonge the company) forrowing the griefe of his fifter, bewrayde his fafetye, and craved pardon. The kinge, to renowne the vertues of *Caffandra*, pardoned both him and *Promos*. The circumftances of this rare Hiftorye, in action lyvelye foloweth.

T H E

THE
HISTORIE
OF
PROMOS and CASSANDRA.

ACTUS I.   SCENA I.

Promos, Mayor, Shirife. Sworde-bearer : *One with a bunche of keyes :* Phallax, Promos Man.

YOU officers which now in *Julio* ftaye,
 Know you our leadge, the King of *Hungarie,*
Sent me *Promos,* to joyne with you in fway,
That ftill we may to Juftice have an eye.
And now to fhow my rule and power at large
Attentivelie his Letters Pattents heare :
Phallax, reade out my Soveraines chardge.
     Phallax.
As you commaunde. I wyl give heedefull eare.
   [Phallax *readeth the Kinge's Letters, which muft be fayre
   written in parchment, with fome great counterfeat zeale.*
     Promos.
 Loe, here you fee what is our foveraignes wyl ;
Loe, heare his wifh that right, not might beare fwaye ;
Loe, heare his care to weede from go d the yll,
To fourge the wights good lawes that difobay.

         Such

Such zeale he beares unto the Common weale,
(How so he bids, the ignorant to save)
As he commaundes, the lewde do rigor feele:
Such is his wish, such is my wyll to have;
And such a Judge, here *Promos* vowes to be.
No wylfull wrong sharpe punishment shall mysse;
The simple thrall shal be judgde with mercie,   *Love, hate*
Each shall be doombde even as his merite is.   *and gaine, the*
Love shall not staye, nor hate revenge procure,   *causes of In-*
Ne yet sha'l coyne corrupt or foster wrong: *justice.*
I doo protest, whylste that my charge indure,
For friende nor foe to singe a partiall song.
    Thus have you heard howe my Commission goes;
He absent, I present our Soveraigne still:
It aunsweres then, each one his dutie showes,
To mee, as him, what I commaunde and wyll.
Mayor.
    Worthy Deputie, at thy chardge we joye,
We doe submitte our selves to worke thy heast:
Receive the sword of Justice to destroy
The wicked impes, and to defend the rest.
Shirife.
    Our Citty keyes take wisht Listenant heare;
We doe committe our safetie to thy head:
Thy wyse foresight will keepe us voyde of feare,
Yet wyll we be assistant still at neede.
Promos.
    Both sworde and keies unto my princes use
I doo receive and gladlie take my chardge.
It resteth nowe, for to reforme abuse,
We poynt a tyme of councell more at lardge;
To treat of which, a whyle we wyll depart.
All speake.
    To worke your wyll we yeelde a wylling hart.

                                    [*Exeunt.*

ACTUS

ACTUS I. SCENA II.

Lamia, a Curtizane, entreth finging.

The SONG.

Al a flaunt now vaunt it, braſe wenche caſt away care
With Layes of Love chaunt it, for no coſt ſee thou ſpare.

Sith nature hath made thee with bewty moſt brave,
Sith fortune doth lade thee with what thou wouldſt have;
Ere pleaſure doth vade thee, thy ſelfe ſet to ſale,
All wantons will trade thee, and ſtowpe to thy ſtale.
   All a flaunt, *ut ſupra.*

Yong Ruflers maintaines thee, defends thee and thine;
Olde Dottrels retaines thee, thy beuties ſo ſhine;
Though many diſdaynes thee, yet none may thee tuch;
Thus envie refraynes thee, thy countinaunce is ſuch.
   All a flaunt, *ut ſupra.*

Shee ſpeaketh.

Triumphe fayre *Lamia* now, thy wanton flag advaunce,
Set foorth thy ſelf to braveſt ſhow, boſt thou of happy chaunce
Gyrle, accompt thou thy ſelfe the cheefe of Lady Pleaſure's
   traine;
Thy face is faire, thy forme content, thy fortunes both doth
   ſtaine.
Even as thou wouldſt thy houſe doth ſtande, thy furniture is
   gay,
Thy weedes are brave, thy face is fine, and who for this doth
   paye?
Thou thy ſelf? no, the ruſhing Youthes that bathe in wanton
   bliſſe,
Yea, olde and dooting fooles ſometimes doo helpe to paye
   for this.
Free coſt betweene them both I have, all this for my behove;
I am the ſterne that gides their thoughts, looke what I like,
   they love.
Few of them ſturre that I byd ſtaie; if I bid go, they flye;
If I on foe purſue revenge, *Alarme* a hundred crye.

                                                    The

The braveſt, I their harts, their handes, their purſes holde at wyl,
Joynde with thé credite of the beſt, to bowlſter mee in yll.
But ſee wheras my truſtie man doth run ; what newes brings he?

ACTUS I.   SCENA III.

Roſko (Lamia's *Man*) Lamia.

Roſko.

Good people ; did none of you my miſtreſſe *Lamia* ſee?
Lamia.
Roſko, what newes, that in ſuch haſt you come blowing?
Roſko.
Miſtreſſe, you muſt ſhut up your ſhops, and leave your oc-
cupying.
Lamia.
What ſo they be, fooliſh knave, tell me true?
Roſko.
Oh yll, for thirtie beſydes you.
Lamia.
For me, good fellowe! I pray thee why ſo ?
Roſko.
Be patient Miſtreſſe, and you ſhall knowe.
Lamia.
Go too, ſay on.
Roſko.
Marrie, right nowe at the Seſſions I was,
And thirtie muſt to *Truſſum corde* go.
Among the which (I weepe to ſhowe) alas :
Lamia.
Why, what's the matter, man ?
Roſko.
O *Andruzio,*
For loving too kindlie, muſt looſe his heade,
And his ſweete hart muſt weere the ſhamefull weedes
Ordainde for Dames that fall through fleſhly deedes.
Lamia.
Is this offence in queſtion come againe ?
Tell, tell no more ; tys tyme this tale were done :
See, ſee, how ſoone my triumphe turnes to paine.

Roſko.

Rosko.

Miſtreſſe, you promiſed to be quiet,
For Gods ſake, for your owne ſake, be ſo.

Lamia.

Alas, poore *Roſko*, our dayntie dyet
Our braverie and all we muſt forgo.

Rosko.

I am ſorie.

Lamia.

Yea, but out alas, ſorrowe wyll not ſerve:
Roſko, thou muſt needes provide thee elſe where;
My gaynes are paſt, yea, I my ſelſe might ſtarve,
Save that I did provide for a deare yeare.

Rosko.

They rewarde fayre (their harveſt in the ſtacke)
When winter comes that byd their ſervaunts packe.
Alas miſtreſſe, if you turne mee off now,
Better then a Roge none wyll me allowe.

Lamia.

Thou ſhalt have a Paſporte.

Rosko.

Yea, but after what ſorte?

Lamia.

Why, that thou wert my man.

Rosko.

O the judge, ſylde ſhowes the favour,
To let one theeſe bayle another:
Tuſh, I know, ere long you ſo wyll ſlyp awaye,
As you, for your ſelfe, muſt ſeeke ſome teſtimony
Of your good lyfe.

Lamia.

Never feare: honeſtly
Lamia nowe meanes to lyve even tyll ſhe dye.

Rosko.

As jumpe as apes in view of nuttes to daunce,
Kytte will to kinde, of cuſtome, or by chaunce:
Well, howe ſo you ſtande upon this holy poynt,
For the thing you knowe, you wyll jeopard a joynt.

Lamia.

Admitte I would, my hazarde were in vaine.

Rosko.

Rosko.
Perhappes I know to turne the fame to gaine.
Lamia.
Thou comforts mee, good *Rosko*, tell me howe?
Rosko.
You wyl be honeft, 'twere fyn to hinder you.
Lamia.
I dyd but jeaft, good fweete fervaunt, tell mee.
Rosko.
Sweete fervaunt now, and late, pack Syr, God bwy ye.
Lamia.
Tufh, to trye thy unwillingneffe, I dyd but jeaft.
Rosko.
And I do but trye how long you would be honeft.
Lamia.
I thought thy talke was too fweete to be true.
Rosko.
Yea, but meant you to byd honeftie a due?
Lamia.
No, I dyd fo long fince, but inforfte by need,
To byd him welcome home againe, I was decreede.
Rosko.
Verie good, miftreffe, I know your minde,
And for your eafe this remedie I finde:
Prying abroade for playfellowes and fuch,
For you miftreffe, I heard of one *Phallax*,
A man efteemde of *Promos* verie much:
Of whofe nature I was fo bolde to axe,
And I fmealt he loved lafe mutton well.
Lamia.
And what of this?
Rosko.
Marry of this, if you the waye can tell
To towle him home, he of you wyll be fayne,
Whofe countenaunce wy'll fo excufe your faultes,
As none, for life, dare of your lyfe complaine.
Lamia.
A good device, God graunt us good fucceffe:
But I praye thee, what trade doth he profeffe?
Rosko.
He is a paltrie petyfogger.

Lamia.

Lamia.

All the better, fufpition wyll be the leffe.
Well, go thy wayes, and if thou him efpye,
Tell him from me that I a caufe or two
Woulde put to him at leyfure wyllinglie.

Rofko.

Hir cafe is fo common, that fmall pleading wyl
ferve,
I go (nay ronne), your commaundement to ob-
ferve.

The ſcurge of lawe (and not zeale) keepeth the lewde in awe.

Lamia.

Aye me alas, leffe *Phallax* helpe poore wench undone I am :
My foes nowe in the winde wyll lye to worke my open fhame :
Now envious eyes will prie abroade offenders to intrap,
Of force nowe *Lamia* muft be chafte, to fhun a more mifhap.
And, wanton girle, how wilt thou fhift for garments fine and
gay ?
For dainty fare, can crufts content ? who fhal thy houferent
pay ?
And that delights thee moft of all, thou muft thy daliaunce
leave ;
And can then the force of lawe or death, thy minde of love
bereave ?
In good faith, no : the wight that once hath taft the fruits of
love,
Untill her dying daye will long Sir *Chaucer's* jefts to prove.

A C T U S I. S C E N A IV.

Lamia's *Mayde*, Lamia.

Mayde.

Forfooth Miftris your thraule ftayes for you at home.
Lamia.
Were you borne in a myll curtole ? you prate fo hye.
Mayde.
The gentelman that came the laft day with Captain *Prie.*
Lamia.
What, young *Hipolito* ?

4

Mayde.

Mayde.

Even he.

Lamia.

Leaſt he be gone, home hye,
And will that *Dalia* pop him in the neather roome,
And keepe the falling doore cloſe tyll I come ;
And tell my thraule his fortune wyll not ſtaye.

Mayde.

Wyll you ought elſe ?   [*Exit.*

Lamia.

Pratyng vixen, away !
Gallants adue, I venter muſt *Hipolito* to ſee,
He is both young and welthy yet, the better ſpoyle for mee.
Note.
My haſſard for his ſake I trowe, ſhall make him pray and pay :
He, he ſhall pranck me in my plumes, and deck mee brave and
gay.
Of Curtiſie, I praye you yet, if *Phallax* come this waye,
Report, to put a caſe with him, heare *Lamia* long dyd ſtay.
                                                      [*Exit.*

ACTUS II.   SCENA I.

Caſſandra, *a Mayd.*

Caſſandra.

AYE mee, unhappy wenche, that I muſt live the day
To ſee *Andrugio* tymeles dye, my brother and my ſtay.
The only meane, God wot, that ſhould our houſe advaunce
Who in the hope of his good hap, muſt dy through wanton
chance.
O blynde affectes in love, whoſe tormentes none can tell,
Yet wantons wyll byde fyre and froſt, yea haſhard   *The force*
death, nay hell,   *of Love.*
To taſte thy ſowre ſweete frutes, digeſted ſtyll with care !
Fowle fall thee Love, thy lightning joyes hath blaſted my
welfare ;
Thou fyerſt affection fyrſt within my brothers breſt :

                                                      Thou

Thou mad'ft *Polina* graunt him (earſt) even what he would re-
queſt:
Thou mad'ft him crave and have a proofe of *Venus* meede,
For which foule act he is adjudg'd eare long to lofe his heade.
The lawe is fo fevere in fcourging fleſhly ſinne
As marriage to worke after mends doth feldome favor win.
A law firſt made of zeale, bur wreſted much amis:
Faults ſhould be meafured by defert, but all is one   *A good lawe*
     in this: *·yll executed.*
The lecher fyerd with luſt is puniſhed no more
Then he which fel through force of love whofe marriage falves
     his fore;
So that poore I difpayre of my *Andrugio's* lyfe,
O would my dayes myght end with his, for to appeafe my
     ſtryfe!

ACTUS II.   SCENA II.

Andrugio *in Priſon.*   Caſſandra.

Caſſandra.

My good fyſter *Caſſandra?*
                    Caſſandra.
Who calleth *Caſſandra?*
                    Andrugio.
Thy wofull brother *Andrugio.*
                    Caſſandra.
Andrugio, o difmall day, what greefes doe mee affayle?
Condempned wretch to fee thee here faſt fettered now in jayle!
How haps thy wits were witched fo that knowing death was
     meede
Thou wouldeſt commit (to ſlay us both) this vile lafcivious
     deede,
                    Andrugio.
O good *Caſſandra,* leave to check, and chide me thraule
     therfore,
If late repentaunce wrought me helpe, I would doe fo no more.
But out alas, I wretch, too late doe forrowe my amys
Unles Lord *Promos* graunt me grace, in vayne is had ywiſt.
          B   Wherfore

Wherfore fweete fifter whylft in hope my dampned lyfe yet
    were,
Affaulte his hart in my behalfe with battering tyre of teares.
If thou by fute doeft fave my lyfe, it both our joyes will be,
If not, it may fuffice thou foughtft to fet thy brother free :
Wherfore fpeede to proroge my dayes, to-morrowe elfe I dye.
Caffandra.
  I wyll not fayle to pleade and praye to purchafe the mercye,
Farewell awhyle, God graunt me well to fpeede.
Andrugio.
  Syfter adew ; tyl thy returne I lyve twene hope and dreede.
Caffandra.
  Oh happy tyme ! fee where Lord *Promos* comes.
Now tongue addreffe thy felfe my mind to wray :
And yet leaft hafte worke wafte, I hold it beft
In covert, for fome advauntage, to ftay.

ACTUS II. SCENA III.

Promos *with the* Shriefe, *and their Officers.*

Promos.

  'Tis ftrange to thinke what fwarms of unthrifts live
Within this towne, by rapine, fpoyle, and theft,
That were it not that juftice ofte them greeve
The juft mans goods by ruflers fhould be reft.
At this our fyfe are thirtye judgde to dye
Whofe falles I fee their fellowes fmally feare,
So that the way is, by feverity
Such wicked weedes even by the rootes to teare.
Wherefore, *Shriefe,* execute with fpeedy pace
The dampned wights, to cutte of hope of grace.
Shriefe.
  It fhal be done.
Caffandra to hirfelfe.
  O cruell words they make my hart to bleede :
Now, now I muft this dome feeke to revoke
Leaft grace come fhort when ftarved is the fteede.

She

She kneeling speakes to Promos.

Moſt mighty lord, a worthy judge, thy judgement ſharpe abate,
Vaile thou thine eares to heare the plaint that wretched I
  relate.
Behold the wofull ſyſter here of poore *Andrugio*,
Whom though that lawe awardeth death, yet mercy do him
  ſhow.
Way his yong yeares, the force of love which forced his amis,
Way, way that mariage works amends for what committed is.
He hath defilde no nuptiall bed, nor forced rape hath mov'd ;
He fel through love who never ment but wive the wight he
  lov'd :
And wantons ſure to keepe in awe theſe ſtatutes firſt were
  made,
Or none but luſtfull leachers ſhould with rygrous law be payd.
And yet to adde intent thereto is farre from my pretence ;
I ſue with teares to wyn him grace that ſorrows his offence. --
Wherefore herein, renowned lorde, juſtice with pitee payſe
Which two, in equall ballance waide, to heaven your fame will
  raiſe.

Promos.

Caſſandra, leave of thy bootleſſe ſute, by law he hath bene
  tride,
Lawe founde his faulte, lawe judgde him death,

Caſſandra.

  Yet this maye be replide,
That law a miſchiefe oft permits to keepe due forme of lawe,
That lawe ſmall faultes, with greateſt doomes, to keepe men
  ſtyl in awe.
Yet kings, or ſuch as execute regall authoritye,
If mends be made, may over-rule the force of lawe with mercie.
Here is no wylful murder wrought which axeth blood againe ;
Andrugio's faulte may valued be, marriage wipes out his ſtayne.

Promos.

  Faire dame, I ſee the naturall zeàle thou beareſt to *Andrugio*,
And for thy ſake (not his deſart) this favour wyll I ſhowe :
I wyll repryve him yet a whyle, and on the matter pawſe ;
To-morrowe you ſhall lycence have afreſh to pleade his cauſe.
Shriſe execute my chardge, but ſtaye *Andrugio*,
Untill that you in this behalfe more of my pleaſure knowe.

Shriefe,

Shriefe.

I wyll performe your wyll.

Caſſandra.

O moſt worthy magiſtrate, myſelfe thy thrall I binde,
Even for this lytle lightning hope which at thy handes I finde.
Now wyl I go and comfort him which hangs twixt death and
　　life.　　　　　　　　　　　　　　　　　　　　[*Exit.*

Promos.

Happie is the man that injoyes the love of ſuch a wife.
I do proteſt hir modeſt wordes hath wrought in me amaze.
Though ſhe be faire, ſhe is not deackt with gariſh ſhewes for
　　gaze;
Hir bewtee lures, hir lookes cut off fond ſutes with chaſt diſ-
　　dain;
O God I feele a ſodaine change that doth my freedome chayne!
What didſt thou ſay? fie *Promos*, fie! of hir avoide the thought,
And ſo I will; my other cares will cure what love has wrought.
Come awaye.　　　　　　　　　　　　　　　　[*Exeunt.*

ACTUS II.　　SCENA IV.

Phallax, *Promos Officer*, Gripax *and* Rapax *Promoters.*

Phallax.

My truſty friendes about your buſineſſe ſtraight,
With ſymple ſhowes your ſubtile meanings bayte:
Promote all faults up into my office,
Then turne me loſe the offenders to fleece.

Gripax.

Tuſh, to finde lawe breakers let me alone,
I have eyes will look into a mylſtone.

Phallax.

God a mercy *Gripax.*

Rapax.

And I am ſo ſubtyll ſighted I trowe,
As I the very thoughts of men doo know.

Gripax.

I fayth, *Rapax* what thought thy wife when ſhe,
To lye with the preeſt by night ſtole from thee?

　　　　　　　　　　　　　　　　　　　　　Rapax,

Rapax.

Marry fhe knew you and I were at fquare;
And leaft we fell to blowes, fhe did prepare
To arme my head, to match thy horned browe.

Gripax.

Goe and a knave with thee.

Rapax.

I ftay for you.

Phallax.

No harme is done, here is but blow for blow,
Byrds of a fether beft flye together:
Then like partners about your market goe:
Marrowes adew: God fend you fayre wether.

Gripax.

Fare you well; for us take no care,
With us this brode fpeeche fildome breedeth fquare.   [*Exeunt.*

Phallax.

Marry Syr, wel fare an office, what fome ever it be,   [*Phallax*
The very countenaunce is great, though flender be the   *alone.*
    fee.
I thanke my good Lord *Promos* now, I am an officer made,
In footh more by hap then defart, in fecret be it fayde.   *Office.*
No force for that, each fhyft for one, for *Phallax* will doo fo;
Well fare a head can take his tyme, noy watch for tyme I trow.
I fmyle to thinke of my fellowes how fome brave it, fome
    waight,
And thinke reward there fervice juft, with offred   *A note for*
    fhifts wyl bayght;   *wayghters.*
When they (poore foules) in troth do falle a myle upon
    account,
For flattery and fervent plefing are meanes to make men mount:
I fpeak on proofe: Lord *Promos* I have pleafed many a day,
Yet am I neither learned, true, nor honeft any way.
What fkyls for that, by wit or wyle, I have an office got,
By force wherof every lycence, warrant, pattent, pafport,
Leace, fyne, fee, *et cetera*, pas and repas, through *Phallax*
    hands
Difordred perfons brybe me wel to efcape from juftice hands.
And welthy churles for to promote, I have now fet a worke
Such hungry lads as foone will fmell where ftatute breakers
    lurk;

    B 3   And

And if they come within our grype, we meane to ſtripe them ſo
As (if they ſcape from open ſhame) their bagges with us ſhall goe.
And truſt me this, we officers of this mylde mould are wrought ;
Agree with us and ſure your ſhame by us ſhal not be ſought.
But ſoft a whyle, I ſee my Lord ; what makes him lowre ſo ?
I wyll intrude into his ſight, perhaps his greeſe to know.

ACTUS II.   SCENA IV.

Phallax.   Promos.

Promos.

Well mette *Phallax*, I long have wyſht to ſhowe
A cauſe to thee which none but I yet know.
         Phallax.
Say on my Lord, a happy man weare I
If any way your wiſh I could ſupply.
         Promos.
Faine would I ſpeake, but oh, a chylling feare
(The caſe is ſuch) makes mee from ſpeech forbeare.
         Phallax.
Theſe wordes my lord (whome ever have bene juſt)
Now makes, me thinke, that you my truth miſtruſt.
But ceaſe ſuſpect, my wyll with yours ſhall gree,
What ſo (or againſt whome) your dealing be.
         Promos.
Againſt a wight of ſmall account it is,
And yet I feare, I ſhall my purpoſe mys.
         Phallax.
Feare not my Lord, the olde proverbe doth ſaye
Faynt harts doth ſteale fayre ladyes ſeld away.
         Promos.
Fayre ladyes ! O, no ladye is my love,
And yet ſhe ſure as coye as they wyl prove.
         Phallax.
I thought as much love did torment you ſo.
But what is ſhe that dare ſaye *Promos* noe ?
         Promos.
Doe what one can, fyre wyll breake forth I ſee,

                                                              My

My words unwares hath fhowen what greeveth me :
My wound is fuch as love muft be my leache,
Which cure wyll bring my gravity in fpeeche.
For what may be a folly of more note,
Then for to fee a man gray beard to dote.

Phallax.

No my lord, *Amor omnia vincit,*
And *Ovid* fayth, *Forma numen habet.*
And for to prove love's fervice feemes the wife,
Set *Sallamon* and *Sampfon,* before your eyes ;
For wyt, and ftrength who wonne the cheefeft prife,
And both lyv'd by the lawes love did devife,
Which proves in love a certaine Godhed lyes :
And Goddes rule yearely by wifdome from the fkyes,
Whofe wyls (thinke I) are wrought beft by the wife.

Promos.

Indeede divine I thinke loves working is,
From reafons ufe in that my fenfes fwarve ;
In pleafure paine, in payne I fynde a blyffe ;
On woe I feede, in fight of foode I ftearve :
.Thefe ftrange effects by love are lodg'd in mee,
My thoughts are bound, yet I myfelfe am free.

Phallax.

Well my good Lord, I axe (with pardon fought)
Who fhe may be that hath your thrauldome wrought.

Promos.

The example is fuch as I fygh to fhowe,
Syfter fhe is to dampned *Andrugio.*

Phallax.

All the better for you the game doth goe ;
The Proverbe fayth that kyt wyll unto kinde :
If this be true, this comfort then I fynde—
Caffandra's flefh is as her brother's frayle ;
Then wyll fhe ftoupe (in cheefe) when lords affayle.

Promos.

The contrary (through feare) doth worke my payne,
For in her face fuch modefty doth raigne,
As cuttes of loving futes with chafte difdayne.

Phallax.

What love wyll not neceffity fhall gayne ;

B 4

Her

Her brother's life will make her glad and fayne.

Promos.

What is it beft *Andrugio* free to fet,
Ere I am fure his fyfter's love to gette?

Phallax.

My lovyng lord, your fervaunt meanes not fo;
But if you wyll, elfe where in fecret goe:
To worke your wyll, a fhift I hope to fhowe.

Promos.

With ryght good wyll, for fuch my ficknes is,
As I fhall dye if her good will I mys.   [*Exeunt.*

A C T U S   II.   S C E N A   V.

The Hangman *with a greate many ropes aboughet his necke.*

The wynd is yl blowes no man's gaine, for cold I neede
   not care, ·
Here is nyne and twenty futes of apparrell for my fhare:
And fome, berlady, very good, for fo ftandeth the cafe
As neyther gentelman nor other lord, *Promos* fheweth grace.
But I marvell much poore flaves, that they are hanged fo foone;
They were wont to ftaye a day or two, now fcarce an after
   noone.
All the better for the hangman, I pardons dreaded fore,
Would cutters fave whofe clothes are good, I never fear'd the
   poore.
Let me fee, I muft be dapper in this my facultie;
Heare are new ropes: how are my knots? I faith fyr, flippery.
At faft or loofe, with my *Giptian*, I meane to have a caft;
Tenne to one I read his fortune by the marymas faft.

Serg.

Away, what a ftur is this, to fee men goe to hanging?

Hangman.

Harke, God bwy ye: I muft be gone, the prifners are a
   comming.   [*Exit.*

ACTUS II.   SCENA VI.

Sixe prifoners bounde with cords.   Two Hackfters, *one* Woman, *one like a* Giptian, *the reft poore* Roges, *a* Preacher, *with other Officers.*

They fing.

With harte and voyce to thee O Lorde,
  At latter gafpe, for grace we crie :
Unto our futes, good God accorde,
  Which thus appeale to thy mercie.
Forfake us not in this diftreffe,
  Which unto thee our finnes confeffe :
Forfake us not in this diftreffe,
  Which unto thee our finnes confeffe.

Firft Hackfter.

Al forts of men beware by us whom prefent death affaults ;
Looke in your confcience what you find, and forow for your
  faults.
Example take by our frefh harmes, fee here the fruites of pride :
I, for my part deferved death, long ere my theft was fpide.
O careles youth lead awrie with everie pleafing toy,
Note well my words, they are of woorth, the caufe though my
  annoy.
Shun to be pranckt in peacocks plumes for gaze which only
  are ;
Hate, hate the dyce even as the divell ; of wanton Dames
  beware.
Thefe, thefe wer they that fuckt my welth ; what folowed them
  in neede,
Twas intift by lawles men on theevifh fpoyles to feede.
And nufled once in wicked deedes I feard not to offende,
From bad, to worfe and worft I fell, I would at leyfure mende.
But oh, prefuming over much ftyll to efcape in hope,
My faultes were found and I adjudgde to totter in a rope :
To which I go with thefe my mates, likewife for breach of
  lawes.
For murder fome, for theeverie fome, and fome for litle caufe.

Second

Second Hackster.

Beware deere friends of quarelling, thirſt ſpoile of no mans
   breath ;
Blood axeth blood; I ſheeding blood untimelie catch my
   death.

A Woman.

Maides and women, ſhun pride and ſloth, the rootes of every
   vice ;
My death ere long wil ſhew their ends ; God graunt it make
   you wiſe !

A Scoffing Catchpole.

How now, *Giptian?* All *a mort* knave, for want of company ?
Be cruſtie man : the *Hangman* ſtraight wil reade fortunes
   with thee.

The Preacher.

With this thy ſcoffing ſpeach, good friend, offend him not,
His faults are ſcorged ; thine ſcape (perhaps) that do deſerve
   his lot.

A poore Roge.

Jeſus ſave me, I am caſt for a purſe with three halfe pence.

A churliſh Officer.

Diſpatch, prating knave and be hang'd, that we were jogging
   hence.

They leyſurablie depart ſynging; the *Preacher* whiſpering
ſome one or other of the Priſoners ſtyll in the eare.

They ſing.

Our ſecrete thoughts, thou Chriſt doſt knowe,
   Whome the worlde doth hate in thrall ;
Yet hope we that thou wilt not ſoe,
   On whome alone we thus do call.
   Forſake us not in this diſtreſſe,
   Which unto thee our ſinnes confeſſe :
   Forſake us not, &c,

ACTUS

ACTUS III.   SCENA I.

Promos *alone.*

Promos.

D O what I can, no reafon cooles defire :
The more I ftrive my fonde affectes to tame,
The hotter (oh) I feele a burning fire
Within my breaft, vaine thoughts to forge and frame,
O ftraying effectes of blinde affected love,
From wifdomes pathes which doth aftraye our wittes ;
Which makes us haunt that which our harmes doth move,
A fickneffe lyke, the fever Etticke fittes,
Which fhakes with colde when we do burne like fire.
Even fo in Love we freefe through chilling feare,
When as our hartes doth frye with hote defire.
What faide I ? lyke to Etticke fittes ? nothing neare ;
In fowreft Love, fome fweete is ever fuckt :
The lover findeth peace in wrangling ftrife,
So that if paine were from his pleafure pluckt,
There were no heaven like to the Lover's life.
But why ftande I to pleade their joye or woe,
And reft unfure of hir I wifh to have ?
I know not if *Caffandra* love, or noe :
But yet admytte fhe graunt not what I crave,
If I be nyce to hir brother lyfe to give :
Hir brother's life too much wyll make her
    yeelde —   *Might ma-*
                                       flers right.
A promife then to let hir brother lyve,
Hath force inough to make her flie the fielde.
Thus though fute fayle, neceffitie fhall wyn
Of lordlie rule the conquering power is fuch :
But (oh fweete fight) fee where fhe enters in :
Both hope and dreade, at once my harte doth tuch.

                                      ACTUS

ACTUS III.   SCENA II.

Caffandra, Promos.

Caffandra fpeakes to herfelfe.

Caffandra.

I fee two thralles, fweete feemes a lytle joye;
For fancies free *Andru io's* breaft hath fcope:
But leaft detract doth rayfe a new annoye,
I nowe will feeke to turne to happe his hope.
See, as I wifht, Lord *Promos* is in place;
Nowe in my fute God graunt I maye finde grace.

Shee kneeling fpeakes to Promos.

Renowned Lorde, whylſt life in me doth laſt,
In homage bondes I binde myfelfe to thee;
And though I did thy goodnefſe latelie tafte,
Yet once againe on knees I mercie feeke
In his behalfe that hanges twene death and life,
Who ſtyll is pieaſt if you the mendes do leeke,
His lawles love to make his lawfull wife.

Promos.

Faire dame, I wel have wayd thy fute, and wiſh to do thee
   good,
But all in vaine, al things conclude to have thy brother's blood.
The ſtricknes of the lawe condempnes an ignorant abufe,
Then wylful faultes are hardlie helpt or cloked with excufe;
And what maye be more wylfull then a maide to violate?

Caffandra.

The force was final when with her wyl he, wretch, the conqueſt gate.

Promos.

Lawe ever at the worſt doth confter evyl intent.

Caffandra.

And lawe even with the worſt awardes them punifhment;
And fith that rigorous lawe adjudg'd him to dye,
Your glorie will be much the more in fhowing him mercie.
The world will think how that you do but graunt him grace
   on caufe:

                                                    And

And where caufe is there mercy fhould abate the force of lawes.
Promos.
Caffandra, in thy brother's halfe thou haft fayde what may be;
And for thy fake it is, if I doe fet *Andrugio* free.
Shart tale to make, thy beauty hath furpryzed me with love,
That maugre wit, I turne my thoughts as blynd affections
    move.
And quite fubdude by *Cupids* might, neede makes me fue for
    grace
To thee *Caffandra* which doeft holde my freedome in a lace.
Yeelde to my will, and then commaund even what thou wilt
    of mee;
Thy brother's life, and all that elfe may with thy liking gree.
        Caffandra.
And may it be, a Judge himfelf the felf fame   [*Caffandra*
    fault fhould ax,   *to herfelf.*
For which he domes an others death ? O crime without ex-
    cufe!
Renowned lorde, you ufe this fpeach (I hope) your thrall to
    trye,
If otherwife my brother's life fo deare I will not bye.
        Promos.
Faire dame my outward lookes my inward thoughts bewray,
If you miftruft, to fearch my harte, would God you had a
    kaye!
        Caffandra.
If that you love (as fo you faye) the force of love you know,
Which felt, in confcience you fhould my brother favour fhow.
        Promos.
In doubtfull warre one prifoner ftill doth fet another free.
        Caffandra.
What fo warre feekes, love unto warre contrary is you fee.
Hate foftreth warre, love cannot hate, then maye it cover force.
        Promos.
The lover ofte fues to his foe, and findeth no remorfe.
Then if he hap to have a helpe to wyn his frowarde foe,
Too kindle a foole I will him holde that lets fuch vantage gee.
        Caffandra.
Well, to be fhort, my felfe wyll dye ere I my honor ftayne ;
You know my minde, leave off to tempt, your offers are in vaine.
        Promos.

Promos.

Bethink yourfelf at price enough I purchafe, fweet, your
 love;
Andrugio's life fuffis'd alone your ftraungenes to remove;
The which I graunt, with any wealth that elfe you wyll re-
 quire:
Who buyeth love at fuch a rate, payes well for his defire.

Caſſandra.

No, *Promos*, no; honor never at value maye be folde;
Honor farre dearer is then life, which paſſeth price of golde

Promos.

To buie this Juel at the full, my wife I may thee make.

Caſſandra.

For unfure hope, that peerelefs pearle I never will forfake.

Promos.

Thefe futes feemes ftrange at firft, I fee wher   [*To him-*
 modefty beares fway;   *felf.*
I therfore wil fet down my wyll, and for hir anfwer ftaye.
    Fayre *Caſſandra*, the juel of my joye,
    Howe fo in fhowe my tale feemes ftraunge to thee,
    The fame well waide, thou need'ft not be fo coye,
    Yet for to give thee refpite I agree.
    I wyll two daies hope ftyll of thy confent;
    Which if thou graunt (to cleare my clowdes of care)
    Cloth'd like a Page (fufpect for to prevent)
    Unto my Court, fome night, fweet wenche, repaire.
Tyl then adue; thou thefe my words in works perform'd fhall
 find.

Caſſandra.

Farewel my Lord, but in this fute you bootles waft your
 wind.
Caſſandra! O moft unhappy, fubject to everie woe,
What tonge can tel, what thought conceive, what pen thy
 gueffe can fhew!
Whom to fcurge, heaven and earth do heapes of thral ordain,
Whofe words in wafte, whofe works are loft, whofe wifhes
 are in vain.
That which to others comfort yeelds, doth caufe my heavy
 cheer,
I meane, my beautie breedes my bale, which many hold fo
 deere.

                                                    I would

I would to God that kinde elfe where beftowed had this blafe,
My vertues then had wrought regard, my fhape now gives
    the gafe.
This forme fo *Promos* fiers with love as wifdom cannot quench
His hote defire, tyll he luft in *Venus'* feas hath drencht.

At thefe wordes *Ganio* muft be readie to fpeake.

ACTUS III.   SCENA III.

Ganio, Andrugio's *boye*. Caffandra.

Ganio.

Miftrefs *Caffandra*, my mafter longs to heare of your good
    fpeed.
Caffandra.
Poore *Ganio*, his death alas, fierce fortune hath decreed.
Ganio.
His death! God forbid all his hope fhould turne to fuch
    fucceffe;
For God's fake, go and comfort him, I forrowe his diftreffe.
Caffandra.
I needes muft go, although with heavy cheere.
Ganio.
Sir, your fyfter *Caffandra* is here.   [*Exit.*

ACTUS III.   SCENA IV.

Andrugio *out of prifon*. Caffandra *on the ftage*.

Andrugio.
My *Caffandra* what newes, good fifter fhowe.
Caffandra.
All thinges conclude thy death, *Andrugio*:
Prepare thy felfe, to hope it ware in vaine.
Andrugio.
My death! alas, what rayfed this new difdayne?
Caffandra.
Not Juftice zeale in wicked *Promos* fure.

                         Andrugio.

Andrugio.

Sweete, fhew the caufe I muſt this doome indure.

Caſſandra.

If thou doſt live, I muſt my honor lofe.
Thy raunfome is, to *Promos* fleſhly wyll
That I do yelde: than which I rather chofe
With torments ſharpe my felfe he firſt ſhould kyll.
Thus am I bent: thou feeſt thy death at hand:
O would my life would fatisfie his yre,
Caſſandra then would cancell foone thy band.

Andrugio.

And may it be a judge of his account
Can fpot his minde with lawles love or luſt?
But more, may he doome any fault with death,
When in fuch faute he findes himfelfe unjuſt?
Syſter, that wife men love, we often fee,
And where love rules, gainſt thornes doth reafon fpurne;
But who fo loves, if he rejected be,
His paſſing love to peeviſh hate will turne.
Deare fiſter then note how my fortune ſtands:
That *Promos* love, the like is oft in ufe;
And fith he crave this kindneſſe at your hands,
Think this, if you his pleafure do refufe,
I, in his rage (poor wretch) ſhall fing *Peccavi.*
Here are two evyls, the beſt harde to digeſt;
But whereas things are driven unto neceſſity,
There are we byd, of both evyls choofe the leaſt.

Caſſandra.

And of thefe evils the leaſt, I hold, is death,
To ſhun whofe dart we can no meane devife;
Yet honor lives when death hath done his worſt;
Thus fame then lyfe is of farre more comprife.

Andrugio.

Nay, *Caſſandra,* if thou thy felfe fubmyt,
To fave my life, to *Promos* fleaſhly wyll,
Juſtice wyll fay thou doſt no cryme commit,
For in forſt faultes is no intent of yll.

Caſſandra.

How fo th' intent is conſtrued in offence,
The Proverbe faies that tenne good turnes lye dead,

And one yll deede tenne tymes beyond pretence
By envious tongues, report abrode doth fpread.
Andrugio, fo my fame fhall vallewed bee;
Difpite will blafe my crime, but not the caufe;
And thus, although I fayne would fet thee free,
Poore wench, I teare the grype of flaunder's pawes.

Andrugio.

Nay fweete fifter, more flaunder would infame
Your fpotles lyfe to reave your brother's breath,
When you have power for to enlarge the fame;
Once in your handes doth lye my lyfe and death.
Way that I am the felfe fame flefh you are;
Thinke, I once gone, our houfe will goe to wrack:
Knowe, forced faultes for flaunder neede not care:
Looke you for blame, if I guaile through your lack.
Confider well my great extremitie;
If other wife this doome I could revoke,
I would not fpare for any jebardye
To free thee, wench, from this fame heavy yoke:
But ah, I fee elfe no way faves my life,
And yet his hope may further thy confent;
He fayde, he maye percafe make thee his wife,
And t' is likelie he cannot be content
With one night's joye: if love he after feekes;
And I difcharg'd, if thou aloofe then be,
Before he lofe thy felfe that fo he leekes,
No dought but he to marryage wyll agree.

Caſſandra.

And fhall I fticke to ftoupe to *Promos* wyll,
Since my brother injoyeth lyfe thereby?
No, although it doth my credit kyll,
Ere that fhe fhould, my felfe would chufe to dye.
My *Andrugio*, take comfort in diftreffe,
Caſſandra is wonne thy raunfome great to paye;
Such care fhe hath thy thraldome to releace
As fhe confentes her honor for to flay.
Farewell, I muft my virgins weedes forfake,
And lyke a Page to *Promos* lewde repayre.   [*Exit.*

Andrugio.

My good fifter, to God I thee betake,
To whome I pray that comforte change thy care.

C   ACTUS

ACTUS III.   SCENA V.

Phallax alone.

Phallax.

Tis more then ftraunge to fee Lord *Promos* plight;
He fryfkes abought as byrdes were in his breech.
Even now he feemes (through hope) to tafte delight;
And ftraight (through feare) where he clawes it doth not ytch.
He mufeth now, ftrayght wayes the man doth fing;
(A fight, in footh, unfeemely for his age)
He longing lookes when any newes fhal bring,
To fpeake with him, without there waytes a Page.
O worthy wit (fyt for a Judges head)
Unto a man to chaunge a fhiftles mayde!
Wyncke not on me; twas his and not my deede:
His, nay his rule, this *Metamorphos* made—
But Holla, tongue, no more of this, I pray:
Non bonus eft ludere cum fanctis.
The quieteft and the thryftieft courfe, they fay,
Is not to checke but prayfe great mens amys.
I finde it true; for foothing *Promos* vaine
None lyke my felfe is lykte in his conceyte:
    Whyle favour laft, then good, I fifh for gaine
    (For grace wyll not byte alwayes at my bayte)
    And as I wifh, at hande, good fortune fee.
    Here coms *Rapax* and *Gripax*, but what's this?
    As good as fayre handfel God graunt it bee:
    The knaves bring a Woman *coram nobis.*

·

ACTUS III.   SCENA VI.

Phallax, Gripax, Rapax, *a* Bedell, *and one with a browne Byll
bring in* Lamia *and* Rofko *her man.*

Lamia.

Teare not my clothes my friends, they coft more then you
are aware.

Bedell.

Bedell.

Tufh, foon you fhal have a blew gown; for thefe take you
no care.

Rofko.

If fhe tooke thy offer, poore knave, thy wife would ftarve
with cold.

Gripax.

Well Syr, whipping fhall keepe you warme.

Phallax.

What meanes thefe knaves to fcolde?

Rapax.

Maifter *Phallax*, we finde you in good time;
A woman here we have brought afore you;
One to be chargde with many a wanton crime,
Which tryall will, with proofe inough, finde true:
A knave of hirs we have ftayed likewife,
Both to be us'd as you fhall us advife.

Phallax.

What call you hir name?

Rapax.

Lamia.

Phallax.

Fayre Dame, hereto what do you faye?

Lamia.

Worfhipfull Sir, my felfe I happy reake
With patience that my aunfwer you will heare.
Thefe naughtie men thefe wordes on mallice fpeake,
And for this caufe yll wyll to me they beare.
I fcornde to keepe, their mindes with money playe;
I meane to keepe my life from open fhame;
Yea, if I liv'd as lewdlie as they faye.
But I that knewe my felfe unworthy blame
Shrunk not to come unto my triall nowe:
My tale is tolde; conceyve as lyketh you.

Phallax.

My friends, what proofe have you againft this dame?
Speake on fure ground, leaft that you reape the fhame:
The wrong is great, and craves great recompence,
To touch her honeft name, without offence.

Gripax.

All *Julio*, Syr, doth ryng of her lewd lyfe.

Byll.

Byll.

Indeede fhe is knowne for an ydle hufwife.

Rofko.

He lyes, fhe is occupied day and night.

Phallax.

To fweare againft her, is there any wight?

Rapax.

No, not prefent; but if you do detayne her,
There wil be found by oth fome that wyll ftayne her.

Phallax.

I fee fhe is then on fufpition ftayde,
Whofe faultes to fearch, upon my charge is layde.
From charge of her I therfore will fet you free;
My felfe will fearch her faultes, if any be.
A Gods name you may depart.

2 or 3 fpeake. God bwy, Syr.

Gripax.

In fuch fhares as this henceforth I will begin,
For all is his, in his clawes, that commeth in.   [*Exeunt.*

Phallax.

Fayre *Lamia,* fince that we are alone,
I plainely wyll difcourfe to you my minde:
I thinke you not to be fo chaft a one
As that your lyfe this favor ought to fynde.
No force, for that, fince that you fcot free goe,
Unpunifhed whofe life is judged yll;
Yet thinke (through love) this grace the Judge doth fhew,
And love with love ought to be anfwered ftyll.

Lamia.

Indeede I graunt (although I could reprove
Their lewde complayntes with goodneffe of my lyfe)
Your curtefy your detter doth me prove,
In that you tooke (my honeft fame in ftryfe)
My aunfwere for difcharge of their report:
For which good turne I at your pleafure reft,
To worke amends, in any honeft fort.

Phallax.

Away with honefty, your anfweare then, in footh,
Fyts me as jumpe as a pudding a Friar's mouth.

Rofko.

He is a craftie childe; dally, but do not.

Lamia.

Lamia.

Tufh, I warrant thee, I am not fo whot.
Your wordes are too harde, fir, for me to confter.

Phallax.

Then to be fhort, your rare bewtie my hart hath wounded fo
As, (fave your love become my leach) I fure fhall die with
woe.

Lamia.

I fee no figne of death in your face to appeare;
Tis but fome ufuall qualme you have pitifull dames to feare.

Phallax.

Faire *Lamia,* truft me I faine not, betimes beftow fom grace.

Lamia.

Well, I admit it fo; onelie to argue in your cafe.
I am maried, fo that to fet your love on me, were vaine.

Phallax.

It fuffifeth me that I may your fecrete friend remaine.

Rofko.

A holie hood makes not a Frier devoute,
He will playe at finall game, or he fitte out.

Lamia.

Though for pleafure, or to prove me, thefe profers you do
move,
You are to wife to haffarde life upon my yeelding love.
The man is painde with prefent death, that ufeth wanton
pleafure.

Phallax.

To fcape fuch paine, wife men thefe joyes without fufpect
can meafure.
Furthermore, I have ben (my Girle) a Lawier to too long,
If at a pinche I cannot wreft the law from right to wrong.

Lamia.

If lawe you do profeffe, I gladlie crave
In a caufe or two your advife to have.

Phallax.

To refolve you, you fhail commaunde my fkyll,
Wherfore like friendes lets common in good wyll.

Lamia.

You are a merie man, but leave to jeaft,
To morrowe night, if you will be my geaft

At

At my poore houfe, you fhall my caufes knowe,
For good caufe, which I meane not here to fhowe.
Phallax.

Willinglie, and for that hafte calles me hence
My fute tyll then fhall remaine in fufpence :
Farewell clyent, to morrowe looke for me.   [*Exit.*

Lamia.

Your good welcome, Sir, your beft cheere will be.

Rofko.

I tolde you earft the nature of *Phallax,*
Money or faire women workes him as waxe.
And yet I muft commend your fober cheere,
You told your tale, as if a Saint you were.

Lamia.

Well (in fecreete be it fayde) how fo I feemd divine,
I feared once a blew gowne would have bene my fhrine.
But nowe that paine is flead, and pleafure keepes his holde,
I knowe that *Phallax* will my fame hence forth upholde :
To entertaine which Geaft I will fome dayntie cheere prepare ;
Yet ere I go, in pleafant fong, I meane to purge my care.

THE SONG.

ADUE, poore care adue,
  Go cloye fome helples wretche ;
My life, to make me rue,
  Thy forces do not ftretche.

Thy harbor, is the harte,
  Whom wrong hath wrapt in woe ;
But wrong doth take my parte
  With cloke of right in fhoe.

My faultes inquirie fcape,
  At them the judges winke ;
Thofe for my fall that gape,
  To fhowe my lewdneffe fhrinke.

Then filly care, go packe,
  Thou art no geaft for me ;
I have, and have no lacke,
  And lacke is fhrowde for thee.   [*Exeunt.*

ACTUS

ACTUS III.   SCENA VII.

Caſſandra, *apparelled like a Page.*

Caſſandra.

Unhappy wretche, I bluſh my ſelfe to ſee
Apparelled thus monſtrous to my kinde :
But oh, my weedes wyll with my fault agree,
When I have pleaſde lewde *Promos* fleſhlie minde.
What ſhall I do ? go proffer what he ſought ?
Or on more ſute ſhall I give my conſent ?
The beſt is ſure, ſince this muſt needes be wrought,
I go, and ſhewe neede makes me to his bent.
My fluddes of teares, from true intent which floe,
May quenche his luſt or ope his muſled eyen
To ſee that I deſerve to be his wife,
Though now conſtrainde to be his concubine.
But ſo or no, I muſt the venter give :
No daunger feares the wight prickt foorth by neede :
And thus lyke one more glad to dye than lyve,
I forewarde ſet ; God graunt me well to ſpeede.   [*Exit.*

ACTUS IV.   SCENA I.

Dalia, Lamia's *Maide going to market.*

Dalia.

WITH my miſtreſſe the worlde is chaunged well,
She fearde of late of whipping cheere to ſmell ;
And nowe againe both gallant, freſh and gaye,
Who in *Julio* flauntes it out lyke *Lamia ?*
A luckie friende (yea one that beareth ſwaye)
Is now become a proppe of ſuch a ſtaye
To hir good name, as who is he dare ſaye
That *Lamia* doth offende nowe any waye ?

C 4

This

This her good friende wyll be hir Geaſt this night;
And that he maye in his welcome delyght,
To market I in haſte am ſent to buye
The beſt cheare that I faſten on my eye.   [*Exit.*

A C T U S IV.   S C E N A   II.

Promos *alone.*

Promos.

   By proofe I finde no reaſon cooles deſire.
Caſſandraes ſute ſuffiſed to remove
My lewde requeſt; but contrarie, the fire
Hir teares inflamd of luſt and filthy love.
And having thus the conqueſt in my handes
No prayer ſervde to worke reſtraint in me,
But needes I would untye the precious bandes
Of this fayre dames ſpotles virginitye.
The ſpoyle was ſweete, and wonne even as I woulde;
And yet ungainde tyll I had given my trothe
To marie hir, and that hir brother ſhoulde
Be free from death; all which I bounde with oathe,
It reſteth now (unleſſe I wrong her much)
I keepe my vowe: and ſhall *Andrugio* live?
Such grace would me with unindifferencie tuch,
To pardon him that dyd commit a rape.
To ſet him free, I to *Caſſandra* ſware,
But no man elſe is privie to the ſame;
And rage of Love for thouſande oathes nyll ſpare,
More then are kept when gotten is the game.
Well, what I ſayde, then Lover like I ſayde,
Now reaſon ſayes, unto thy credite looke;
And having well the circumſtaunces wayde,
I finde I muſt unſweare the oathe I tooke.
But double wrong I ſo ſhould do *Caſſandra*;
No force for that my might commaundeth right;
Hir privie maime hir open cryes will ſtaye,
Or if not ſo, my frowning will hir fright:
And thus ſhall rule conceale my filthy deede.
Nowe foorthwith I wyil to the Gayler ſende

                                    That

That fecretelie *Andrugio* he behead,
Whofe head he fhall with thefe fame wordes commend
" To *Caffandra*, as *Promos* promift thee,
" From prifon loe, he fendes thy Brother free.

ACTUS IV.   SCENA III.

Caffandra.

Caffandra.

Fayne would I wretch conceale the fpoyle of my virginity,
But o my gilt doth make me blufh chaft virgins here to fee.
I, monfter now, no mayde nor wyfe, have ftoupte to *Promos*
    luft;
The caufe was, nether fute nor teares could quench his
    wanton thurft.
What cloke wyl fcufe my crime? my felfe my confcience
    doth accufe:
And fhall *Caffandra* now be turned, in common fpeeche, a
    ftewes?
Shall fhe, whofe vertues bare the bell be calld a vicious dame?
O cruell death, nay hell, to her that was conftraynd to fhame.
Alas few wyll give foorth I fynd to fave my brothers lyfe,
But fayntly I through *Promos* othe, doo hope to be his wife.
For lovers feare not how they fweare to wyn a lady fayre,
And having wonne, what they did wifh, for othes nor lady
    care:
But to be juft or no, I joy *Andrugio* yet fhall lyve;—
But ah I fee a fight that doth my hart as under ryve.

ACTUS IV.   SCENA. IV.

Gayler *with a dead mans head in a charger.*   Caffandra.

Gayler.

This prefent wil be galle I know to fayre *Caffandra*,
Yet if fhe knewe as much as I, moft fwete I dare well fay.
In good tyme fee where fhe doth come to whome my arrand is.
                                                    Caffandra.

Caſſandra.

Alas his haſty pace to me, ſhowes ſomewhat is amys.

Gayler.

Fayre *Caſſandra*, my Lord *Promos* commends him unto thee,
To keepe his word, who ſayes from priſon he ſends thy brother
   free.

Caſſandra.

Is my *Andrugio* done to death? fye, fye, o faythles truſt!

Gayler.

Be quiet, Lady, law found his fault, then was his judgment
   juſt.

Caſſandra.

Wel my good friend, ſhow *Promos* this, ſince law hath don
   this deed,
I thank him yet he would vouchſaf on me my brother's head;
Loe this is all: now geve me leave to rew his loſſe alone.

Gayler.

I wyll perform your will, and wiſh you ceaſe your mone.

Caſſandra.

Farewell.

Gayler.

I ſure had ſhowen what I had done, her teares I pittied ſo,
But that I wayde that women ſyld do dye with greefe and woe:
And it behoves me to be ſecret, or elſe my necke-verſe cun:
Well, now to pack my dead man hence it is hye tyme I run.

Caſſandra.

Is he paſt ſight? then have I tyme to wayle my woes alone:
Andrugio, let mee kis thy lippes yet ere I fall to mone.
O would that I could waſt to teares to waſh this bloody face,
Which fortune farre beyond deſart hath followed with diſgrace.
O *Promos* falce and moſt unkinde, both ſpoyld of love and ruth!
O *Promos* thou doſt wound my hart to thinke on thy untruth!
Whoſe plyghted fayth is tournd to frawd, and words to works
   unjuſt!
Why doe I lyve, unhappy wench, ſyth treaſon quites my truſt?
O death, devorſe me wretch at once from this ſame worldly
   lyfe!
But why do I not ſlay myſelfe for to appeaſe this ſtryfe?
Perhaps within this womoe of myne another *Promos* is;
I ſo by death ſhal be avengd of him in murthring his;

                      And

And ere I am affured that I have revengde this deede,
Shall I difpatch my lothed life? that haft weare more than
    fpeede.
So *Promos* would triumphe that nowe his tiranny fhould know;
No, no, this wicked fact of his fo flightly fhall not goe.
The King is juft and mercyfull, he doth both heare and fee,
See mens defarts, heare their complaynts to judge with equity.
My wofull cafe with fpeede I wyll unto his grace addreffe,
And from the firft unto the laft the truth I wyll confeffe.
So *Promos*, thou by that fame lawe fhalt lofe thy hated breth,
Through breach wherof thou didft condemne *Andrugio* unto
    death.
So doing yet, the world will fay I broke *Diana's* lawes:
But what of that? no fhame is myne when truth hath fhewne
    my caufe.
I am refolved the King fhall knowe of *Promos* injury;
Yet ere I go, my brother's head I wyll ingraved fee.   [*Exit.*

ACTUS IV. SCENA V.

Gayler. Andrugio.

Gayler.

Andrugio, as you love our lives, forthwith poft you away:
For Gods fake to no lyving friend your fafety yet bewraye;
The proverbe fayth two may keepe counfell if that one be gone.
Andrugio.
Affure thy felf, moft faithful friend, I wyl be knowne to
    none.
To none alas! I fee my fcape yeeldes mee but fmall releefe;
Caffandra and *Polina* wyll deftroye themfelves with greefe,
Through thought that I am dead: they dead, to live what
    helpeth me?
Gayler.
Leave of thefe plaints of fmal availe, thank God that you are
    free,
For God it was within my mind that did your fafety move,
And that fame God no doubt wyl worke for your and their
    behove.
Andrugio.

Andrugio.

Moſt faithfull friend, I hope that God wyl worke as you do ſay,
And therfore to ſome place unknowne I wyl my ſelfe convaye.
Gayler, farewel : for thy good deede I muſt remayne thy
    debter ;
In meane whyle yet receyve this gyft, tyll fortune ſends a better.

Gayler.

God bwy Syr, but kepe your mony, your need you do not
    know.

Andrugio.

I pas not now for fortuns threats, yea though hir force ſhe
    ſhow,
And therfore ſtyck not to receyve this ſmale reward in part.

Gaylar.

I wyll not ſure ſuch proffers leaſe ; tys time you doe depart.

Andrugio.

Since ſo thou wilt, I wyl be gone : adue tyl fortune ſmile.
                                                    [*Exit.*

Gayler.

Syr, fare you wel, I wyl not fayle to pray for you the while.
Well, I am glad that I have ſent him gone,
For, by my fayth, I lyv'd in perlous feare :
And yet, God wot, to ſee his bytter mone
When he ſhould dye, would force a man forbeare
From harming him, if pitty might beare ſway.
But ſee how God hath wrought for his ſafety :
A dead man's head that ſuffered th'other day,
Makes him thought dead, throughout the citie.
Such a juſt, good, and righteous God is he,
Although a whyle he let the wicked rayne,
Yet he releeves the wretch in miſery ;
And in his pryde he throwes the tyraunt downe.
I uſe theſe wordes upon this onely thought
That *Promos* long his rod cannot eſcape,
Who hath in thought a wylfull murder wrought,
Who hath in act perform'd a wicked rape.
Gods wyll be done, who well *Andrugio* ſpeede ;
Once well, I hope to heare of his good lucke ;
For, God, thou knoweſt my conſcience dyd this deede,
And no deſire of any worldly muck.   [*Exit.*

            3   ACTUS

ACTUS IV. SCENA VI.

Dalia from market.

Dalia.

In good fweete footh I feare I fhal be fhent,
It is fo long fince I to market went ;
But truft me, wyld fowle are fuch coftly geare,
Specially woodcocks out of reafon deare,
That this houre I have the market bett,
To drive a bargaine to my moft profyt ;
And in the end, I chaunc'd to light on one
Hyt me as pat as a pudding *Pope Jone.*
Other market mades pay downe for their meate,
But that I have bought on my fcore is fet.
Well fare credit when mony runneth low,
Marry, yet Butchers the which do credit fo,
(As much good meate as they kyll) may perchaunce
Be glad and fayne at heryng cobs to daunce.
What force I that ? every man fhyft for one ;
For if I ftarve, let none my fortune mone.

She faynes to goe out.

ACTUS IV. SCENA VII.

Grimball, Dalia; *cyther of them a Bafket.*

Grimball.

Softe *Dalia*; a woorde with you, I praye.

Dalia.

What, friend *Grimbal*; welcome as I maye faye.

Grimball.

Sayft thou me fo ? then kyffe me for acquaintaunce.

Dalia.

If I lyke your manhoode, I may do fo perchaunce.

She faynes to looke in his bafket.

Grimball.

Bate me an afe, quoth *Boulton :* Tufh your minde I know :
Ah Syr, you would, belike, let my cocke fparrowes goe.

Dalia

Dalia.

I warrant thee *Grimball.*   [*She takes out a white pudding.*

Grimball.

Laye off handes *Dalia.*
You powte me, if that you got my pudding awaye.

Dalia.

Nay good, fweete, honny *Grimball,* this pudding give me.

Grimball.

Iche were as good geete hir, for fhe wyll hate, I fee,
Well, my nown good harte roote, I freelie give thee this,
Upon condition that thou give me a kys.

Dalia.

Nay, but firft wafh your lippes with fweete water you fhall.

Grimball.

Why ych was ryte now for my pudding, hony fweet *Grimbal.*
Well *Dalia,* you will floute fo long, tyll (though I faye)
With kindneffe you wyll caft a proper handfome man away :
Wherefore, foote Conny, even a little fpurte.

Dalia.

Laye off handes, Sir.

Grimball.

Good do not byte, for ych meane thee no hurte :
Come off, Pyggefnie, prefarre me not a jote.

Dalia.

What would the good foole have?

Grimball.

Why you woot whote.
Hearke in your eare.

Dalia.

You fhall commaunde, fo proper a man ye are,
That for your fake I wyll not flicke to ware
A blew Caffocke during my lyfe forfoothe :
Mary, for my fake, I woulde be verie lothe
So goodlie a handfome man fhould lofe his head.

Grimball.

Nay, for my head, care not a tinker's torde,
For fo God judge me, and at one bare worde,
Yle lofe my death, yea, and my great browne Cowe,
I love you fo filtlilie, law ye nowe.

Dalia.

Dalia.

Thou fayeſt valiantlie, now ſing as well too,
And thou ſhalt quicklie knowe what I meane to doo.

Grimball.

Yes by Gogs foote, to pleaſure thee, ych ſhall
Both ſyng, ſpring, fight and playe the dewle and all.

Dalia.

O luſtilie.

THE SONG.

Grimball.

Come ſmack me, come ſmack me, I long for a ſmouch.

Dalia.

Go pack thee, go pack thee, thou filthie fine ſlouch.

Grimball.

Leard, howe I love thee.

Dalia.

This cannot move me.

Grimball.

Why pretie Pyſney, my harte, and my honny.

Dalia.

Becauſe, goodman Hogs face, you woe without money.

Grimball.

I lacke money, chi graunt.

Dalia.

Then *Grimball* avaunt.

Grimball.

Cham yong, ſweete hart, and feate; come kyſſe me for love.

Dalia.

Crokeſhanke, your jowle is to great ſuch lyking to move.

Grimball.

What meane you by this?

Dalia.

To leave thee, by Gys.

Grimball.

Firſt ſmack me, firſt ſmack; I dye for a ſmouch.

Dalia.

Go pack thee, go pack thee, thou filthie fine ſlouch. [*Exit.*

Grimball.

Grimball.

Dalia, arte thou gone? what wolt ferve me foe?
O God, cham readie to raye myfelfe for woe.
Be valiaunt, *Grimball;* kyl thy felfe man.
Nay, bum ladie, I will not by Saint *Anne.*
Ich have hearde my great Granfier faye,
Maide will faye naye, and take it; and fo fhe maye.
And therfore chyll to Miftreffe *Lamia.*
With thefe Puddings and cock fparowes by and by;
And in the darke againe ych will hir trye.

ACTUS V.   SCENA I.

Phallax *alone.*

Phallax.

I marvell much what worketh to my Lord *Promos* unreft,
He fares as if a thoufand devils were gnawing in his breft.
There is fure fome worme of griefe that doth his confcience
      nip,
For fince *Andrugio* loft his head, he hath hung downe the lippe:
And truth to fay, his fault is fuch as well may greve his mynd,
The devill himfelfe could not have ufde a practife more unkind.
This is once, I love a woman, for my life, as well as he,
But (fayre dames) with her that loves me, I deale well with,
      truft mee.
Well, leave I now my Lord *Promos* his owne deeds to aunfwere:
Lamia, I know, lookes, and double lookes, when I come to
      fupper:
I thought as much: fee, to feeke me heare coms her aple fquier.

ACTUS V.   SCENA II.

Rofko, Phallax.

Rofko.

O that I could find Mafter *Phallax,* the meate burnes at
      the fire.

                                                    And

And, by your leave, *Andrugio's* death doth make my miftris
    fweate.

Phallax.

How now *Rofko?*

Rofko.

Ift you Syr? my miftris doth intreate
That with all fpeede your worfhip will come away to fupper;
The meate and all is ready to fet upon the borde, Syr.

Phallax.

Gramercy for thy paynes; I was even comming to her.

Rofko.

You are the welcomft man alyve to her I know,
And truft me at your commaundement remayneth poore *Rofko.*

Phallax.

It is honeftly fayd, but now tell mee
What quality haft, that I may ufe thee.

Rofko.

I am a Barbour, and when you pleafe, Syr,
Call (and fpare not) for a caft of rofe water.

Phallax.

But heare me, canft thou heale a greene wound well?

Rofko.

Yea, greene and ould.

Phallax.

Then thy beft were to dwel
In fome ufuall place or ftreete, where through frayes
Thou mayft be fet a worke with wounds alwayes.

Rofko.

I thanke my Miftris I have my hands full,
To trym gentelmen of her acquayntaunce;
And I truft, Syr, that if your worfhip chaunce
To have neede of my helpe, I fhall earne your mony
Afore an other.

Phallax.

That thou fhalt truly.
But fyrra, where dwels *Lamia?*

Rofko.

Even heare Syr, enter I pray.

Phallax.

That I wyl fure, if that my way be cleare.

      D
                                            Rofko.

Rosko.

Yes Sir, her doores be open all the yeare.   [*Exeunt.*

ACTUS V.   SCENA III.

Polina *(the mayde that* Andrugio *lov'd) in a blew gowne.*

Polina.

Polina curſt, what dame alyve hath cauſe of griefe lyke thee,
Who, (wonne by love) haſt yeeld the ſpoyle of thy virginity?
And he for to repayre thy fame, to marry thee that vowde,
Is done to death for firſt offence the ſecond mends not lowde.
Great ſhame redounds to thee, o love, in leaving us in thrall;
Andrugio and *Polina* both, in honoryng thee did falle.
Thou ſo didſt wytch our wits, as we from reaſon ſtrayed
    quight,
Provockt by thee we dyd refuſe no vauntage of delight.
Delight! what did I ſay? nay death, by raſh and fowle abuſe,
Alas I ſhame to tell thus much, though love doe worke excuſe.
So that (fayre dames) from ſuch conſent, my accydents of
    harme
Forewarneth you to keepe aloofe though love your harts do
    arme.
But ah *Polina*, whether runnes thy words into adviſe,
When others harmes, in forſt by love, could never make the
    wiſe.
The cauſe is plaine, for that in love no reaſon ſtands in ſteade,
And reaſon is the only meane, that others harmes we dreade.
Then, that the world hereafter may to love inferre my yll,
Andrugios tombe with dayly teares *Polina* worſhip wyll:
And furthermore I vowde whylſt life in me doth foſter breth
No one ſhall vaunt of conquered love by my *Andrugios* death.
Theſe ſhameful weedes which forſt I were, that men my fault
    may know,
Whilſt that I live ſhall ſhow I morne for my *Andrugio.*
I wyll not byde the ſharpe aſſaultes from ſugred words yſent,
I wyll not truſt to careles othes which often wyn conſent:
I wyll cut off occaſions all which hope of myrth may move;
With ceaſeles teares yle quench each cauſe that kindleth coles
    of love:

                                                    And

And thus tyl death, *Polina* wyll ettraunge her felfe from joy,
Andrugio to reward thy love which dyd thy life deftroy. [*Exit.*

ACTUS V. SCENA IV.

Rofko *alone.*

Rofko.

A Syr, in fayth, the cafe is altred quight,
My miftris late that lived in wretched plight
Byds care adue and every caufe of woe,
The feare is fled that made her forrow fo.
Mafter *Phallax* fo underprops her fame
As none for lyfe dare now her lewdnes blame.
I feare (nay hope) fhe hath bewicht him fo
As haulfe his brybes unto her fhare will goe:
No force for that; who others doth deceyve
Deferves himfelfe lyke meafure to receyve.
Well, leave I *Lamia*, for herfelfe to pray
Better then I can fhewe who knowes the way.
It ftands me on for my poore felfe to fhyfte,
And I have founde a helpe at a dead lyfte.
My ould friend *Grimball's* purce with pence is full,
And if I empty it not, *Dalia* wull.
The flavering foole, what he can rap and rend
(He loves her fo) upon the fylth wyll fpend:
But bye your leave, yle barre her of this match,
My net and all is fet, the foole to catch.
Forfooth before his amorous fute he move
He muft be trim'd to make her more to love
And in good footh the world fhal hardly fall
But that he fhal be wafht, pould, fhavd and all.
And fee the luck, the foole is faft I know,
In that with *Rowke* he doth fo fadly goe.

SCENA V. Grymball, Rowke, Rofko.

Grymball.

God bores, as fayft, when fomewhat handfome ch'am,
I faith fhe wyll come off for very fhame.

Rowke.

Rowke.

Yea without doubt, for I fweare by Saint *Anne*
My felfe loves you, you are fo cleane a young man.

Grimball.

Nay, thou woult fay fo when my face is fayre wafht.

Rofko.

Good luck a Gods name, the wodcocke is mafht.

Rowke.

And who barbes ye *Grimball* ?

Grimball.

A dapper knave, one *Rofko.*

Rofko.

Well letherface ; we fhall have you affe, ere you goe.

Rowke.

I know him not : is he a deaft barber?

Grimball.

O yea, why he is Miftris *Lamia's* Powler :
And looke fyrra, yen is the lyttel knave.
How doft *Rofko* ?

Rofko.

Whope, my eye fight God fave
What ould *Grimball!* welcome, fit you downe heare.
Boye.

Boy.

Anon.

Rofko.

Bay leaves in warme water, quick, bring cleane   *Boy in the*
        geare.   *Houfe.*

Boy.

Strayght.

Rowke.

As thou faydft *Grimball*, this is a feate knave indeede.

Rofko.

How fay' Syr ? oyntments for a fcab do you neede?

Rowke.

Scab ! fcurvy Jack ! Ile fet you a worke Syr.

Grimball.

Nay Gogs foote, good nowe, no more of this ftur.

Rowke.

I faith Barber, I wyll pyck your teeth ftraight.

                                            Rofko.

Rofko.

Nay, to pick my purfe I feare thou doft wayght.

Rowke.

Yea Gogs hart.

Grimball.

Nay, Gogs foote.

Rofko.

Nowe come Ruffen.

Grimball.

Leave, if you be men,
Heare ye me now? be friendes, and by my trothe,
Chill fpende a whole quarte of ale on you bothe.

Rofko.

Well Maffe *Grimball*, I lytle thought I wus,
You would a brought a knave to ufe mee thus.

Grimball.

Why, knoweft him not? why it is luftie *Rowke.*

Rofko.

A ftrong theefe, I warrant him by his looke.

Rowke.

Go to, no more, Barber, leaft copper you catch.

Grimball.

What wilt give thy nofe awaye? beware that match.
For chy fee no copper unleft be there.

Boy.

Mafter, here is delicate water and cleane geare.   *Boy brings*

Rofko.   *water.*

Well to quiet my houfe, and for *Grimball's* fake,
If it pleafeth you as friendes, we hands will fhake.

Grimball.

I, I, do fo.

Rowke.

And for his fake I agree.

Grimball.

Well then that we may drinke, ftraight wayes wafh mee.

Rofko.

Good Syr, here's water as fweete as a rofe.
Now whyles I wafh, your eyes harde you muft clofe.

Grimball.

Thus?

D 3

Rofko.

Rosko.

Harder yet.

Grimball.

O, thus.

Rosko.

Yea marry so.
Howe syrra, you knowe what you have to doe,

Rowke, *cuttes* Grimball's *purse.*

Rosko.

Winke harde, *Grimball.*

Grimball.

Yes, yes, I shall.

Rowke.

Heare's the toothpick and all.   [*Exit.*

Rosko.

Departe then, tyll I call.
Verie well Syr, your face is gayly cleane ;
Were your teeth nowe pickt, you maye kisse a queane.

Grimball.

Sayst thou mee so ? Good nowe dispatch and awaye :
I even fyssill untyl I smouch *Dalia.*

Rosko.

O doo you so ? I am right glad you tell :
I else had thought, tad bene your teethe dyd smell.

Grimball.

O Lorde, gogs foote, you picke me to the quicke.

Rosko.

Quiet yourselfe, your teeth are furred thicke.

Grimball.

O, oh no more : O God, I spattel blood.

Rosko.

I have done : spyt out ; this doth you much good.
Boye.

Boy.

Anon.   *Boy within.*

Rosko.

Bring the drinke in the porringer,
To gargalis his teeth.

Boy.

Boy.

It is here, Syr. [*Exit.*

Rosko.

Wash your teeth with this, good maister *Grimball.*

Grimball.

I am poyfoned ; ah, it is bytter gall.

Rosko.

Eate thefe Comfyts, to fweeten your mouth with all.

Grimball.

Yea mary Syr, thefe are gay fugred geare.

Rosko.

Their fweetneffe ftraight wyll make you ftinke I feare.

Grimball.

Well nowe, what muft I paye, that chy were gone.

Rosko.

What you wyll.

Grimball.

Sayft me fo ? O cham undone.

Rosko.

Howe nowe *Grimball ?*

Grimball.

O Leard, my purfe is cutte.

Rosko.

When ? where ?

Grimball.

Nowe, here.

Rosko.

Boye, let the doore be fhutte :
If it be here we wyll ftraight wayes fee.
Where's he that came with you ?

Grimball.

I can not tell.

Rosko.

What is hee ?

Grimball.

I knowe not.

Rosko.

Where doth he dwell ?

Grimball.

O Leard, I ken not I.

D 4

Rosko.

Rosko.

You have done well :
This knave, your pence in his pocket hath purst :
Let's seeke him out.

Grimball.

Nay hearke, I muft neades tirft.
O Leard, Learde, cham ficke : my belly akes too too.

Rosko.

Thou lookft yll : well Yle tell thee what to doo.
Since thou art fo ficke, ftraight wayes get thee home,
To finde this Jacke my felfe abroade wyll rome :
The rather, for that he playde the Knave with mee.

Grimball.

Cham ficke in deede, and therfore ych thanke thee.

Rosko.

I fee fometime the blinde man hits a crowe;
He maye thanke me that he is plagued foe.

Grimball.

Well, well, *Dalia,* the love ych bare to thee
Hath made me ficke and pickt my purfe from mee.   [*Exit.*

Rosko.

A, is he gone ? a foole company him :
In good footh Sir, this match fadged trim.
Well I will trudge to find my feilewe *Rowke,*
To fhare the price that my devife hath tooke.   [*Exit.*

ACTUS V.   SCENA VI.

Caffandra *in blacke.*

Caffandra.

The heavy chardge that Nature byndes me to
I have perform'd ; ingrav'd my brother is :
I woulde to God (to eafe my ceafeles woo)
My wretched bones intombed were with his,
But o in vaine this bootelefle wifh I ufe,
I, poore I muft lyve in forrowe joynde with fhame.
And fhall he lyve that dyd us both abufe ?
And quench, through rule, the coles of juft revenge?

O no :

O no: I wyll nowe hye me to the King,
To whom I wyll recount my wretched ſtate ;
Lewde *Promos* rape, my brother's death, and all :
And (though with ſhame I maye this tale relate)
To proove that force enforced me to fall.
When I have ſhowne Lorde *Promos* fowle miſdeedes,
This knife, foorthwith ſhall end my woe and ſhame :
My gored harte which at his feete then bleedes,
To ſcorge his faultes, the Kyng wyll more inflame.
In deedes to doo that I in woordes pretende,
I now adviſe my journey to the King :
Yet ere I go, as ſwans ſing at their ende
In ſolemne ſong I meane my knell to ryng.

Caſſandraes *Song*.

Sith fortune thwart doth croſſe my joyes with care,
   Sith that my bliſſe is chaungde to bale by fate ;
Sith frowarde chaunce my dayes in woe doth weare,
   Sith I, alas, muſt mone without a mate ;
I wretch have vowde to ſing both daye and night,
O ſorrowe, ſlaye all motions of delight !

Come, grieſlie griefe, torment this harte of mine,
   Come, deepe diſpaire, and ſtoppe my loathed breath ;
Come, wretched woe, my thought of hope to pine,
   Come, cruell care, preferre my ſute to death :
Death, ende my wo, which ſing both daye and night,
O ſorrowe, ſlaye all motions of delight !   [*Exit.*

G. W.

F I N I S.

THE

S E C O N D E   P A R T

OF THE FAMOUS

H I S T O R I E

OF

PROMOS and CASSANDRA:

Set forth in a Comicall Discourse.

By GEORGE WHETSTONE Gent.

Formæ nulla Fides.

THE

SECONDE PARTE

OF THE

HISTORIE

OF

PROMOS AND CASSANDRA

ACTUS I.   SCENA I.

Polina *in a blewe Gowne, shadowed with a blacke Sarcenet, going to the Temple to praye upon* Andrugio's *Tombe.*

PROMISE is debt, and I my vowe have paît
    Andrugio's tombe to wafh with daylie teares ;
Which facrifice (although God wot, in wafte)
I wyll performe ; my altar is of cares.
Of fuming fighes my offring incence is,
My pittious playntes in fteede of prayers are :
Yea, woulde to God, in penaunce of my mys,
I with the reft, my loathed lyfe might fhare !
But oh in vaine I wifh this welcomde ende ;
Death is to flowe to flaye the wretched wight :
And all to foone he doth his forces bende
To wounde their hartes which wallowe in delight.

5

Yet

Yet in my eare ftyll goes my paffing bell,
So ofte as I *Andrugio's* death doo minde,
So ofte as men with poynted fingers tell
Their friendes my faultes which by my weedes they finde.
But oh the caufe with death which threats me moft,
I wifh to dye, I dye through wretched woe;
My dying harte defires to yeelde the ghoft,
My traunces ftraunge a prefent death forefhewe.
But as the reede doth bow at every blaft,
To breake the fame when rowgheft ftormes lackes might,
So wretched I with every woe doe wafte,
Yet care wants force to kyll my hart outryght.
O gratious God, and is my gilt fo great
As you the fame with thoufand deathes muft wreake?
You will it fo, elfe care I could intreate,
With halfe theie woes my thryd of lyfe to breake.
But what meanft thou, *Polina* moft accurft?
To mufe why God this pennaunce joynes thee to?
Whofe correction, although we take at worft,
To our great good he doth the fame beftow.
So that, fyth greefe can not relyve my friend,
Syth fcorching fighes my forrowes cannot drye,.
Syth care himfelfe lackes force my lyfe to ende,
Syth ftyll I lyve that every howre doe dye;
Syth mighty God appoyntes my pennaunce fo,
In mornefull fong I wy'll my patience fhow.

Polina's *Song.*

Amyd my bale, the lightning joy that pyning care doth bring,
With patience cheares my heavy hart, as in my woes I fing.
I know my gilt, I feele my fcurge, my eafe is death I fee;
And care (I fynde) by pecemeale weares my hart to fet me
        free.

O care, my comfort and refuge, feare not to worke thy wy'll;
With patience I thy corfives byde; feede on my life thy fyll:
Thy appetyte with fyghes and teares I dayly wyl procure,
And wretched I will vaile to death, throw when thou wilt
        thy Lure.   [*Exit* Polina.

                              A C T U S

ACTUS I.   SCENA II.

Enter a Meffenger from the King.

I have at length (though weery come in troth)
Obtaynd a fight of *Julio's* ftately walles :
A king's meffage can not be done in floth :
Whome he bids goe, muft runne through myre and dyrt :
And I am fent to Lord *Promos* in poft
To tell him that the King wy'll fee him ftrayght ;
But much I feare that *Promos* needes not boft
Of any gayne by his foveraignes receyte.
But *Holla* tongue, of lavyfh fpeeche beware.
Though fubjects oft in Princes' meaning prye
They muft their wordes and not their myndes declare:
Unto which courfe I wyll my tongue apply,
Lord *Promos* fhall my Prince's comming know,
My Prince himfelfe the caufe thereof fhall fhow.   [*Exit.*

ACTUS I.   SCENA III.

Rofko, Lamia's *man.*

Rofko.

Ift poffible that my miftris *Lamia*
Over the fhooes fhould b'yn love with *Phallax ?*
Why, by I—(as fhe her felfe doth faye)
With pure good wyll her harte doth melt lyke waxe :
And this I am fure, every howre they themfelves
By their fweete felves, or by their letters greete :
But the fport is, to fee the loving elves
Byll together when they in fecret meete.
She lowres, he lauffes, fhe fyghes throwe pure love;
Nay, nay, fayes he (good pugges) no more of this :
Well, fayes fhee, and weepes, my griefe you do   *The ftrumpets*
        not prove :   *and croco-*
Then ftrayght this ftorme is cleared with a kys.   *diles alyke.*
And then a both fides three wordes and a fmouch ;
Within her eare then whifpereth this flouch,

                                                       And

And by the way he ftumbleth on her lyppes.
Thus eyther ftryves moft loving fignes to fhow;
Much good do it them, fyth they are both content:
Once I am fure, how fo the game doth goe.
I have no caufe their lyking to repent.
I fyldome doe between them meffage beare,
But that I have an Item in the hande:
Well, I muft trudge to doe a certain chare,
Which, take I tyme, cocke for my gayne doth ftand.

ACTUS I.   SCENA IV.

Phallax. Dowfon, *a Carpenter*.

Phallax.

Difpatch *Dowfon*; up with the frame quickly;
So fpace your roomes, as the nyne worthyes may
Be fo inftauld as beft may pleafe the eye.
Dowfon.

Very good, I fhall.
Phallax.

Nay, foft; *Dowfon*, ftay:
Let your man, at Saint *Annes* croffe, out of hande
Ereckt a ftage, that the Wayghts in fight may ftande.
Dowfon.

Wyll you ought elfe?
Phallax.

Soft a whyle: let me fee:
On Jefus gate, the foure vertues, I trow,
Appoynted are to ftand.
Dowfon.

I Syr, they are fo.
Phallax.

Wel then, about your charge: I will forefee
The Confort of Mufick well plaft to be.
Dowfon.

I am gone, Syr.   [*Exit.*

ACTUS

ACTUS I.   SCENA V.

The Bedell *of the Taylers*, Phallax.

Bedell.

Heare you, Maifter *Phallax?*
The Wardens of the Marchant Taylers axe
Where (with themfelves) they fhall their Pageaunt place?
Phallax.
With what ftrange fhowes doo they their Pageaunt grace?
Bedell.
They have *Hercules* of monfters conqueryng,
Huge great *Giants* in a foreft fighting
With *Lyons, Beares, Wolves, Apes, Foxes* and *Grayes,*
Baiards, Brockes, &c.
Phallax.
O wondrous frayes.
Marry Syr, fince they are provided thus
Out of their wayes, God keepe Maifter *Pediculus.*
Bedell.
You are plefaunt Syr, but with fpeede I pray
You aunfwere mee; I was charged not to ftay.
Phallax.
Becaufe I know you have all things currant,
They fhall ftand where they fhal no viewers want:
How fay you to the ende of Ducke Alley?
Bedell.
There all the beggers in the towne will be.
Phallax.
O, moft attendaunce is where beggers are:
Farewell, away.
Bedell.
I wyll your wyll declare.

E   ACTUS

A C T U S I.   S C E N A VI.

Phallax. *Two men apparrelled lyke greene men at the Mayor's feaſt, with clubbes of fyreworke.*

Phallax.

This geare fadgeth now that theſe fellowes peare:
Friendes where waight you ?

Firſt.

In Jeſus ſtreete to keepe a paſſadge cleare.
That the King and his trayne maye paſſe with eaſe.

Phallax.

O, very good.

Second.

Ought elſe, Syr, do you pleaſe ?

Phallax.

No, no : about your charge.

Both.

We are gone.   *[Exeunt.*

Phallax.

A Syr, heare is ſhort knowledge, to entertayne a kyng ;
But O, O, *quid non pecunia ?* yea at a dayes warning ?
The King in proviſion that thought to take us tardy,
As if we had a yeare bene warnd, ſhall by his welcome ſee.
I have yet one chare to do : but ſoft here is *Roſko*,
I muſt needes delyver him a meſſadge before I goe.

A C T U S I.   S C E N A VII.

Roſko.   Phallax.

Roſko.

I fayth I have noble newes for *Lamia.*

Phallax.

Nay ſoft, friend *Roſko*, take myne in youre waye.

Roſko.

Mayſter *Phallax*, O Syr I cry you mercy.

Phallax.

Phallax.

Rofko, with fpeede tell thy Miſtris from me,
The king ſtraight wayes wyll come to the Cytie,
In whofe great trayne there is a company
Within her houfe with mee ſhall mery be.
Thereforc, for my fake, wyll her to forefee
To welcome them, that nothing wanting be :
This is all I wyll, for want of leyfure.   [*Exit.*

Rofko.

I wyl not fayle Syr to ſhow your pleafure.
Mary, in fayth, thefe newes falles jumpe with the reſt,
They ſhal be welcome and fare of the beſt :
But although they well fyll their bodyes thus,
Their purfes will be dryven to a *non plus.*
No force a whyt, each pleafure hath his payne,
Better the purce then body ſtarve of twayne.
Well, I wyll trudge my welcome newes to tell,
But then abroade, good company to fmell.   [*Exit.*

ACTUS I.   SCENA VIII.

Corvinus *the King*; Caſſandra; *two Counfellors*, and Udiſtao
a young nobleman.

King.

Caſſandra we draw neare unto the Towne,
So that I wyll that you from us depart,
Tyll further of our pleafure you doe heare.
Yet reſt aſſured that wycked *Promos,*
Shall abyde fuch punifhment, as the world
Shall hould mee juſt, and cleare thee of offence.

Caſſandra.

Dread Soveraigne, as you wyl, *Caſſandra* goeth hence. [*Exit.*

King.

I playnely fee it tendes to great behove
That Prynces oft doo vayle their eares to heare
The mifer's playnt : for though they doe appoynt
Such as they thynke will juſtice execute,
Auƈthority is fuch a commaunder,

E 2

At

As whereas men by office beareth fway,
If they their rule by confcience meafure not,
The poore man's right is overcome by might :
If love, or hate, from juftice leave the judge,
Then money fure may overrule the cafe.
Thus one abufe is caufe of many moe,
And therefore none in judges ought to be.
How rulers wrong, fewe tales are tould the King :
The reafon is, their power keepes in awe
Such men as have great caufe for to complayne.
If *Caffandra* her goodes, nay life, prefer'd
Before revenge of *Promos* treachery,
I had not knowne his deteftable rape,
The which he forft to fave her brother's lyfe.
And furthermore, *Andrugio's* raunfome payde,
I had not knowne he put him unto death :
For when (good foule) fhe had this treafon tould,
Through very fhame her honour fo was fpoyld,
She drewe her knyfe to wound her felfe to death ;
Whofe pytious plyght my hart provockt to wrath
At *Promos* wyles.
So that, to ufe indifferency to both,
Even in the place where all thefe wronges were done,
Myfelfe am come to fyt upon the caufe.
But fee where *Promos* and the Mayor waight
To welcome mee with great folemnity.
With cheereful fhowe I fhaddowe wyll the hate
I beare to him for his infolency ;
Perhaps I may learne more of his abufe,
Whereby the more his punifhment may be.
Come my Lords, to the towne hafte we apace.
    All fpeake. We all are preft to wayght upon your grace.

ACTUS

ACTUS I.   SCENA IX.

Promos, Maior, *three* Aldermen *in red gownes, with a* Sworde bearer, *awayghtes the Kinge's comming.*

Promos *his briefe Oration.*

Promos.

Renowned King, lo here your faithful subjects preast to show
The loyall duetie which (in ryght) they to your highnesse owe.
Your presence cheares all sorts of us; yet ten times more we joye
You thinke us stoarde, our warning short, for to receyve a Roye.
Our wyll is such as shall supplie, I trust, in us all want,
And where good wyll the welcome geves, provysion syld is scant.
Loe this is all, yea for us all that I in wordes bestowe;
Your Majestie our further zeale in ready deedes shall knowe.
And first, dreade King, I render you the swoorde of justice heare,
Which as your lieutenant, I trust, uprightlie I dyd beare.

The King *delyvers the swoorde to one of his counsell.*

King.

Promos, the good report of your good government I heare ;
Or at the least the good conceyte that towards you I beare,
To incourage you the more in justice to perseaver,
Is the cheefe cause I dyd addresse my progresse heather.

Promos.

I thanke your Highnesse.

The Maior *presentes the* King *with a fayre Purse.*

Maior.

Renowned King, our ready wylles to showe
In your behalfe our goodes (nay lyves) to spende,
In all our names I freelie here bestowe
On your Highnes this Purse ; unto this ende

E 3   To

To poſſeſſe your moſt royall majeſtie,
In all our wealth therto bounde by duetie.

King.
Your great good wyls, and gyfts with thankes I take;
But keepe you ſtyll your goodes to do you good.
It is inough and all that I do crave,
If needes compels for your and our ſafety,
That you in part your proffers large performe;
And for this time, as outward ſhowes make proofe,
It is inough (and all that I deſire),
That your harts and tongues (alyke) byd me welcome.
All. Lord preſerve your Majeſty.

Five or ſixe, the one halfe men, the other women, neare unto the Muſick, ſinging on ſome ſtage erected from the ground. During the firſt parte of the ſong, the King faineth to talke ſadlie with ſome of his Counſel.

The Kings Gentleman Uſher.   Forwards my Lords.

They all go out leyſurablie while the reſt of the ſong is made an ende.

ACTUS II.   SCENA I.

Lamia *the Curtiſan.*

Lamia.
The match goes harde which rayſeth no man's gaine;
The vertue rare, that none to vice maye wreaſt:
And ſure, the lawe that made me late complaine,
Allureth me many a wanton geaſt.
Dames of my trade ſhutte up their ſhoppes for feare,
Their ſtuffe prov'd *Contra formam Statuti:*
Then I, which lycenſt am to ſell fine ware,
Am lyke to be well cuſtomed, perdy.

And

And nowe tyme ferves, leaft cuftome after fayle,
At hyeft rate my toyes I vallue muft :
Let me alone to fet my toyes to fale,
Yong Ruflers I, in faith, wy'll ferve of truft.
Who wayes me not, him wyll I fayne to love ;
Who loves me once, is lymed to my heart ;
My cullers fome, and fome fhall weare my glove,
And be my harte whofe payment lykes me beft.
And here at hande are cuftomers I trowe ;
Thefe are the friendes of *Phallax*, my fweete friende.
Now wyll I go, and fet my wares to fhowe,
But let them laugh that wynneth in the ende.   [*Exit.*

ACTUS II.   SCENA II.

Apio and Bruno, *two Gentlemen ftraungers* ; *with* Rofko.

Apio.
Come on good friende: where dwels Lady *Lamia?*
Rofko.
Even by, Syr.
Apio.
Well then, go thy waye.
Showe who fent us, and what our meaning is,
Leaft fhe, not knowing us, doo take amys
That thus boldlye we come to vifite hir.
Rofko.
No bolder then welcome, I warrant you Sir.
Bruno.
Well, thy meffage doo.
Rofko.
I go.   [*Exit.*

Fowre Women *bravelie apparelled, fitting finging in* Lamia's *windowe, with wrought fmockes and cawles in their hands, as if they were a working.*

The Quyre.

If pleafure be treafure.
E 4   *Apio.*

Apio.

Harke.

The golden worlde is here, the golden worlde is here.
Refufe you, or chufe you,
But welcome who drawes neare; but welcome who drawes neare.

Bruno.

They be the *Mufes* fure.

Apio.

Naye *Syrens* lure,

Firft fings. Here lyves delyght.
Second. Here dyes defpight.
Both.   Defyre here hath his wyll,

Third. Here loves reliefe
Fourth. Deftroyeth griefe
Laft two.   Which carefull hartes doth kyll.

Bruno.

Attende them ftyll.

Apio.

That, as you wyll.

Firft. Here wyfh in wyll doth care deftroye.
Second.   Playe here your fyll, we are not coye:
Third. Which breedes much y'll we purge annoy,
Fourth. Our lyves here ftyll we leade in joye.

The Quyre,

If pleafure be treafure,
  The golden worlde is here, the golden worlde
   is here:
Refufe you, or chufe you,
  But welcome who coms neare; but welcome
   who coms neare.

Firft. Wantons drawe neare,
Second. Tafte of our cheare,
Both.   Our cates are fine and fweete;

Third.

Third.	Come, be not coye
Fourth.	To worke our joye;
	We fall wyll at your feete.

Bruno.

A, good kinde wormes.

Apio.

Harke.

Firſt.	Loe here we be, good wyll which move
Second.	We lyve, you ſee, for your behove:
Third.	Come, we agree to let you prove,
Fourth.	Without a fee, the fruites of love.

The Quire all.

If pleaſure be treaſure, the golden worlde is here, &c.

Bruno.

Upon this large warrant we maye venter.
The doore opes alone; come let us enter.

Apio.

Agreede.

Enter a Sergeaunt *bearing a Mace, another Offycer with a Paper lyke a Proclamation; and with them the Cryer.*

Officer.

Cryer, make a noyſe.

Cryer.

O yes. *And ſo thriſe.*

Officer.

All manner of perſonnes here preſent —

Cryer.

All manner of perſonnes here preſent —

Officer.

Be ſylent, on payne of impriſonment.

Cryer.

Be ſylent, on payne of impriſonment.

The officer reades the Proclamation.

Corvinus, the hye and mightie King of Hungarie and Boemia: Unto all his loving fubjects of *Julio*, fendeth greeting;

And therwithall giveth Knowledge of his princelie favour towards every fort of them.

Firft, if any perfon, officer, or other, hath wronged any of his true fubjects by the corruption of brybes, affecting or not favouring of the perfon, through ufurie, extortion, wrong imprifonment, or with any other unjuit practife. His Majeftie wylles the partie fo grieved to repayre to Syr *Ulrico*, one of his Highnefle privie Counfell; who (finding his or their injuries) is commaunded to certifie them, and their proove unto the Kings Majeftie; where incontinentlie he wylle order the controverfie, to the releafe of the partie grieved, and the punifhment of the offenders.

Further, if any of his faithfull fubjectes can charge any perfon, officer, or other, with any notable or haynous offence, as Treafon, Murder, Sacriledge, Sedicion, or with any fuch notorious cryme; for the fafetie of his Royal Perfon, benefyte and quiet of his Realme and fubjectes, on Fridaye nexte, his moft excellent Majeftie (with the advife of his honorable Counfell) wyl in open Court fyt; to heare and determine all fuch offences. Therfore he ftrayghtlie chargeth all and everie of his fubjectes that knowe any fuch haynous offenders, on the forenamed daye that he prefent both the offender and his faulte. Dated at his Royall Court in *Julio*, the 6 of Februarie.

GOD fave the K I N G.   '   [*Exeunt.*

A C T U S II.   S C E N A IV.

Rofko.

Roflo.

See howe we are croft! we thought the King for pleafure
Came to vifite us: when to his paine
And our plagues, I feare he beftowes his leyfure
To heare the wronges of fuch as wyll complayne

4

Of

Of any man : But the fport is, to fee
Us officers, one looke of another ;
I at Lorde *Promos*, Lorde *Promos* at mee ;
The *Lawiers* at the *Shriefe* and *Maior :*
They gafe as much on the ruling Lawier ;
For to be plaine, the cleareft of all
Peccavi fing, to heare the grievous call
Againft ufurie, brybrie, and barrating,
Suborning, extorcion and boulftring.
Some faultes are hearde, fome by Proclamation ftaye,
Before the King to be hearde on Fridaye.
I yet have fcapte, and hope to go fcot free :
But fo, or no, whylft leyfure ferves mee,
To have my aunfwers frefh if I be cauld,
Of merry mates I have a meeting ftauld,
To whom, my fences to refrefh, I wend ;
Who gets apace as meryly may fpend.   [*Exit.*

ACTUS II.   SCENA V.

Sir Ulrico *with divers papers in his hand; two poore Cityfiens
foliciting complayntes.*

Ulrico.

As thou complaynft; agaynft all equity
Houldes *Phallax* thy houfe by this extremity ?
Firft.
Yea fure, and he hath bound me fo fubtylly
As leffe you helpe, lawe yeeldes me no remidy.
Ulrico.
Well, what fay you ? is *Phallax* mony payd ?
Second.
Save fyve pound, Syr.
Ulrico.
For which your bond is ftayde.
Second.
Nay mary, the fame I would gladly pay,
But my bonde for the forfeyt he doth ftay.

Ulrico.

Ulrico.

Summmum jus, I fee, is *fumma injuria.*
So thefe wronges muft be falved fome other way.

Firft.

Yea, more then this, moft men fay—

Ulrico.

What?

Firft.

To be playne, he keepes Miftris *Lamia.*

Ulrico.

Admyt he doe, what helpe have you by this?

Second.

Yes mary, it prooves a double knave he is,
A covetous churle and a lecher too.

Ulrico.

Well, well, honeft men, for your witneffe go;
And as on proofe I fynd your injuries,
So I wyl move the king for remedyes.

Both.

We thanke your honour.   [*Exeunt.*

Ulrico.

Tys more then ftraunge, to fee with honeft fhow
What fowle deceytes lewde officers can hyde :
In every cafe, their craite they collour fo,
As ftyll they have ftryckt lawe upon their fide.
Thefe cunning Theeves with lawe can lordfhips fteale,
When for a fheepe the ignoraunt are truft :
Yea, who more rough with fmall offenders deale
Then thefe falfe men to make themfelves feeme juft?
The tirant *Phallaris* was prayfed in this
When *Perillus* the brafen torment made,
He founde the wretch ftrayght wayes in fome amys,
And made him firft the fcourge thereof to tafte :
A juft reward for fuch as doe prefent
An others fault, himfelfe the guiltyeft man :
Well, to our weale, our gratious king is bent
To tafte thefe theeves to ufe what meanes he can.
But as at Cheaftes though fkylful players play
Skylleffe vewers may fee what they omyt,
So though our King in fearching judgment may

Geffe

Geffe at their faultes which fecret wronges commit,
Yet, for to judge by trueth, and not by ame,
Myfelfe in cheele his highneffe doth auctorife
On proofe for to returne who meryts blame,
And as I fynde, fo he himfelfe will punifh ;
So that to ufe my charge indyfferently,
My clyents' wronges I wyll with wytneffe trye.

As he is going out, Pimos, *a young Gentleman, fpeaks to him.*

ACTUS II.   SCENA VI.

Pimos.

Sir *Ulrico,* I humbly crave to know
What good fucceffe my honeft fute enfues.
Ulrico.
Mafter *Pimos,* in breefe the fame to fhowe,
I feare you both my order wyll refufe.
Lyros, that thinkes he geves more then he fhould,
And you, for that you have not what you would.
Pimos.
It fhall goe hard if that your award miflikes mee.
Ulrico.
Wel, goe with me, and you the fame fhall fee.
Pimos.
I waight on you.   [*Exeunt.*

ACTUS III.   SCENA I.

Phallax.

Phallax.

MY troubled hart with guiltyneffe agrev'd
Lyke fyre doth make my eares and cheekes to glow :
God graunt I fcape this blacke day unreprev'd,
I care not how the game goe to-morrow.
                                        Well,

Well, I wyll fet a face of braffe on it,
And with the reft upon the King attend,
Who even anon wyll heare in judgement fyt,
To heaven or hell fome officers to fend.
But foft, a pryze; *Gripax* and *Rapax* I fee,
A fhare of their venture belonges to mee.

ACTUS III.   SCENA. II.

Gripax, Rapax, *Promoters.* John Adroynes, *a Clowne;*
Phallax.

John.
Nay good honeft *Promoters*, let mee go.
Gripax.
Tufh *John Adroynes*, we muft not leave you fo:
What, an ould hobclunch a wanton knave.
You fhal to the King.
John.
Marry *John Adroynes*, God fave
The King: why he wyll not looke on poore men.
Rapax.
Yes, yes; and wyll fpye a knave in your face.
John.
Wyll he fo? then good you be gone apace.
Gripax.
And why?
John.
Leaft in my face he fpye you too.
Phallax.
Have you feene a dawe bebob two crowes fo?
Rapax.
Well, come awaye, Syr Patch.
John.
Leave, or by God yle fcratch.

They fawle a fighayng.
Gripax.
What wilt thou fo?
John.
Yea, and byte too.

Gripax.

Gripax.

Helpe *Rapax,* play the man.

John.

Nay, do both what you can.

Phallax.

If that in bobs theyr bargayne be,
In fayth they fhare alone for mee.

Rapax.

What byteft thou, hobclunch?

John.

Yea, that chull, and punch.

Gripax.

O Lorde God, my hart.

John.

Knaves, Ile make you fart.

Rapax.

Hould thy hands, Lob.

John.

Fyrft, take this bob.

Phallax.

To parte this fraye it is hye time I can tell,
My *Promoters* elfe of the roſte wyll fmell.

Rapax.

O, my neck thou wylt breake.

John.

Yea Gods ames, cryſt thou creake?

Phallax.

How now, my friends! why what a ftur is this!

Gripax.

Marry.

Phallax.

What?

John.

Eare they part, yle make them pys.

Phallax.

Houlde ; no more blowes.

John.

Knaves, this honeft man thanke
That you fcape fo well.

Phallax.

Phallax.

Friende be not to cranke ;
I am an officer, and meane to know
The caufe why you brauld thus, before I go ;
Your bobs fhow that the fame you beft can tell.

Rapax.

I would your worfhip felt the fame as well,
I then am fure this blockhed led flave
For both his faultes double punifhment fhould have.

Phallax.

What faultes ?

Rapax.

Marry.

John.

He wyll lye lyke a dogge.

Phallax.

How now ycu churle, your tongue would have a clog.
Say on.

Rapax.

To fhowe his firft and chiefeft faughte.
His father's maide and he, are naught.

John.

What I ?

Rapax.

I.

John.

By my Grandfire's foule, you lye.

Phallax.

Peace.
Friende, for this faulte thou muft dye.

John.

Dye ? Leard fave us you fqwade knave ; yle bum yee.
For reforming a lye thus againft mee.

Phallax.

Tufh, tufh, it helpeth not if they can prove this.

Gripax.

For fome proufe, I fawe him and the maide kys.

John.

Can not foke kys, but they are naught by and by ?

Phallax.

Phallax.

This prefumption, friende, wyll touch the fhrowdlie.
If thou fcape with lyfe, be thou fure of this,
Thou fhalt be terriblie whipped for this kys.

John.

Whypt! mary God fhielde ; chy had rather be hangde,

Rapax.

Growte nowle, come to the king.

John.

Art not well bangde?

Phallax.

Well, good fellowes, lets take up this matter.

Gripax.

Nay firft *John Adroines* fhal be truft in a halter.

Phallax.

Why, helpes it you to fee the poore man whypt?
I praye you, friendes, for this tyme let him goe.

John.

Stande ftyll, and chull whether they wyll or no.

Rapax.

Nay, but we charge him in the King's name, ftaye thee.

Phallax.

Harke, honeft man, I warrant thee fet free,
Greafe them well in their handes, and fpeake them fayre.

John.

O Leard God, our tallow potte is not here.

Phallax.

Tufh, clawe them with money.

John.

Who fo? my nayles are fharpe.

Phallax.

I fee, for Clownes *Pan's* pype is meeter then *Apollo's* harpe:
They can no fkyll in muficke but plaine fong.

Gripax.

I praye lets goe ; we tryfle tyme too long.

Phallax.

Strayght.
Cockes foule, knave, ftoppe his mouth with money.

John.

O, I ken you nowe Syr ; chi crie you mercie.

F

Rapax.

Rapax.

Come on, flouch, wylt pleafe you be jogging hence?

John.

Here is all; tenne fhyllinges and thyrtene pence.

Phallax.

Harke ye, my friendes.

Gripax.

We muft not let him goe.

Phallax.

Harke once more.

John.

Give them the money.

Phallax.

It fhall be fo.

Rapax.

Well, although he deferves great punifhment,
For your fake, for this tyme we are content:
John Adroines farewell; henceforth be honeft,
And for this faulte wyll paffe it ore in jeaft.   [*Exeunts*

John.

Then gives our money.

Phallax.

Why?

John.

Why they dyd but jeaft.

Phallax.

Yea, but they tooke thy money in earneft.   [*Exit.*

John.

Art gone? now the Dewle choake you all with it:
How chy kiffe againe the knaves have taught me wyt;
But by faint *Anne*, chy do fee burlady,
Men maye do what them woll that have money.
Ich furely had bene whipt, but for my golde,
But chull no more with fmouches be fo bolde.
Yea, and Ich wifh all lovers to be wyfe.
There be leaning knaves abroade have cattes eyes.
Why, by Gods bores they can bothe fee and marke,
If a man fteale but a fmouch in the darke.
And nowe the worlde is growne to fuch jollie fpye,
As if foke doo kyffe the'are nought by and by.

3

Well,

Well, ych wyll home, and tell my father *Droyne*,
Howe that two theeves robd mee of my coyne.   [*Exit.*

Enter the King, Promos, Ulrico, Maior, Gonsago, Phallax,
with two other attendantes.

King.

Sir *Gonsago,* if that we henceforth heare
With will, or wealth, you doe our subjects wrong,
Looke not agayne this favour for to fynde ;
We use this grace to wyn you to amende :
If not, our wrath shall feare you to offende.
God speede you.
                    [Gonsago *doth reverence and departeth.*

King.

I see by proofe that true the proverbe is,
Myght maisters right, wealth is such a canker,
As woundes the conscience of his maister,
And devoures the hart of his poore neyghbour :
To cure which sore, justice his pryde must pyne,
Which justice ought in princes most to shine :
And syth subjects lyve by their princes law,
Whose lawes in cheefe the rytch should keepe in awe.
The poore in wronges but sildome doth delyght,
They have inuffe for to defende their right.
It much behoves the maker of these lawes
(This mony findes in them so many flawes)
To see his lawes observd as they are ment,
Or else good lawes wyll turne to evyll intent.
Well, ere I leave, my poorest subjects shall
Both lyve and lyke, and by the richest stawl.

Promos.

Regarded and most mightie Prince, your clemency herein
Those harts your rule commands through feare, to faithful love
    shall win.

Ulrico.

Renowned King, I am for to complaine
Of *Phallax,* Lord *Promos* secondary,
Whose hainous wronges many poore men doth paine,
By me, who pray your highnes remedy.
                    F 2   King.

King.

My Lord *Promos*, it feemes you rule at large,
When as your clarkes are officers unjuft.

Promos,

Dread King, I thinke he can thefe wrong difcharge.

King.

Doe you but thinke Syr? a fure fpeare to truft,
A dum death and blynde judge can do as much.
Well, well, God graunt your owne lyfe byde the tuch.
Syr *Ulrico*, your complaynt continew.

Ulrico.

Gratious King, his wronges be thefe, in few.
Firft, *Phallax* is a common Barriter,
In office, a lewd extortioner.
The crafty man oft puts thefe wronges in ure
If poore men have that lykes his fearching eye;
He fhoweth gould the needy foules to lure;
Which if they take, fo faft he doth them tye,
That by fome bonde or covenaunt for fayted
They are in forft (farre beneath the vallew)
To let him have what his eye coveyted:
And for to prove that this report is true,
I fhowe no more then witnefie prov'd by oth,
Whofe names and handes defends it heare as troth.

[Ulrico *delivers the King a writing with names at it.*

King.

How now *Promos?* how thinke you of your man?
Ufe both your wyttes to cleare him if you can.

Promos.

Dread King, my hart to heare his faultes doth bleede.

King.

How farde it then to fuffer it indeede?
It dyde, I trow, or now you fpeake in jeft.
Thy mafter's mute, *Phallax*, I houlde it beft
That thou fpeake for thyfelfe.

Phallax.

I humbly crave
Of your grace, for aunfwere refpyt to have.

King.

King.

Why ? to devife a cloke to hyde a knave ?
Friend, *veritas non quærit angulos* ;
And if yourfelfe you on your truth repofe,
You may be bould thefe faultes for to deny ɣ
Some lyttel care upon their othes to lye.
See if any in your behalfe will fweare.

Phallax.

O Lord God, is there no Knyghtes of the pofte heare ?
Well then, of force I muft fing *Peccavi*,
And crye out ryght to the King for mercy,
  O King I am in faulte I muft confeffe,
  The which I wyll with repentaunce redreffe.

King.

Thy confeffion doth meryt fome favour,
But repentaunce payes not thy poore neyghbour ;
Wherefore, Syr *Ulrico*, his goods feafe you,
And thofe he wrong'd, reftore you to their due.

Ulrico,

Looke, what he gettes, moft thinke he waftes ftraight waye
Upon a leawde harlot named *Lamia :*
So that his goods wyll fcarfe pay every wight,

King.

Where naught is left, the king muft lofe his right.
Pay as you may, I hould it no offence
If eache pay fomewhat for experience.
But by the way, you rule the citty well
That fuffer, by your nofe, fuch dames to dwell.
And now, *Phallax*, thy further pennaunce ys,
That forthwith thou do refigne thy office.
Ulrico, to his account lykewife fee.

Ulrico.

It fhal be done.

King.

Phallax, further heare mee :
Becaufe thou didft thy faultes at firft confeffe
From punifhment thy perfon I releafe.

Phallax.

I moft humbly do thanke your majefty.

Promos.

Ah ! out alas ! *Caffandra* heare I fee.

Caffandra

Caſſandra *in a bleuve gowne ſhadowed with black*

Caſſandra.

O would the teares myght tel my tale, I ſhame ſo much my
    fall,
Or elſe Lord *Promos* lewdnes ſhowen, would death would ende
    my thrall!

Promos.

Welcome my ſweete *Caſſandra.*

Caſſandra,

Murdrous varlet, away!
Renowned King, I pardon crave for this my bould attempt
In preaſing thus ſo neare your grace, my ſorrow to preſent;
And leaſt my foe, falſe *Promos* heare, do interrupt my tale,
Graunt, gratious King, that uncontroul'd I may report my bale.

King.

How now *Promos?* how lyke you of this ſong?
Say on fayre dame, I long to heare thy wrong.

Caſſandra.

Then knowe dread Soverayne, that he this doome did geve,
That my brother for wantonneſſe ſhould loſe his head,
And that the mayde which ſin'd ſhould ever after lyve
In ſome religious houſe, to ſorrowe her miſdeede.
To ſave my brother jug'd to dye, with teares I ſought to
    move
Lord *Promos* hart to ſhowe him grace; but he with lawles love
Was ſyred by and by; and knowing neceſſity
To ſave my brother's lyfe, would make me yeeld to much,
He crav'd this raunſome, to have my virginitie;
No teares could worke reſtraynt, his wicked luſt was ſuch;
Two evils here were, one muſt I chuſe, though bad were very
    beſt,
To ſee my brother put to death, or graunte his lewde requeſt,
In fyne, ſubdude with naturall love, I did agree
Upon theſe two poyntes, that marry me he ſhould,
And that from priſon vyle he ſhould my brother free.
All this with monſtrous othes he promiſed he would.
But oh this perjurd *Promos* when he had wrought his wyll,
Fyrſt caſt me of, and after caus'd the Gailer for to kill

          My

My brother, raunfomde with the fpoyle of my good name:
So that for companing with fuch a hellifh feende
I have condemnde myfelf to weare thefe weedes of fhame,
Whofe cognifance doth fhewe that I have (flefhly) fin'd.
Loe thus, hie and renowned king, *Caffandra* endes her tale,
And this wicked *Promos* that hath wrought her endles bale.

King.

If this be true, fo fowle a deede fhall not unpunifht goe,
How fayft thou *Promos* to her playnte? arte giltye? yea or noe?
Why fpeakft thou not? a faulty harte thy fcilence fure doth
    fhowe.

Promos.

My gilty hart commaunds my tongue, O King, to tell a
    troth,
I doe confeffe this tale is true, and I deferve thy wrath.

King.

And is it fo? this wicked deede thou fhalt ere long buy deare.
Caffandra, take comfort in care, be of good cheere:
Thy forced fault was free from evill intent,
So long, no fhame can blot thee any way:
And though at full I hardly can content thee
Yet as I may, affure thyfelfe I wyl.
Thou wycked man, might it not thee fuffice
By worfe then force to fpoyle her chaftitie,
But heaping finne on finne againft thy oth,
Haft cruelly her brother done to death.
This over proofe ne can but make me thinke
That many waies thou haft my fubjectes wrongd;
For how canft thou with juftice ufe thy fwaie
When thou thy felfe doft make thy will a lawe?
Thy tyranny made mee this progreffe make
How fo for fport tyl nowe I colloured it,
Unto this ende, that I might learne at large
What other wronges by power thou haft wrought,
And heere I heare: the ritche fuppreffe the poore
So that it feemes the beft and thou art friendes:
I plafte thee not to be a partiall judge.
Thy offycers are covetous, I finde,
By whofe reportes thou over-ruleft futes:
Then who that gives an Item in the hande

In

In ryght, and wrong, is fure of good fucceffe.
Well, varlet, well, too flowe I hether came
To fcourge thy faultes, and falve the fores thou mad'ft.
On thee vyle wretche this fentence I pronounce;
That forthwith thou fhalt marrie *Caffandra*,
For to repayre hir honour thou dydft wafte;
The next daye thou fhalt lofe thy hated lyfe
In penaunce that thou mad'ft hir Brother dye.

Promos.

My faultes were great, O King, yet graunt me mercie,
That nowe with bloody fighes lament my finnes too late.

King.

Hoc facias alteri quod tibi vis fieri.
Pittie was no plee, Syr, when you in judgement fate:
Prepare your felfe to dye, in vaine you hope for lyfe.
My Lordes, bring him with mee: *Caffandra* come you in like
cafe;
My felfe wyll fee thy honour falv'd in making thee his wife,
The fooner to fhorten his dayes.

All the company.   We wayte upon your grace.

As the King is going out, a poore man fhall kneele in his waye.

King.

Syr *Ulrico*, I wyld commiffion fhould be made
To Syr *Anthony Alberto*, and *Juftice Diron*,
To heare and determine all futes to be had
Betwene Maifter *Proftro*, and this poore man: is it done?

Ulrico.

Renowned King it is ready.

King.

Repayre to Syr *Ulrico* for thy commiffion.

All. God preferve your Majeftie.

They all depart fave the Clowne.

Clowne.

Bones of me, a man were better fpeak to great Lords they
fee,
Then to our proude Juftlers of peace that byn in the cuntry.

He

He that is rytch, as my dame fayth, goes away with the hare :
This two yeere they have hard my matter, and yet cham nere
    the neere.
And at firft dafh, a good fatte Lorde, God in heaven fave his
    life,
Fayth, for nothing, teld the King of Mas *Proftros* and my ftryfe.
O Leard, ych thought the King could not bide or poore men
    to looke ;
But God fave his grace, at fyrft dafh, my fupplycation he tooke.
And you hard how gently he call'd mee poore man, and wild
    me goe
For my paffport, I kenne not what, to good Syr *Ulrico.*
Well, chull go for't, and hope to be with Mafter *Proftros* to
    bring ;
But ere ych goe, chul my Ballat of good King *Cornyne* fing.

The Clownes *Song.*

You barrons bolde and luftie lads,
   Prepare to welcome our good King,
Whofe comming fo his fubjectes glads
   As they for joye the belles doo ryng.
     They fryfke and fkippe in everie place,
     And happy he can fee his face,
     Who checks the rytch that wrong by might
     And helpes the poore unto his right.

The love that rygour gettes, through feare,
   With grace and mercie he doth wyn ;
For which we praye thus everie where
   Good Lorde preferve our King Corvin.
     His favour raignes in everie place,
     And happy he can fee his face.   [*Exit.*

ACTUS

ACTUS IV. SCENA I.

Grefco, a good fubftantiall Offycer; Two Beadelles in blew Coates, with Typeftaves.

Grefco.

COME loytring knaves, fpeede about your bufineffe;
Fetche mee in all ydle vacaboundes.

Firft.

Yes, Syr, yes.

Grefco.

Searche Ducke alley, Cocke lane, and Scouldes corner:
About your charge; lets fee howe you can fturre.

Second.

Yes, I have winges in my heeles to flee.

Firft.

Who gives two pence a ftraunge Monfter to fee?

Second.

What monfter?

Firft.

A horned beaft with winges upon his heeles.

Second.

Out, dronken dreule.

Grefco.

What! runnes your head on wheeles?
Be packing bothe, and that betymes, you were beft.

Firft.

We are gone, Syr; we dyd but fpeake in jeaft.

[*Excunt Beadelles.*

Grefco.

The King, I fayth, hath fet us all a worke,
To fearche odde holes where ydle varlettes lurke;
He fo nypped our *Maior* for yll rule,
As ever fince he hath bene lyke to whule;
And in a rage, the man is nowe fo whotte
As lewde perfonnes, tagge and ragge, goes to potte.

But

But in chiefe he ſtormes at fyne miſtriſſe *Lamia*,
She drinkes for all; come ſhe once in his waye:
And leaſt ſhe ſcape, myſelfe forſooth he wylles
Worſhipfullie to fetche hir with fortie Bylles.
Well, I muſt goe and worke our *Maior's* heaſt,
No force, for once ſhe wyll never be honeſt.   [*Exit.*

ACTUS IV.   SCENA II.

Andrugio, *as out of the wooddes, with Bowe and Arrowes, and
a Cony at his gyrdle.*

Andrugio.

This ſavage life were hard to brooke, if hope no comfort
    gave;
But I (whoſe life from tyrant's wrath God's providence did
    ſave)
Do take in worth this miſery, as penaunce for my mys,   ×
Stil fed with hope to chaunge this ſtate when God's good
    pleaſure is.
A hollow cave for houſe and bed, in worth *Andrugio* takes;   ×
Such ſorie foode as fortune ſendes, he ſyldome nowe forſakes.
I am my ſelfe forſoothe nowe butcher, cooke, cater and all,
Yea often tymes I fall to ſleepe with none, or ſupper ſmall.
Then in my denne I call to minde the lyfe I lyv'de in bliſſe,
And by the want, I freedome judge the greateſt joye that is.
The freeman is in viewe of friendes, to have releaſe in neede,
The exyle, though he have no lacke, yet lyves he ſtyll in
    dreede
That his myſdeedes wyll hardly ſcape the puniſhment of lawe,
And lyving he were better dead that lyveth in this awe.
Beſides this feare which never fayles the baniſht man in want,
As ofte he is, is ſure to finde his ſuccors verie ſcant.
Then who is he ſo mad, that friendes and freedome doth
    enjoye,
That wyll adventure breach of lawe, to lyve in this annoye?
And not annoye to him alone, but to his friendes and kyn:
                                                    Great

Great be the cares *Caſſandra* and *Polina* lyveth in,
Through thought of me whom long agone beheaded they
    ſuppoſe:
For my offence thus are they ſcorgde, yet dare I not diſcloſe
My ſafetie, for theer helpe: but harke! who commeth here?
This chaunce ſeemes ſtrange: God graunt good newes; I
    hope, and yet I feare.

John Adroynes, a Clowne: Andrugio.

John.

If che could finde my mare, che would be ruſty by the rood,
And cham ſure the hoorechup is peaking in this wood.
Chy wyl ſeeke every corner, but che wyll find her.

He whiſtlyng lookes up and downe the ſtage.

Andrugio.

This clowne can hardly mee bewray, and yet ſuch dunghyll
    churles
Such newes as is in market tounes about the country whorles.
What ſeekes thou, good fellow?

John.

My ſqawde Mare: doſt her know?

Andrugio.

No.

John.

Then ſcummer me not; in haſte ych goe
Seeke my mare, to ſee the ſport at *Julio.*

Andrugio.

What ſport?

John.

A lyttel ſport.

Andrugio.

What?

John.

Nay ſkyl not a whit?

Andrugio.

What meanes this aſſe?

I

John.

John.

T'wyll teache the hoorecup wyt.
H'yll hang handfome young men for the foote finne of love,
When fo his knavery himfelfe a bawdy Jack doth prove.

Andrugio.

His wordes feemeth ftraunge ; fomewhat is awry.

John.

Wel, chyll fee his fhoulders from's jowle to flye.

Andrugio.

Whofe fhoulders, friend ?

John.

As though you dyd know ?

Andrugio.

Whome ?

John.

Lord *Promos.*

Andrugio.

Yes, my moft accurfed foe :
But what of him ?

John.

Thou kenft.

Andrugio.

No.

John.

Sayft not, yes.

Andrugio.

Yes.

John.

So.

Andrugio.

But friend, thou took'ft my wordes amys,
I know nothing in what ftate *Promos* is.

John.

Thou know'ft and thou knoweft not : out horfon foole!
Leave ftealing Cunnyes and get thee to fcoole.
Farewell.

Andrugio.

Soft.

John.

O th' arte no foole, good theefe :
Save my mony, take my life.

Andrugio.

Andrugio.

Tufh, be breefe.
Some newes of lewde Lord *Promos* tell mee,
And wyth lyfe and mony, yle fet thee free.

John.

I wyll. Thou knowſt the King now at *Julio*.

Andrugio.

Very well.

John.

Thou canſt tell as wel as I.
Let me goe.

Andrugio.

Nay yle fee if thou doſt lye.
If thou doſt, yle whip thee when thou haſt done.

John.

Kiſſyng and lying, ich fee is all one,
And chave no mony, chul tell true therfore.

Andrugio.

Difpatch then.

John.

Then, lying Promoter, this more.
Caſgandra fcufde *Promos* of honeſtie,
And killyng *Ramfſtrugio* for baudry.

Andrugio.

What more?

John.

The King at *Promos* great pleaſure did take;
And *Caſgandra* an honeſt woman to make,
The King maunded him her ſtrayght to marry,
And for killyng her brother, he muſt dye.

Andrugio.

Is this true?

John.

Why how fay you? do I lye?

Andrugio.

Well, fo or noe, for thy newes have this connie.

John.

Gods bores, gave it me; to be fwete tis to cheape:
Burlady, yet tyll Sunday it will keepe.
Well, now, God bwye, Mas lying Promoter:
Weos fee at the fport?

Andrugio.

Andrugio.

I, peradventure.

John.

Since can not finde my mare, on foote chull go :
Ych thinke each daye a nowre to be at *Julio*.   [*Exit.*

Andrugio.

Straunge are the newes the Clowne hath showne to me ;
Not ftraunge a whyt, if they well fcanned be,
For God we fee, ftyll throwes the tyraunt downe,
Even in the heyght and pride of his renowne.
Lorde *Promos* rule, nay tyranny in deede
For Judges is a mirror worthy heede.
The wretched man, with fhowe of Juftice zeale
Throughly dyd with poore offenders deale.
The wicked man both knewe and judgde abufe,
And none fo much as he, her faultes dyd ufe.
He fellons hang'd, yet by extorcion ftoale ;
He wantons plag'd, himfelfe a doating foole :
He others checkt, for fuing for their right,
And he himfelfe mayntaynęd wrongs by might.
But fee the rule of mifchiefe ; in his pride
He headlong falles, when leaft he thought to flide.
Well, by his fall I maye perhaps aryfe :
Andrugio, yet in clyming be thou wyfe.
What ? ftyll unknowne fhall I live in this wood ?
Not fo.
Go wraye thefe newes, no doubt, unto my good.
Yet ere I go, I wyll my felfe difguife,
As in the towne, in fpite of linxes eyes,
I will, unknowne, learne howe the game doth go :
But ere I go, fyth eafed is my woe,
My thankes to God I fyrft in fong wyll fhoe.

Andrugio's *Song.*

To thee, O Lorde with harte and voyce I fyng,
  Whofe mercie great, from mone to fweete delight,
From griefe to joye my troubled foule doeft bring ;
  Yea more, thy wrath hath foylde my foe in fyght,
    Who fought my lyfe (which thou, o God, didft fave)
    Thy fcorge hath brought untimelie to his grave.

Whofe

Whofe griefe wyll gawle a thoufand judges moe,
 And wyll them fee themfelves, and fentence juft,
When blacke reproche this thundring fhame fhall fhoe,
 A judge condemde for murder, thefte and lufte.
   This fcorge, O God, the lewde in 'feare wyll bring;
   The juft, for joye, thy praifes lowde wyll fyng.

                                              [*Exit*

Grefco, *with three other, with bylles, bringing in* Lamia *prifoner.*

                Grefco.
Come on faire dame, fince faire words works no heede,
Now fowle meanes fhall in you repentaunce breede.
                Lamia.
Maifter *Grefco,* where you maye helpe, hurt not.
                Grefco.
And nothing but chaftment wyll helpe you to amende:
Well, I wyll not hurt you your lewdnes to defende.
                Lamia.
My lewdnes, Syr! what is the difference
Betwixt wantons, and hoorders of pence ?
                Grefco.
Thou haft winde at wyll, but in thy eyes no water:
Tho' arte full of grace : how fhe blufheth at the matter !
                Lamia.
Howe fample I your wyfe and daughter, Syr ?
                Grefco.
Axe mee, when whypping hath chaung'd thy nature.
                Lamia.
What whypping? why am I a horfe or a mare ?
                Grefco.
No ; but a beaft that meetelie well wyll bare.
                Lamia.
Indeede (as nowe) perforce I beare this flowt:
But ufe me well, elfe I fayth, gette I out
Looke for quittaunce.
                Byl.
Binde hir to the peace, Syr,   [*Firft Byl.*
So maye your worfhip be out of daunger.
                Grefco.
Bring hir awaye ; I knowe howe to tame hir.

                                              Lamia.

Lamia.

Perhaps, Syr, no: the worſt is but ſhame hir.
Byl.

Come ye drab.   [*Second Byl.*

Lamia.

Howe nowe ſcab! handes of my gowne.
Byl.

Care not for this; yuſe have a blew one ſoone. [*Third Byl.*
                                                 [*Exeunt.*

Caſſandra.

Caſſandra.

Unhappy wench, the more I ſeeke for to abandone griefe
The forder off I wretched finde both comfort and reliefe.
My brother firſt, for wanton faultes condempned was to dye,
To ſave whoſe life my ſute wrought hope of grace, but
    haples I
By ſuch requeſt my honor ſpoyld and gayned not his breath,
For which deceite I have purſude Lorde *Promos* unto death,
Who is my huſbande nowe become, it pleas'd our ſoveraigne ſo
For to repayre my craſed fame, but that which workes my wo
This day he muſt (oh) leſe his head my brother's death to
    quite,
And therin fortune hath, alas! ſhowne me hir greateſt ſpyte.
Nature wyld mee my brother love; now dutie commaundes mee
To preferre before kyn or friend, my huſband's ſafetie.
But O! aye me, by fortune I am made his chiefeſt foe,
Twas I, alas! even onely I that wrought his overthroe.
What ſhall I doo to worke amends for this my haynous deede?
The tyme is ſhort, my power ſmall, his ſuccors axeth ſpeede.
And ſhall I ſecke to ſave his blood that latelie ſought his lyfe?
O yea, I then was ſworne his foe, but now as faithfull wife
I muſt and wyll preferre his health, God ſende me good
    ſucceſſe,
For now unto the King I wyll my chaunged minde to expreſſe.
                                                  [*Exit.*

Phallax.

Phallax.

Was ever man ſet more freer than I?
Firſt went my goodes, then my Offyce dyd flye.

G   But

But had the King set me free from flattrie,
The next deare yeare I might have starv'd perdie.
But Lorde *Promos* hath a farre more freer chaunce,
He free from landes, goodes, and office doth daunce ;
And shall be free from life, ere long, with a launce.
The officers and chiefe men of *Julio*
Vengeaunce lyberall themselves lykewise shoe ;
Poore knaves and queanes that up and downe do goe
These horesen kinde crustes in houses bestoe :
But yet. poore cheere they have ; marry for heate
They whyp them untyl verie blood they sweate.
But see their cost bestowde of fyne *Lamia* ;
To save hir feete from harde stones and colde waye,
Into a carte they dyd the queane convaye,
Apparelled in colours verie gaye ;
Both hoode and gowne of greene and yellowe saye.
Her garde weare typstaves all in blewe arraye ;
Before hir a noyse of Basons dyd playe :
In this triumphe she ryd well nye a daye.
Fie, fie ! the citie is so purged nowe,
As they of none but honest men allowe ;
So that farewell my parte of thriving there :
But the best is, flattrers lyve everie where.
Set cocke on hoope ; *Domini est terra.*
If thou cannot where thou wouldst, lyve where thou maye.
Yes, yes, *Phallax* knoweth whether to go ;
Nowe God bwy ye all honest men of *Julio :*
As the devilles lykes the company of friers,
So flattrers loves as lyfe to joyne with lyers.

ACTUS V.   SCENA I.

Andrugio, disguised in some longe blacke cloake.

Andrugio.
These two dayes I have bene in court disguis'd,
Where I have learn'd the scorge that is devis'd

For

For *Promos* faulte ; he my fyfter fpowfed hath
To falve her fame crackt by his breache of fayth :
And fhortlie he muft lofe his fubtyll head,
For murdring me, whome no man thinkes but dead :
His wyll was good, and therefore, befhrewe mee
If (mov'd with ruthe) I feeke to fet him free.
But foftlie ; with fome newes thefe fellowes come :
I wyll ftande clofe, and heare both all and fome.

ACTUS V.   SCENA II.

Enter Ulrico, Marfhall.

Ulrico.

Marfhall, heare your warrant is ; with fpeede
The king commaunds that *Promos* you behead.
Marfhall.
Sir, his highneffe wyll fhal be forthwith done.
                                    [*Exit* Marfhall.
Ulrico.
The king welnye to pardon him was wonne,
His heavy wyfe fuch ftormes of teares did fhowre,
As myght with rueth have moyft a ftony hart ;
But *Promos* guylt dyd foone this grace devoure.
Our gratious king, before hir wretched fmart,
Prefer'd the helth of this our common weale.——
But fee, again to fue for him fhe comes ;
Her ruthfull lookes, her greefe, doth force me feele.
With hope, I muft her forrowes needes delay,
Tyll *Promos* be difpatcht out of the way.

ACTUS V.   SCENA   III.

Caffandra.

Caffandra.
Syr *Ulrico*, if that my unknowne greefe
May move good mindes to helpe mee to releefe,
                    G 2   Or

Or bytter fyghes of comfort cleane difmayde,
May move a man a fhiftleffe dame to ayde,
Rue of my teares from true intent which flowe;
Unto the king with me yet once more goe.
See if his grace my hufband's lyfe wyll fave,
If not, with his death fhall my corps ingrave.

Ulrico.

　What fhall I doe, her forrowes to decreace?
Feede her with hope:—fayre dame, this mone furceafe;
I fee the king to grace is fomewhat bent,
We once agayne thy forrowes wyll prefent:
Come, we wyl wayght for tyme thy fute to fhow.

Caffandra.

　Good knight, for time do not my fute foreflowe;
Whylft graffe doth growe, ofte fterves the feely fteede.

Ulrico.

　Feare not; your lorde fhal not dye with fuch fpeede.

[*Exeunt.*

Enter Andrugio.

Andrugio.

　Lord God, how am I tormented in thought!
My fifter's woe fuch rueth in me doth grave,
As fayne I would (if ought fave death I caught)
Bewray myfelfe, Lord *Promos* life to fave.
But lyfe is fweete, and naught but death I eye,
If that I fhould my fafety now difclofe;
▓that I chufe, of both the evels, he dye:
Time wyll appeafe, no dought, *Caffandra's* woes.
And fhall I thus acquite *Caffandra's* love?
To worke her joy, and fhall I feare to dye,
Whylft that fhe lyve no comforte may remove
Care from her harte, if that her hufband dye?
Then fhall I ftycke to hafard lym, nay lite,
To falve hir grcefe, fince in my cure it refts?
Nay firft, I wil be fpoyld with blooddy knife
Before I fayle her plunged in diftres.
Death is but death, and all in fyne fhall dye:
Titus (being dead) my fame fhall live alway.

Well,

Well, to the king *Andrugio* now wyll hye,
Hap lyfe, hap death, his fafety to bewray.   [*Exit.*

ACTUS V.   SCENA IV.

The Marfhall ; *three or fowre with halbards, leading* Promos *to execution.*

Bylman.

Roome, friends ; what meane you thus to gafe on   *A Byl-*
us ?   *man.*
A comes behinde makes all the fport, I wus.

Promos.

Farewell, my friendes, take warning by my fall,
Difdaine my life but liften to my ende;
Frefh harmes, they fay, the viewers fo apall,
As oft they win the wicked to amend.
I neede not heare my faultes at large refyte,
Untimely death doth witneffe what I was,
A wicked man whiche made eache wrong feeme right ;
Even as I would was wrefted every cafe.
And thus, long tyme I lyv'd and rul'd by wyl ;
Whereas I lov'd, their faultes I would not fee :
Thofe I did hate, tenne tymes beyond there yll
I did perfue, vyle wretch, with cruelty.
Yea dayly I from bad to worfe did flyde,
The reafon was, none durft controule my lyfe ;
But fee the tall of mifcheeve in his pride :
My faultes were knowne, and loe, with bloddy axe   *k*
The headfeman ftrayght my wronges with death wyll quite ;
x The which in worth I take, acknowledging
The doome was geven on caufe, and not on fpyte ;
Withing my ende might ferve for a warning
For fuch as rule and make their will a lawe :
If to fuch good my faynting tale might tend,
Wretched *Promos*, the fame would longer draw ;
But if that wordes prevayle, my wofull ende
From my huge faultes, then tenne tymes more wyll warne.

                    G 3   Forgeveneffe

Forgevenefle now of all the world I crave;
Therwith, that you, in zealous prayer, wyll
Befeeche of God that I the grace may have
At latter gafpe, the feare of death to kyll.

Marfhall.

Forwards, my Lord ; me thinkes you fayntly goe.

Promos.

O Syr, in my cafe your felfe would be as flowe.

Enter Caffandra, Polina, *and one mayde.*

Caffandra.

Aye me, alas ! my hope is untimely.
Whether goes my good Lord ?

Promos.

Sweete wife, to dye.

Caffandra.

O wretched wench, where may I firft complayne,
When heaven and earth agrees upon my payne ?

Promos.

This mone, good wife, for Chriftes fake, forfake ;
I, late refolv'd, through feare of death now quake ;
Not fo much for my haynous finnes forepaft,
As for the greefe that prefent thou doft taft.

Caffandra.

Nay, I vile wretch. fhould moft agreeved be,
Before thy time, thy death which haftened have :
But (O fweete hufband) my fault forgeve mee,
And, for amends, Iie helpe to fyll thy grave.

Promos.

Forgeve thee, ah ! nay, for my foule's releefe,
Forget, fweete wyfe, this thy moft guyltles greefe.

Marfhall.

My Lord *Promos,* thefe playntes but move hir mone,
And your more greefe : it is beft you ware gone.
Good Maddame, way by lawe your Lord doth dye,
Wherefore make vertue of neceffity.

5   Delay

Delay but workes your forrowes and our blames:
So that now, to the comfort of thefe dames,
And your wifdome, inforced we leave you.
My Lord *Promos*, byd your wife and friends adew.

Promos.

Farewell, farewell; be of good cheare, deare wyfe,
With joy for woe, I fhall exchange this life.—
Andrugio's death, *Polina* forgeve mee.

Polina.

I doe, and pray the Lord to releeve yee.

Caffandra.

Yet ere we part, fweete hufband, let us kis :—
O, at his lyppes why tayleth not my breath?

Promos.

Leave mone, fwete wife; I doe deferve this death.
Farewell, farewell.

They all depart, fave Polina, Caffandra, *and her woman.*

Caffandra.

My loving Lorde, farewell.
I hope, ere long, my foule with thine fhall dwell.

Polina.

Now, good Madame, leave of this bootelefle griefe.

Caffandra.

O *Polina*, forrowe is my reliefe;
Wherfore, fweete wenche, helpe me to rue my woe;
With me, vyle wretche, thy bytter plaintes beftowe,
To hatten lyngring death who wanteth might
I fee, alone to fley the wretched wight.

Polina.

Nay firft powre foorth your playntes to the powers divine,
When hate doth clowde all worldly grace whofe mercies ftyll
    do fhine.

Caffandra.

O, fo or no, thy motion doeth well,
Swan lyke in fong to towle my pafling bell.

G 4

The

The Song of Caffandra.

Deare dames, divorfe your minds from joy, helpe to bewayle
 my wo ;
Condole with me whofe heavy fighs the pangs of death do
 fhoe :
Rend heairs, fhed teares, poore wench diftreft, to haft the
 means to dye,
Whofe joye, annoy ; reliefe, whofe griefe hath fpoyl'd with
 crueltie.

My brother flaine, my hufband, ah ! at poynt to lofe his
 head—
Why lyve I then unhappy wench, my fuckers being dead ?
O time, O cryme, O caufe, O lawes, that judgd them thus
 to dye,
I blame you all, my fhame .my thrall, you hate that harmeleffe trye.

This tragidy they have begun, conclude I wretched muft ;
O welcome care, confume the thread thereto my life doth
 truft :
Sound bell, my knell ; away delaie, and geve mee leave to
 dye,
Left hope have fcope unto my hart, afrefh for ayde to flye,

Enter Ganio *fometime* Andrugio's *Boye.*

    Ganio.
O fweete newes for *Polina* and *Caffandra.*
Andrugio lyves.
    Polina.
What doth poore *Ganio* faye ?
    Ganio.
Andrugio lyves and *Promos* is repriv'd.
    Caffandra.
Vaine is thy hope, I fawe *Andrugio* dead.
    Ganio.
Well then, from death he is againe revyv'd,
Even nowe I fawe him in the market ftead.
         Polina.

Polina.

His wordes are ftraunge.

Caſſandra.

Too fweete, God wot, for true.

Ganio.

I praye you, who are thefe here in your view ?

Caſſandra.

The King.

Ganio.

Who more ?

Polina.

O, I fee *Andrugio.*

Caſſandra.

And I, my Lorde *Promos* ; adue forrowe.

Enter the King, Andrugio, Promos, Ulrico, *the* Marſhall.

Polina.

My good *Andrugio !*

Andrugio.

My fweete *Polina !*

Caſſandra.

Lyves *Andrugio* ; welcome fweete brother.

Andrugio.

Caſſandra !

Caſſandra.

I.

Andrugio.

Howe fares my deare fyſter ?

King.

Andrugio, you fhall have more leyfure
To greete one another : it is our pleafure
That you forthwith, your fortunes here declare,
And by what meanes you thus preferved weare.

Andrugio.

My faulte through love, and judgment for my faulte,
Lorde *Promos* wronges unto my fiſter done ;
My death fuppofde, dread King, were vaine to tell,
Caſſandra heare thofe dealings all hath fhowne :

The

The reft are thefe.
When I fhould dye, the Gayler mov'd to ruth
Declard to mee what *Promos* pleafure was;
Amaz'd wherat, I tolde him all the trueth,
What betwene *Caffandra* and him dyd paffe.
He much agriev'd Lorde *Promos* guylt to heare
Was verie lo e, mee (woful man) to harme:
At length, juft God, to fet me (wretched) cleare,
With this defence his wylling minde dyd arme.
Two da es afore, to death were divers done,
For feveral faultes by them committed;
So that of them he tooke the head from one,
And to *Caffandra* the fame prefented,
Affirming it to be her brother's head.
Which done, by night he fent me poft away;
None but fuppofed that I indeede was dead,
When as in trueth in uncouth hauntes I laye.
In fine, a Clowne came, peaking through the wood
Wherin I lyvd, your Graces being here,
And *Promos* death by whom I underftood:
Glad of which newes, howe fo I lyv'd in feare,
I ventured to fee his wretched fall.
To free fufpect, yet ftraunger lyke arayde,
I hether came: but loe the inwarde thrall
Of *Caffandra* the hate fo fore difmayde,
Which I conceyved agaynft my brother *Promos*,
That loe I chews'd to yeeld myfelf to death
To fet him free; for otherwyfe I knew
His death ere long would fure have ftopt her breath.
Loe gratious King, in breefe I have here fhowne
Such adventures as wretched I have paft,
Befeeching you with grace to thinke upon
The wight that wayles his follyes at the laft.
King.
A ftrange difcourfe as ftrangely come to light;
God's pleafure is that thou fhouldft pardon'd be:
To falve the fault thou with *Polina* mad'it,
But marry her, and heare I fet thee free.
Andruzio.
Moft gratious Prince, thereto I gladly gree.

Polina.

Polina.

Polina! the happyeſt newes of all for thee.

Caſſandra.

Moſt gratious King, with theſe my joye to match,
Vouchſafe to geve my dampned huſbande lyfe.

King.

If I doo ſo, let him thanke thee, his wife.
Caſſandra, I have noted thy diſtreſſe,
Thy vertues eke, from firſt unto the laſt;
And glad I am, without offence it lyes
In me to eaſe thy griefe and heavines.
Andrugio ſav'd the juel of thy joye,
And for thy ſake I pardon *Promos* faulte:
Yea let them both thy vertues rare commende,
In that their woes with this delyght doth ende.

Company.

God preſerve your Majeſtie.

Promos.

Caſſandra, howe ſhall I diſcharge thy due?

Caſſandra.

I dyd but what a wife ſhould do for you.

King.

Well, ſince all partes are pleaſed as they woulde,
Before I parte, yet, *Promos,* this to thee:
Henceforth, forethinke of thy forepaſſed faultes,
And meaſure grace with Juſtice evermore.
Unto the poore have evermore an eye,
And let not might out countenaunce their right.
Thy officers truſt not in every tale,
In cheife, when they are meanes in ſtrifes and ſutes:
Though thou be juſt, yet coyne maye them corrupt;
And if by them thou doſt injuſtice ſhowe,
Tys thou ſhalt beare the burden of their faultes.
Be loving to good *Caſſandra* thy wife,
And friendlie to thy brother *Andrugio,*
Whom I commaund as faythfull for to be
To thee, as befeemes the duety of a brother.
And now agayne thy government receyve;
Injoye it ſo as thou in juſtice joye.
It thou be wyſe, thy fall maye make thee ryſe:

The

The loft fheepe founde, for joye the feaft was made.
Well; here an ende of my advife I make :
As I have fayde; be good unto the poore,
And juftice joyne with mercie evermore.

Promos.

Moft gratious King, I wyll not fayle my beft,
In thefe preceptes to followe your beheaft.

                                        · G. WHETSTONE.

                F I N I S,

Imprinted at London by *Richarde Jhones*, and are to be folde
over agaynft Saint Sepulchres Church, without Newgate.
Auguft 20, 1578.

M E N Æ C M I.

A pleasant and fine conceited

C O M Œ D I E,

Taken out of the most excellent wittie

P O E T *P L A U T U S.*

Chosen purposely from out the rest, as least harmefull,
and yet most delightfull.

Written in ENGLISH, by W. W.

L O N D O N,
Printed by Tho. Creede, and are to be sold by WILLIAM
BARLEY, at his shop in *Graticus-streete.*
1595.

The PRINTER to the READERS.

THE writer hereof (loving Readers) having diverse of this Poettes Comedies Englished, for the use and delight of h's private friends, who in Plautus owne words are not able to understand them: I have prevailed so far with him as to let this one go further abroad, for a publike recreation and delight to all those, that affect the diverse sorts of bookes compiled in this kind, whereof (in my judgement) in harmlesse mirth and quicknesse of fine conceit, the most of them come far short of this. And although I found him very loath and unwilling to hazard this to the curious view of envious detraction, (being as he tels mee) neither so exactly written, as it may carry any name of a Translation, nor such libertie therin used, as that he would notoriously varie from the Poets owne order: yet sith it is onely a matter of meriment, and the litle alteration therof, can breede no detriment of importance, I have over-ruled him so farre, as to let this be offred to your curteous acceptance, and if you shall applaude his litle labour heerein, I doubt not but he will endevour to gratifie you with some of the rest better laboured, and more curiously polished.

Farewell.

* Where you finde this marke, the Poets conceit is somewhat altred, by occasion either of the time, the country, or the phrase.

THE

THE ARGUMENT.

* *TWO twinborne fonnes, a Siciil marchant had,*
Menechmus one, and Sosicles the other:
The firft his father loft a litle lad,
The **Grandfire** *namde the latter like his brother.*
This (growne a man) long travell tooke to fecke
His Brother, and to Epidamnum came,
Where th'other dwelt inricht, and him fo like,
That Citizens there take him for the fame:
Father, wife, neighbours, each miftaking either,
Much pleafant error, ere they meete togither.

A pleafant

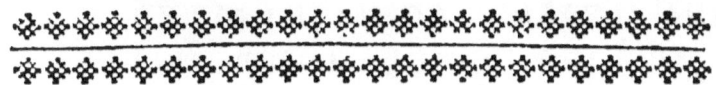

A pleasant and fine conceited

C O M Œ D I E,

CALLED

M E N E C H M U S,

Taken out of the moſt excellent

POET *PLAUTUS.*

ACT I.   SCENE I.

Enter Peniculus *a Paraſite.*

PENICULUS was given mee for my name when I was
yong, bicauſe like a broome I ſwept all cleane away,
where ſo ere 1 become : Namely all the vittels which are
ſet before mee. Now in my judgement, men that clap iron
bolts on ſuch captives as they would keepe ſafe, and tie
thoſe ſervants in chaines, who they thinke will run away,
they commit an exceeding great folly : my reaſon is, theſe
poore wretches enduring one miſerie upon an other, never
ceaſe deviſing how by wrenching aſunder their gives, or by
ſome ſubtiltie or other they may eſcape ſuch curſed bands.
If then ye would keep a man without all ſuſpition of running
away from ye, the ſureſt way is to tie him with meate, drinke
and eaſe : Let him ever be idle, eate his belly full, and
H caroufe

caroufe while his fkin will hold, and he fhall never, I warrant ye, ftir a foote. Thefe ftrings to tie one by the teeth, paffe all the bands of iron, fteele, or what metall fo ever, for the more flack and eafie ye make them, the fafter ftill they tie · the partie which is in them. I fpeake this upon experience of my felfe, who am now going for *Menechmus*, there willingly to be tied to his good cheare: he is commonly fo exceeding bountifull and liberall in his fare, as no marveyle though fuch gueftes as my felfe be drawne to his table, and tyed there in his difhes. Now becaufe I have lately bene a ftraunger there, I meane to vifite him at dinner: for my ftomacke mee-thinkes even thrufts me into the fetters of his daintie fare. But yonder I fee his doore open, and himfelfe readie to come foorth.

S C E N E   II.

Enter Menechmus·*talking backe to his wife within.*

If ye were not fuch a brabling foole and mad-braine fcold as yee are, yee would never thus croffe your hufbande in all his actions. 'Tis no matter, let her ferve me thus once more, Ile fend her home to her dad with a vengeance. I can never go foorth a doores, but fhee afketh mee whither I go? what I do? what bufines? what I fetch? what I carry? * As though fhe were a Conftable or a Toil-gatherer. I have pamperd her too much: fhe hath fervants about her, wooll, flax, and all things neceffary to bufie her withall, yet fhe watcheth and wondreth whither I go. Well fith it is fo, fhe fhall now have fome caufe, I mean to dine this day abroad with a fweet friend of mine.

Peniculus.

Yea marry now comes hee to the point that prickes me: this laft fpeech gaules mee as much as it would doo his wife; If he dine not at home, I am dreft.

Menechmus.

We that have Loves abroad, and wives at home, are miferably hampred, yet would every man could tame his fhrewe as well as I doo mine. I have now filcht away a fine
ryding

ryding cloake of my wives, which I meane to beflow upon one that I love better. Nay, if fhe be fo warie and watchfull over me, I count it an almes deed to deceive her.

Peniculus.

Come, what fhare have I in that fame?

Menechmus.

Out alas, I am taken.

Peniculus.

True, but by your friend.

Menechmus.

What, mine owne *Peniculus?*

Peniculus.

Yours (i'faith) bodie and goods if I had any.

Menechmus.

Why thou haft a bodie.

Peniculus.

Yea, but neither goods nor good bodie.

Menechmus.

Thou couldft never come fitter in all thy life.

Peniculus.

Tufh, I ever do fo to my friends, I know how to come alwaies in the nicke. Where dine ye to-day?

Menechmus.

Ile tell thee of a notable pranke.

Peniculus.

What did the Cooke marre your meate in the dreffing? would I might fee the reverfion.

Menechmus.

Tell me didft thou fee a picture, how *Jupiters* Eagle fnatcht away *Ganimede,* or how *Venus* ftole away *Adonis?*

Peniculus.

Often, but what care I for fhadowes, I want fubftance.

Menechmus.

Looke thee here, looke not I like fuch a picture?

Peniculus.

O ho, what cloake have ye got here?

Menechmus.

Prethee fay I am now a brave fellow.

Peniculus.

But hearke ye, where fhall we dine?

H 2

Menechmus.

Menechmus.

Tufh, fay as I bid thee man.

Peniculus.

Out of doubt ye are a fine man.

Menechmus.

What? canft adde nothing of thine owne?

Peniculus.

Ye are a moft pleafant gentleman.

Menechmus.

On yet.

Peniculus.

Nay not a word more, unlefle ye tell mee how you and your wife be fallen out.

Menechmus.

Nay I have a greater fecret then that to impart to you.

Peniculus.

Say your minde.

Menechmus.

Come farther this way from my houfe.

Peniculus.

So, let me heare.

Menechmus.

Nay farther yet.

Peniculus.

I warrant ye man.

* *Menechmus.*

Nay yet farther.

Peniculus.

'Tis pittie ye were not made a water-man to row in a wherry.

Menechmus.

Why?

Peniculus.

Becaufe ye go one way, and looke an other, ftil leaft your wife fhould follow ye. But what's the matter, Ift not almoft dinner time?

Menechmus.

Seeft thou this cloake?

Peniculus.

Not yet. Well what of it?

Menechmus.

Menechmus.

This fame I meane to give to *Erotium.*

Peniculus.

That's well, but what of all this?

Menechmus.

There I meane to have a delicious dinner prepard for her and me.

Peniculus.

And me.

Menechmus.

And thee.

Peniculus.

O fweet word. What, fhall I knock prefently at her doore?

Menechmus.

I knocke. But ftaie too *Peniculus,* let's not be too rafh. Oh fee fhee is in good time comming forth.

Peniculus.

Ah, he now lookes againft the fun, how her beames dazell his eyes.

Enter Erotium.

Erotium.

What mine owne *Menechmus,* welcome fweete heart.

Peniculus.

And what am I, welcome too?

Erotium.

You Sir? ye are out of the number of my welcome guefts.

* *Peniculus.*

I am like a voluntary fouldier, out of paie.

Menechmus.

Erotium, I have determined that here fhal be pitcht a field this day; we meane to drinke for the heavens: And which of us performes the braveft fervice at his weapon the wine boll, yourfelfe as captaine fhall paie him his wages according to his deferts.

Erotium.

Agreed.

Peniculus.

I would we had the weapons, for my valour pricks me to the battaile.

Menechmus.

Menechmus.

Shall I tell thee fweete moufe? I never looke upon thee, but I am quite out of love with my wife.

Erotium.

Yet yee cannot chufe, but yee muft ftill weare fomething of hers: what's this fame?

Menechmus.

This? fuch a fpoyle (fweete heart) as I tooke from her to put on thee.

Erotium.

Mine owne *Menechmus*, well woorthie to be my deare, of all deareft.

Peniculus.

Now fhe fhowes her felfe in her likeneffe, when fhee findes him in the giving vaine, fhe drawes clofe to him.

Menechmus.

I thinke *Hercules* got not the garter from *Hypolita* fo hardly, as I got this from my wife. Take this, and with the fame, take my heart.

Peniculus.

Thus they muft do that are right lovers: efpecially if they mean to be beggers with any fpeed.

Menechmus.

I bought this fame of late for my wife, it ftood mee (I thinke) in fome ten pound.

Peniculus.

There's tenne pounde beftowed verie thriftily.

Menechmus.

But knowe yee what I woulde have yee doo?

Erotium.

It fhall bee done, your dinner fhall be readie.

* *Menechmus.* .

Let a good dinner be made for us three. Harke ye, fome oyfters, a mary-bone pie or two, fome artichockes, and potato rootes, let our other difhes be as you pleafe.

Erotium.

You fhall Sir.

Menechmus.

I have a little bufineffe in this Cittie, by that time dinner will be prepared. Farewell till then, fweete *Erotium:* Come *Peniculus.*

Peniculu.

Peniculus.

Nay I meane to follow yee: I will fooner leefe my life,
then fight of you till this dinner be done.   [*Exeunt.*

Erotium.

Who's there? Call me *Cylindrus* the Cooke hither.

Enter Cylindrus.

Cylindrus, take this hand-bafket, and heere, there's ten fhil-
lings, is there not?

Cylindrus.

Tis fo miftreffe.

Erotium.

Buy me of all the daintieft meates ye can get, ye know
what I meane: fo as three may dine paffing well, and yet no
more then inough.

Cylindrus.

What guefts have ye to day miftreffe?

Erotium.

Here will be *Menechmus* and his Parafite, and myfelfe,

Cylindrus.

That's ten perfons in all.

Erotium.

How many?

Cylindrus.

Ten, for I warrant you that Parafite may ftand for eight at
his vittels.

Erotium.

Go difpatch as I bid you, and looke ye returne with all fpeed.

Cylindrus.

I will have all readie with a trice.   [*Exeunt.*

H 4   A C T

ACT II.   SCENE I.

Enter Menechmus Soficles Meſſenio *his ſervant, and ſome Saylers.*

Menechmus.

SURELY *Meſſenio*, I thinke Sea-fairers never take ſo comfortable a joy in any thing as when they have been long toſt and turmoyld in the wide ſeas, they hap at laſt to ken land.

Meſſenio.

Ile be ſworn, I ſhuld not be gladder to ſee a whole Country of mine owne, then I have bene at ſuch a ſight.   But I pray, wherfore are we now come to *Epidamnum?* muſt we needs go to ſee everie Towne that we heare off?

Menechmus.

Till I finde my brother, all Townes are alike to me : I muſt trie in all places.

Meſſenio.

Why then let's even as long as wee live ſeeke your brother : ſix yeares now have we roamde about thus, *Iſtria, Hiſpania, Maſſylia, Ilyria,* all the upper ſea, all high *Greece,* all Haven Towns in *Italy.*   I think if we had ſought a needle all this time, we muſt needs have found it, had it bene above ground. It cannot be that he is alive ; and to ſeek a dead man thus among the living, what folly is it?

Menechmus.

Yea, could I but once find any man that could certainly en-forme me of his death, I were ſatisfied ; otherwiſe I can never deſiſt ſeeking : Litle knoweſt thou *Meſſenio* how neare my heart it goes.

Meſſenio.

This is waſhing of a Blackamore.   Faith let's goe home, unleſſe ye meane we ſhould write a ſtorie of our travaile.

Menechmus.

Menechmus.

Sirra, no more of thefe fawcie fpeeches, I perceive I muft teach ye how to ferve me, not to rule me.

Meffenio.

I, fo, now it appeares what it is to be a fervant. Wel I muft fpeake my confcience. Do ye heare fir? Faith I muft tell ye one thing, when I looke into the leane eftate of your purfe, and confider advifedly of your decaying ftocke, I hold it verie needful to be drawing homeward, left in looking your brother, we quite lofe ourfeves. For this affure your felfe, this Towne *Epidamnum*, is a place of outragious expences, exceeding in all ryot and lafcivioufneffe : and (I heare) as full of Ribaulds, Parafites, Drunkards, Catchpoles, Cony-catchers, and Sycophants, as it can hold. Then for Curtizans, why here's the curranteft ftamp of them in the world. Ye muft not thinke here to fcape with as light coft as in other places. The verie name fhews the nature, no man comes hither *fine damno*.

Menechmus.

Yee fay very well indeed: give mee my purfe into mine owne keeping, becaufe I will fo be the fafer, *fine damno*.

Meffenio.

Why Sir?

Menechmus.

Becaufe I feare you wil be bufie among the Curtizans, and fo be cozened of it: then fhould I take great paines in belabouring your fhoulders. So to avoid both thefe harms, Ile keep it my felfe.

Menechmus.

I pray do fo Sir : all the better.

Enter Cylindrus.

* I have tickling geare here yfaith for their dinners: It grieves me to the heart to think how that cormorant knave *Peniculus* muft have his fhare in thefe daintie morfels. But what? Is *Menechmus* come alreadie, before I could come from the market? *Menechmus*, how do ye Sir? how haps it ye come fo foone?

Menechmus.

Menechmus.

God a mercy my good friend, doeſt thou know mee ?

Cylindrus.

Know ye ? no not I.   Where's mouldichappes that muſt dine with ye ? A murrin on his manners.

Menechmus.

Whom meaneſt thou, good fellow ?

Cylindrus,

Why *Peniculus* worſhip, that whorſon lick-trencher, your paraſiticall attendant.

Menechmus.

What *Peniculus ?* what attendant ? my attendant ? Surely this fellow is mad.

Meſſenio.

Did I not tell ye what cony-catching villaines you ſhould finde here ?

Cylindrus.

Menechmus, harke ye Sir, ye come too ſoone backe againe to dinner, I am but returned from the market.

Menechmus.

Fellow, here thou ſhalt have money of me, goe get the Prieſt to ſacrifice for thee.   I know thou art mad, els thou wouldſt never uſe a ſtranger thus.

Cylindrus.

Alas ſir, *Cylindrus* was wont to be no ſtranger to you. Know ye not *Cylindrus ?*

Menechmus.

Cylindrus, or *Coliendrus,* or what the divell thou art, I know not, neither do I care to know.

Cylindrus.

I know you to be *Menechmus.*

Menechmus.

Thou ſhouldſt be in thy wits, in that thou nameſt me ſo right ; but tell me, where haſt thou knowne me ?

Cylindrus.

Where ? even here, where ye firſt fell in love with my miſ-treſſe *Erotium.*

Menechmus.

I neither have lover, neither knowe I who thou art.

Cylindrus,

Cylindrus.

Know ye not who I am? who fills your cup and dieffes your meat at our houfe?

Meffenio.

What a flave is this? that I had fomewhat to breake the Rafcals pate withal.

Menechmus.

At your houfe, when as I never came in *Epidamnum* till this day.

Cylindrus.

Oh that's true. Do ye not dwell in yonder houfe?

Menechmus.

Foule fhame light upon them that dwell there, for my part.

Cylindrus.

Queftionleffe, he is mad indeede, to curfe himfelfe thus. Harke ye *Menechmus.*

Menechmus.

What faift thou?

Cylindrus.

If I may advife ye, ye fhall beftow this money which ye offred me, upon a facrifice for your felfe: for out of doubt you are mad that curfe your felfe.

Meffenio.

What a verlet art thou to trouble us thus?

Cylindrus.

Tufh, he will many times jeft with me thus.   Yet when his wife is not by, 'tis a ridiculous jeft.

Menechmus.

Whats that?

Cylindrus.

This I fay.   Thinke ye I have brought meate inough for three of you? If not, Ile fetche more for you and your wench, and fnatcheruft your Parafite.

Menechmus.

What wenches? what Parafites?

Meffenio.

Villaine, Ile make thee tell me what thou meaneft by all this talke?

Cylindrus.

Away Jack Napes, I fay nothing to thee, for I know thee not, I fpeake to him that I know.

Menechmus.

Menechmus.

Out, drunken foole, without doubt thou art out of thy wits.

Cylindrus.

That you fhall fee by the dreffing of your meat.   Go, go,
ye were better to go in and finde fomewhat to do there, whiles
your dinner is making readie.   Ile tell my miftreffe ye be
here.

Menechmus.

Is he gone ? *Meffenio* I thinke uppon thy words alreadie.

Meffenio.

Tufh marke I pray.   Ile laie fortie pound here dwels fome
Curtizan to whom this fellow belongs.

Menechmus.

But I wonder how he knowes my name.

Meffenio.

Oh Ile tell yee.   Thefe Courtizans affoone as anie ftraunge
fhippe arriveth at the Haven, they fende a boye or a wench to
enquire what they be, what their names be, whence they come,
wherefore they come, &c.   If they can by any meanes ftrike
acquaintance with him, or allure him to their houfes, he is
their owne.   We are here in a tickle place maifter : tis beft to
be circumfpect.

Menechmus.

I miflike not thy counfaile *Meffenio.*

Meffenio.

I, but follow it then.   Soft, here comes fomebodie forth.
Here firs, Marriners, keep this fame amongft you.

Enter Erotium.

Let the doore ftand fo.   Away, it fhall not be fhut.   Make
hafte within there ho : Maydes looke that all things be readie.
Cover the boord, put fire under the perfuming pannes : let
all things be very handfome.   Where is hee that *Cylindrus*
fayd ftood without here ? Oh what meane you fweet heart,
that ye come not in ? I truft you thinke yourfelfe more welcome to this houfe then to your owne, and great reafon why
you fhould do fo.   Your dinner and all things are readie as
you willed.   Will ye go fit downe ?

Menechmus.

I

Menechmus.

Whom doth this woman fpeake to?

Erotium.

Even to you Sir : to whom elfe fhould I fpeake?

Menechmus.

Gentlewoman, ye are a ftraunger to me, and I marvell at your fpeeches.

Erotium.

Yea Sir, but fuch a ftraunger, as I acknowledge ye for my beft and deareft friend, and well you have deferved it.

Menechmus.

Surely *Meffenio,* this woman is alfo mad or drunke, that ufeth all this kindneffe to me uppon fo fmall acquaintance.

Meffenio.

Tufh, did not I tell ye right? thefe be but leaves that fall upon you now, in comparifon of the trees that wil tumble on your necke fhortly. I told ye, here were filver tong'de hacfters. But let me talke with her a litle. Gentlewoman, what acquaintance have you with this man? where have you feene him?

Erotium.

Where he fawe me, here in *Epidamnum.*

Meffenio.

In *Epidamnum?* who never till this day fet his foote within the towne?

Erotium.

Go, go, flowting Jack. *Menechmus* what need all this? I pray go in.

Menechmus.

She alfo calls me by my name.

Meffenio.

She fmels your purfe.

Menechmus.

Meffenio, come hither : here take my purfe. Ile know whether fhe aime at me or my purfe, ere I go.

Erotium.

Will ye go in to dinner, Sir?

Menechmus.

A good motion ; yea, and thanks with all my heart.

Erotium.

Erotium.

Never thanke me for that which you commaunded to be provided for yourfelfe.

Menechmus.

That I commaunded?

Erotium.

Yea for you and your Parafite.

Menechmus.

My Parafite?

Erotium.

Peniculus, who came with you this morning, when you brought me the cloake which you got from your wife.

Menechmus.

A cloake that I brought you, which I got from my wife?

Erotium.

Tufh, what needeth all this jefting? Pray leave off.

Menechmus.

Jeft or earneft, this I tell ye for a truth. I never had wife, neither have I; nor never was in this place till this inftant; for only thus farre am I come, fince I brake my faft in the fhip.

Erotium.

What fhip do ye tell me off?

* *Meffenio.*

Marry Ile tell ye: an old rotten weather-beaten fhip, that we have failed up and downe in thefe fixe yeares. Ift not time to be going homewards thinke ye?

Erotium.

Come, come, *Menechmus*, I pray leave this fporting and go in.

Menechmus.

Well Gentlewoman, the truth is, you miftake my perfon; it is fome other you looke for.

Erotium.

Why, thinke ye I know ye not to be *Menechmus*, the fonne of *Mofchus*, and have heard ye fay, ye were borne at *Siracufis* where *Agathocles* did raigne; then *Pythia*, then *Liparo*, and now *Hiero*.

Menechmus.

All this is true.

Meffenio.

Meſſenio.

Either ſhee is a witch, or elſe ſhee hath dwelt there and knew ye there.

Menechmus.

Ile go in with her, *Meſſenio*, Ile ſec further of this matter.

Meſſenio.

Ye are caſt away then.

Menechmus.

Why ſo? I warrant thee, I can loſe nothing; ſomething I ſhall gaine, perhaps a good lodging during my abode here. Ile diſſemble with her an other while. Nowe when you pleaſe let us go in. I made ſtraunge with you, becauſe of this fellow here, leaſt he ſhould tell my wife of the cloake which I gave you.

Erotium.

Will ye ſtaie any longer for your *Peniculus*, your Paraſite ?

Menechmus.

Not I, Ile neither ſtaie for him, nor have him let come in, if he do come.

Erotium.

All the better. But Sir, will ye doo one thing for me ?

Menechmus.

What is that ?

Erotium.

To beare that cloake which you gave me to the Diars, to have it new trimd and altred.

Menechmus.

Yea that will be well, ſo my wife ſhall not know it. Let mee have it with mee after dinner. I will but ſpeake a word or two with this fellowe, then Ile follow ye in. Ho, *Meſſenio*, come aſide. Goe and provide for thyſelfe and theſe ſhip boyes in ſome inne; then looke that after dinner you come hither for me.

Meſſenio.

Ah maiſter, will yee be conycatcht thus wilfully ?

Menechmus.

Peace fooliſh knave, ſeeſt thou not what a ſot ſhe is; I ſhall coozen her I warrant thee.

Meſſenio.

Ay Maiſter.

Menechmus.

Menechmus.

Wilt thou be gone?

* *Messenio.*

See, fee, fhe hath him fafe inough now. Thus he hath
efcaped a hundreth Pyrates hands at fea; and now one land-
rover hath bourded him at firft encounter. Come away
fellowes.

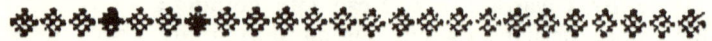

A C·T III.

Enter Peniculus.

TWENTIE yeares I thinke and more, have I plade the
knave, yet never playd I the foolifh knave as I have done
this morning. I follow *Menechmus,* and he goes to the Hall
where now the Seffions are holden; there thrufting our felves
into the preafe of people, when I was in midft of all the
throng, he gave me the flip, that I could never more fet eye
on him, and I dare fweare, came directly to dinner. That I
would he that firft devifed thefe Seffions were hang'd, and all
that ever came of him, 'tis fuch a hinderance to men that
have belly bufineffes in hand. If a man be not there at his
call, they amearce him with a vengeance. Men that have
nothing elfe to do, that do neither bid anie man, nor are
themfelves bidden to dinner, fuch fhould come to Seffions, not
we that have thefe matters to looke too. If it were fo, I had
not thus loft my dinner this day; which I thinke in my confcience he did even purpofely couzen me off. Yet I meane
to go fee. If I can but light upon the reverfion, I may perhaps get my penny-worthes. But how now? Is this *Menechmus* comming away from thence? Dinner done, and all dif-
pacht? What execrable luck have I?

Enter Menechmus *the Travailer.*

Tufh, I warrant ye, it fhall be done as ye would wifh.
Ile have it fo altered and trimd anew, that it fhall by no
meanes be knowne againe.

Peniculus.

Peniculus.

He carries the cloake to the Dyars, dinner done, the wine drunke up, the Parafite fhut out of doores. Well, let me live no longer, but Ile revenge this injurious mockerie. But firft Ile harken awhile what he faith.

Menechmus.

Good goddes, who ever had fuch lucke as I? Such chearc, fuch a dinner, fuch kinde entertainment? And for a farewell, this cloake which I meane fhall go with me.

Peniculus.

He fpeakes fo foftly, I cannot heare what he faith. I am fure he is now flowting at me for the loffe of my dinner.

Menechmus.

She tels me how I gave it her, and ftole it from my wife. When I perceived fhe was in an error, tho I knew not how, I began to foothe her, and to fay every thing as fhe faid. Meane while, I far'd well, and that at free coft.

Peniculus.

Well, I'le go talk with him.

Menechmus.

Who is this fame that comes to me?

Peniculus.

O, well met fickle-braine, falfe and treacherous dealer, craftie and unjuft promife-breaker. How have I deferved, you fhould fo give me the flip, come before, and difpatch the dinner, deale fo badly with him that hath reverenft ye like a fonne?

Menechmus.

Good fellow what meaneft thou by thefe fpeeches? Raile not on mee, unleffe thou intendft to receive a Railers hire.

Peniculus.

I have received the injury (fure I am) alreadie.

Menechmus.

Prethee tell me, what is thy name?

Peniculus.

Well, well mock on Sir, mock on; doo ye not know my name?

Menechmus.

In troth I never fawe thee in all my life, much leffe do I know thee.

I   *Peniculus.*

Peniculus.

Awake, *Menechmus*, awake; ye overfleepe your felfe.

Menechmus.

I am awake, I know what I fay.

Peniculus.

Know you not *Peniculus?*

Menechmus.

Peniculus, or *Pediculus,* I know thee not.

Peniculus.

Did ye fi'ch a cloake from your wife this mornírg, and bring it hither to *Erotium?*

Menechmus.

Neither have I wife, neither gave I my cloake to *Erotium,* neither filcht I any from any bodie.

Peniculus.

Will ye denie that which you did in my company?

Menechmus.

Wilt thou fay I have done this in thy company?

Peniculus.

Will I faÿ it? yea I will ftand to it.

Menechmus.

Away filthie mad drivell away; I will talke no longer with thee.

Peniculus.

Not a world of men fhall ftaie me, but Ile go tell his wife of all the whole matter, fith he is at this point with me. I will make this fame as unbleft a dinner as ever he eate.

Menechmus.

It makes mee wonder, to fee how every one that meetes me cavils thus with me. Wherefore comes foorth the mayd now?

Enter Ancilla, Erotium's *mayd.*

Menechmus, my miftreffe commends her hartily to you, and feeing you goe that way to the Dyars, fhe alfo defireth you to take this chaine with you, and put it to mending at the Goldfmythes, fhe would have two or three ounces of gold more in it, and the fafhion amended.

Menechmus.

Menechmus.

Either this or any thing elfe within my power, tell her, I am readie to accomplifh.

Ancilla.

Do ye know this chaine, Sir?

Menechmus.

Yea I know it to be gold.

Ancilla.

This is the fame you once tooke out of your wives cafket.

Menechmus.

Who, did I?

Ancilla.

Have you forgotten?

Menechmus.

I never did it.

Ancilla.

Give it me againe then.

Menechmus.

Tarry: yes I remember it: 'tis it I gave your miftres.

Ancilla.

Oh, are you advifed?

Menechmus.

Where are the bracelets that I gave her likewife?

Ancilla.

I never knew of anie.

Menechmus.

Faith, when I gave this, I gave them too.

Ancilla.

Well Sir, Ile tell her this fhall be done?

Menechmus.

I, I, tell her fo, fhe fhall have the cloake and this both togither.

Ancilla.

I pray, *Menechmus* but a litle jewell for my eare to making for me: ye know I am alwaies readie to pleafure you.

Menechmus.

I will, give me the golde, Ile paie for the workemanfhip.

Ancilla.

Laie out for me; Ile paie it ye againe.

I 2

Menechmus.

Menechmus.

Alas I have none now.

Ancilla.

When you have, will ye?

Menechmus.

I will. Goe bid your miftrefle make no doubt of thefe. I warrant her, Ile make the beft hand I can of them. Is fhe gone? Doo not all the Gods confpire to loade mee with good lucke? well I fee tis high time to get mee out of thefe coafts, leaft all thefe matters fhould be lewd devifes to draw me into fome fnare. There fhall my garland lie, becaufe if they feeke me, they may thinke I am gone that way. *I wil now goe fee if I can finde my man *Meffenio*, that I may tell him how I have fped.

A C T   IV.

Enter Mulier, *the Wife of* Menechmus *the Citizen, and* Peniculus.

Mulier.

THINKES he I will be made fuch a fot, and to be ftill his drudge, while he prowles and purloynes all that I have, to give his Trulles?

Peniculus.

Nay hold your peace, wee'll catch him in the nicke. This way he came, in his garland forfooth, bearing the cloake to the Dyars. And fee I pray, where the garland lyes; this way he is gone. See, fee, where he comes againe without the cloake.

Mulier.

What fhall I now do?

Peniculus.

What? that which ye ever do; bayt him for life.

Mulier.

Surely I think it beft fo.

Peniculus.

Peniculus.

Stay, wee will ſtand aſide a little; ye ſhall catch him unawares.

Enter Menechmus *the Citizen.*

Menechmus.

It would make a man at his wittes end, to ſee how brabbling cauſes are handled yonder at the Court. If a poore man never ſo honeſt, have a matter come to be ſcan'd there is he outfaſte, and overlaide with countenance: if a rich man never ſo vile a wretch, come to ſpeake, there they are all readie to favour his cauſe. What with facing out bad cauſes for the oppreſſors, and patronizing ſome juſt actions for the wronged, the Lawyers they pocket up all the gaines. For mine owne part, I come not away emptie, though I have bene kept long againſt my will: for taking in hand to diſpatch a matter this morning for one of my acquaintaunce, I was no ſooner entered into it, but his adverſaries laide ſo hard unto his charge, and brought ſuch matter againſt him, that do what I could, I could not winde my ſelfe out til now. I am ſore afrayd *Erotium* thinks much unkindnes in me that I ſtaid ſo long; yet ſhe will not be angry conſidering the gift I gave her to day.

Peniculus.

How thinke ye by that?

Mulier.

I thinke him a moſt vile wretch thus to abuſe me.

Menechmus.

I will hie me thither.

Mulier.

Yea go pilferer, goe with ſhame inough; no bodie ſees your lewd dealings and vile theevery.

Menechmus.

How now wife, what ail yee? what is the matter?

Mulier.

Aſke yee mee whats the matter? Fye uppon thee.

Peniculus.

Are ye not in a fit of an ague, your pulſes beate ſo ſore? to him, I ſay.

Menechmus.

Menechmus.

Pray wife why are ye fo angry with me?

Mulier.

Oh, you know not?

Peniculus.

He knows, but he would diflemble it.

Menechmus.

What is it?

Mulier.

My cloake.

Menechmus.

Your cloake!

Mulier.

My cloake, man; why do ye blufh?

Peniculus.

He cannot cloake his blufhing. Nay I might not go to dinner with you, do you remember? To him, I fay.

Menechmus.

Hold thy peace, *Peniculus.*

Peniculus.

Ha, hold my peace; looke ye he beckons on mee to hold my peace.

Menechmus.

I neither becken nor winke on him.

Mulier.

Out, out, what a wretched life is this that I live.

Menechmus.

Why what aile ye, woman?

Mulier.

Are ye not afhamed to deny fo confidently, that which is apparant?

Menechmus.

I proteft unto before all the Goddes (is not this inough) that I beckond not on him.

Peniculus.

Oh Sir, this is another matter: touch him in the former caufe.

Menechmus.

What former caufe?

Peniculus

Peniculus.

The cloake, man, the cloake: fetch the cloake againe from the Dyars.

Menechmus.

What cloake?

Mulier.

Nay Ile fay no more, fith ye know nothing of your owne doings.

Menechmus.

Tell me wife, hath any of your fervants abufed you? Let me know.

Mulier.

Tufh, tufh.

Menechmus.

I would not have you to be thus difquietted.

Mulier.

Tufh, tufh.

Menechmus.

You are fallen out with fome of your friends.

Mulier.

Tufh, tufh.

Menechmus.

Sure I am, I have not offended you.

Mulier.

No, you have dealt verie honeftly,

Menechmus.

Indeed wife, I have deferved none of thefe words. Tell me, are ye not well?

Peniculus.

What, fhall he flatter ye now?

Menechmus.

I fpeak not to thee, knave. Good wife, come hither.

Mulier.

Away, away; keep your hands off.

Peniculus.

So, bid me to dinner with you againe, then flip away from me; when you have done, come forth bravely in your garland, to flout me. Alas you knew not me even now.

Menechmus.

Why affe, I neither have yet dined, nor came I there, fince we were there together.

I 4

Peniculus.

Peniculus.

Who ever heard one fo impudent? Did yee not meete me here even now, and would make me believe I was mad, and faid ye were a ftraunger, and ye knew me not?

Menechmus.

Of a truth, fince we went togither to the Seffions Hall, I never returned till this very inftant, as you two met me.

Peniculus.

Go too, go too, I know ye well inough. Did ye think I would not cry quittance with you: yes faith: I have told your wife all.

Menechmus.

What haft thou told her?

Peniculus.

I cannot tell: afk her?

Menechmus.

Tell me, wife, what hath he told ye of me? Tell me, I fay; what was it?

Mulier.

As though you knew not my cloake is ftolne from me?

Menechmus.

Is your cloake ftolne from ye?

Mulier.

Do ye afke me?

Menechmus.

If I knew, I would not afke.

Peniculus.

O craftie companion! how he would fhift the matter? Come, come, deny it not: I tell ye. I have bewrayd all.

Menechmus.

What haft thou bewrayd?

Mulier.

Seeing ye will yield to nothing, be it never fo manifeft, heare mee, and ye fhall know in fewe words both the caufe of my griefe, and what he hath told me. I fay my cloake is ftolne from me.

Menechmus.

My cloake is ftolne from me?

Peniculus.

Looke how he cavils: fhe faith it is ftolne from her.

Menechmus.

I

Menechmus.

I have nothing to fay to thee : I fay wife tell me.

Mulier.

I tell ye, my cloake is ftolne out of my houfe.

Menechmus.

Who ftole it ?

Mulier.

He knowes beft that carried it away.

Menechmus.

Who was that ?

Mulier.

Menechmus.

Menechmus.

'Twas very ill done of him.   What *Menechmus* was that ?

Mulier.

You.

Menechmus.

I, who will fay fo ?

Mulier.

I will.

Peniculus.

And I, that you gave it to *Erotium.*

Menechmus.

I gave it ?

Mulier.

You.

Peniculus.

You, you, you: fhall we fetch a kennel of beagles that may cry nothing but you, you, you.   For we are wearie of it.

Menechmus.

Heare me one word, wife.   I proteft unto you by all the Gods, I gave it her not: indeed I lent it her to ufe a while.

Mulier.

Faith Sir, I never give nor lend your apparell out of doores. Methinkes ye might let mee difpofe of mine owne garments as you do of yours.   I pray then fetch it mee home againe.

Menechmus.

You fhall have it againe without faile.

Mulier.

'Tis beft for you that I have : otherwife thinke not to rooft within thefe doores againe.

Peniculus.

Peniculus.

Harke ye, what fay ye to me now, for bringing thefe matters to your knowledge?

Mulier.

I fay, when thou haft anie thing ftolne from thee, come to me, and I will helpe thee to feek it. And fo farewell.

Peniculus.

God a mercy for nothing, that can never be, for I have nothing in the world worth the ftealing. So now with hufband wife and all, I am cleane out of favour. A mifchiefe on ye all.   [*Exit.*

Menechmus.

My wife thinks fhe is notably reveng'd on me, now fhe fhuttes me out of doores, as though I had not a better place to be welcome too. If fhe fhut me out, I know who wil fhut me in. Now will I entreate *Erotium* to let me have the cloake againe to ftop my wives mouth withal; and then will I provide a better for her. Ho, who is within there? Some bodie tell *Erotium* I muft fpeake with her.

Enter Erotium.

Erotium.

Who calls?

Menechmus.

Your friend more then his owne.

Erotium.

O *Menechmus*, why ftand ye here? pray come in.

Menechmus.

Tarry, I muft fpeake with ye here.

Erotium.

Say your minde.

Menechmus.

Wot ye what? my wife knowes all the matter now, and my comming is, to requeft you that I may have againe the cloake which I brought you, that fo I may appeafe her: and I promife you, Ile give ye an other worth two of it.

Erotium.

Why I gave it you to carry to your Dyars; and my chaine likewife, to have it altered.

Menechmus.

Menechmus.

Gave mee the cloake and your chaine? In truth I never
fawe ye fince I left it heere with you, and fo went to the
Seffions, from whence I am but now returned.

Erotium.

Ah then, Sir, I fee you wrought a device to defraude mee
of them both. Did I therefore put yee in truft? Well, well.

Menechmus.

To defraude ye? No: but I fay, my wife hath intelli-
gence of the matter.

Erotium.

Why, Sir, I afked them not; ye brought them of your owne
free motion. Now ye require them againe, take them, make
fops of them, you and your wife together. Thinke ye I
efteeme them or you either? Goe; come to mee againe when
I fend for you.

Menechmus.

What fo angry with mee, fweete *Erotium?* Staie, I pray
ftaie.

* Erotium.

Staie? Faith no Sir: thinke yee I will ftaie at your requeft?

Menechmus.

What gone in chafing, and clalt to the doores? now I am
everie way fhut out for a very benchwhiftler: neither fhall I
have entertainment heere nor at home. I were beft go trie
fome other friends, and afk eounfaile what to do.

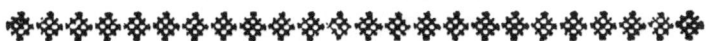

A C T V.

Enter Menechmus *the Traveller,* Mulier.

Menechmus.

MOST foolifhly was I overfeene in giving my purfe and
money to *Meffenio,* whom I can no where find. I feare he is
fallen into fome lewd companie.

Mulier.

Mulier.

I marvaile that my hufband comes not yet; but fee where he is now, and brings my cloake with him.

Menechmus.

I mufe where the knave fhould be.

Mulier.

I will go ring a peale through both his eares for this dif-honeft behaviour.   Oh Sir, ye are welcome home with your theevery on your fhoulders.   Are ye not afhamed to let all the world fee and fpeake of your lewdneffe?

Menechmus.

How now? what lackes this woman?

Mulier.

Impudent beaft, ftand ye to queftion about it? For fhame hold thy peace.

Menechmus.

Wha: offence have I done, woman, that I fhould not fpeake to you?

Mulier.

Afkeft thou what offence? O fhameleffe boldneffe!

Menechmus.

Good woman, did ye never heare why the Grecians termed *Hecuba* to be a bitch?

Mulier.

Never.

Menechmus.

Becaufe fhe did as you do now; on whom foever fhe met withall, fhe railed, and therfore well deferved that dogged name.

Mulier.

Thefe foule abufes and contumelies, I can never endure, nay rather will I live a widowes life to my dying day.

Menechmus.

What care I whether thou liveft as a widow, or as a wife? This paffeth, that I meet with none, but thus they vexe me with ftraunge fpeeches.

Mulier.

What ftraunge fpeeches? I fay I will furely live a widowes life, rather then fuffer thy vile dealings.

Menechmus.

Menechmus.

Prethee for my part, live a widow till the worldes end, if thou wilt.

Mulier.

Even now thou deniedft that thou ftoleft it from me, and now thou bringeft it home openly in my fight. Art not afhamde?

Menechmus.

Woman, you are greatly to blame to charge me with ftealing of this cloake, which this day an other gave me to carry to be trimde.

Mulier.

Well, I will firft complaine to my father. Ho boy, who is within there? *Vecio* go runne quickly to my father; defire him of all love to come over quickly to my houfe. Ile tell him firft of your prankes; I hope he will not fee me thus handled.

Menechmus

What a Gods name meaneth this mad woman thus to vexe me?

Mulier.

I am mad becaufe I tell ye of your vile actions and lewde pilfring away my apparell and my jewels, to carry to your filthie drabbes.

Menechmus.

For whome this woman taketh mee I knowe not. I know her as much as I know *Hercules* wives father.

Mulier.

Do ye not know me? That's well. I hope ye know my father: here he comes. Looke do ye know him?

Menechmus.

As much as I knew *Calcas* of *Troy.* Even him and thee I know both alike.

Mulier.

Doeft know neither of us both, me nor my father?

Menechmus.

Faith, nor thy grandfather neither.

Mulier.

This is like the reft of your behaviour.

Enter

Enter Senex.

Senex.

* Though bearing fo great a burthen as olde age, I can make no great hafte, yet as I can, I will goe to my daughter, who I know hath fome earneft bufineffe with me, that fhee fends in fuch hafte, not telling the caufe why I fhould come. But I durft laie a wager, I can geffe neare the matter : I fuppofe it is fome brabble betweene her hufband and her. Thefe yoong women that bring great dowries to their hufbands, are fo mafterfull and obftinate, that they will have their owne wils in everie thing, and make men fervants to their weake affections : and yoong men too, I muft needs fay, be naught now a dayes. Well Ile go fee, but yonder mee thinks ftands my daughter, and her hufband too.   Oh tis even as I geffed.

Mulier.

Father, ye are welcome.

Senex.

How now daughter ? What ? is all well ; why is your hufband fo fad ? have ye bin chiding ? tell me, which of you is in fault ?

Mulier.

Firft father know, that I have not any way mifbehaved my felfe ; but the truth is, that I can by no meanes endure this bad man to die for it ; and therefore defire you to take me home to you againe.

Senex.

What is the matter ?

Mulier.

He makes me a ftale and a laughing ftocke to all the world.

Senex.

Who doth ?

Mulier.

This good hufband here, to whom you married me.

Senex.

See, fee ; how oft have I warned you of falling out with your hufband ?

Mulier.

I cannot avoid it, if he doth fo fowly abufe me.

Senex.

Senex.

I alwaies told ye, ye muſt beare with him, ye muſt let him alone; ye muſt not watch him, nor dog him, nor meddle with his courſes in any ſort.

Mulier.

Hee hauntes naughtie harlottes under my noſe.

Senex.

He is wiſer, becauſe hee cannot bee quiet at home.

Mulier.

There hee feaſtes and bancquets, and ſpendes and ſpoiles.

Senex.

Wold ye have your huſband ſerve ye as your drudge? Ye will not let him make merry, nor entertaine his friendes at home.

Mulier.

Father will ye take his part in theſe abuſes, and forſake me?

Senex.

Not ſo, daughter; but if I ſee cauſe, I wil as well tel him of his dutie.

Menechmus.

I would I were gone from this prating father and daughter.

Senex.

Hitherto I ſee not but hee keepes ye well, ye want nothing, apparell, mony, ſervants, meate, drinke, all thinges neceſſarie. I feare there is fault in you.

Mulier.

But he filcheth away my apparrell and my jewels, to give to his trulles.

Senex.

If he doth ſo, tis verie ill done; if not, you doo ill to ſay ſo.

Mulier.

You may believe me father, for there you may ſee my cloake which now he hath fetcht home againe, and my chaine which he ſtole from me.

Senex.

Now will I goe talke with him to knowe the truth. Tel me *Menechmus*, how is it that I heare ſuch diſorder in your life? Why are ye ſo ſad, man? wherein hath your wife offended you?

Menechmus.

Menechmus.

Old man (what to call ye I know not) by high *Jove*, and by all the Gods I fweare unto you, whatfoever this woman here accufeth mee to have ftolne from her, it is utterly falfe and un-. true ; and if ever I fet foote within her doores, I wifhe the greateft miferie in the worlde to light uppon me.

Senex.

Why fond man, art thou mad, to deny that thou ever fetft foote within thine owne houfe where thou dwelleft ?

Menechmus.

Do I dwell in that houfe ?

Senex.

Doeft thou denie it ?

Menechmus.

I do.

Senex.

Harke yee daughter; are ye remooved out of your houfe ?

Mulier.

Father he ufeth you as he doth me : this life I have with him.

Senex.

Menechmus, I pray leave this fondneffe ; ye jeft too per-verfly with your friends.

Menechmus.

Good old father, what I pray have you to do with me? or why fhould this woman thus trouble me, with whom I have no dealings in the world ?

Mulier.

Father, marke I pray how his eies fparkle : they rowle in his head ; his colour goes and comes : he lookes wildly. See, fee.

Menechmus.

What? they fay now I am mad : the beft way for me is to faine my felfe mad indeed, fo fhall I be rid of them.

Mulier.

Looke how he ftares about! how he gapes.

Senex.

Come away daughter : come from him.

* *Menechmus.*

Bachus, Appollo, Phœbus, do yee call mee to come hunt in the woods with you ? I fee, I heare, I come, I flie ; but I can-

not

ot get out of thefe fields.   Here is an old maftiffe bitch ftands
..rking at mee; and by her ftandes an old goate that beares
..lfe witneffe againft many a poore man.

Senex.

Out upon him Bedlam foole.

Menechmus.

Harke, *Appollo* commaunds me that I fhoulde rende out hir
eyes with a burning lampe.

Mulier.

O father, he threatens to pull out mine eyes. ·

Menechmus.

Good Gods, thefe folke fay I am mad, and doubtleffe they
are mad themfelves.

Senex.

Daughter.

Mulier.

Here father: what fhall we do?

Senex.

What if I fetch my folkes hither, and have him carried in
before he do any harme.

Menechmus.

How now? they will carry me in if I looke not to my felfe:
I were beft to fkare them better yet.   Doeft thou bid me,
Phœbus, to teare this dog in peeces with my nayles?   If I laie
hold on him, I will do thy commandment.

Senex.

Get thee into thy houfe, daughter; away quickly.

Menechmus.

She is gone: yea *Appollo*, I will facrifice this olde beaft unto
thee; and if thou commandeft mee, I will cut his throate with
that dagger that hangs at his girdle.

Senex.

Come not neare me, Sirra.

Menechmus.

Yea I will quarter him, and pull all the bones out of his
flefh, and then will I barrell up his bowels.

Senex.

Sure I am fore afraid he will do fome hurt.

Menechmus.

Many things thou commandeft me, *Appollo:* wouldft thou
have me harneffe up thefe wilde horfes, and then clime up into

K   the

the chariot, and fo over-ride this old ftincking toothleffe Lyon.
So now I am in the chariot, and I have hold on the raines :
here is my whip; hait; come ye wilde jades make a hideous
noyfe with your ftamping : hait, I fay : will ye not go?

Senex.

What? doth he threaten me with his horfes?

Menechmus.

Harke! now *Appollo* bids me ride over him that ftands there,
and kill him. How now? who pulles mee downe from my
chariot by the haires of my head. O fhall I not fulfill *Appolloes*
commandment?

Senex.

See, fee, what a fharpe difeafe this is, and how well he was
even now.   I will fetch a Phyfitian ftrait, before he grow too
farre into this rage.   [*Exit.*

Menechmus.

Are they both gone now? Ile then hie me away to my
fhip : tis time to be gone from hence.   [*Exit.*

Enter Senex *and* Medicus.

Senex.

My loines ake with fitting, and mine eies with looking,
while I ftaie for yonder laizie Phifitian : fee now where the
creeping drawlatch comes.

Medicus.

What difeafe hath hee, faid you? Is it a letarge or a lunacie,
or melancholie, or dropfie?

Senex.

Wherfore I pray do I bring you, but that you fhuld tell me
what it is, and cure him ot it?

Medicus.

Fie, make no queftion of that. Ile cure him, I warrant ye.
Oh here he comes.   Staie let us marke what he doth.

Enter Menechmus *the Citizen.*

Menechmus.

Never in my life had I more overthwart fortune in one day,
and all by the villanie of this falfe knave the Parafite, my *Uliffes*
that workes fuch mifchiefs againft mee his king. But let me
live

live no longer but Ile be revengde uppon the life of him. His life? nay, tis my life, for hee lives by my meate and drinke. Ile utterly withdraw the flave's life from him. And *Erotium* fhee plainly fheweth what fhe is; who becaufe I require the cloake againe to carrie to my wife, faith I gave it her, and flatly falles out with me. How unfortunate am I?

Senex.

Do ye heare him?

Medicus.

He complaines of his fortune.

Senex.

Go to him.

Medicus.

Menechmus, how do ye, man? why keepe you not your cloake over your arme? It is verie hurtfull to your difeafe. Keepe ye warme, I pray.

Menechmus.

Why hang thyfelf, what careft thou?

Medicus.

Sir, can you fmell anie thing?

Menechmus.

I fmell a prating dolt of thee.

Medicus.

Oh, I will have your head throughly purged. Pray tell me *Menechmus,* what ufe you to drinke? white wine, or claret?

Menechmus.

What the divell careft thou?

Senex.

Looke, his fit now begins.

Menechmus.

Why doeft not as well afke mee whether I eate bread, or cheefe, or beefe, or porredge, or birdes that beare feathers, or fifhes that have finnes?

Senex.

See what idle talke he falleth into.

Medicus.

Tarry; I will afke him further. *Menechmus,* tell me, be not your eyes heavie and dull fometimes?

Menechmus.

What, doeft thinke I am an Owle?

K 2

Medicus,

Medicus.

Doo not your guttes gripe ye, and croake in your belly?

Menechmus.

When I am hungrie they do, elfe not.

Medicus.

He fpeakes not like a madman in that. Sleepe ye foundly all night?

Menechmus.

When I have paid my debts I do. The mifchiefe light on thee, with all thy frivoleus queftions.

Medicus.

Oh now he rageth upon thofe words : take heed.

Senex.

Oh this is nothing to the rage he was in even now. He called his wife bitch, and all to nought.

Menechmus.

Did I?

Senex.

Thou didft, mad fellow, and threatenedft to ryde over me here with a chariot and horfes, and to kill mee, and teare me in peeces. This thou didft : I know what I fay.

Menechmus.

I fay, thou ftoleft *Jupiters* crowne from his head, and thou wert whipt through the Towne for it, and that thou haft kild thy father, and beaten thy mother. Doo ye thinke that I am fo mad that I cannot devife as notable lyes of you as you do of me?

Senex.

Maifter Doctor, pray heartily make fpeede to cure him. See you not how he waxeth?

Medicus.

Ile tell ye. He fhall be brought over to my houfe, and there I will cure him.

Senex.

Is that beft?

Medicus.

What elfe? there I can order him as I lift.

Senex.

Well, it fhall be fo.

Medicus.

Medicus.

Oh Sir, I will make you take neefing powder this twentie dayes.

Menechmus.

Ile beate yee firft with a baftanado this thirtie dayes.

Medicus.

Fetch men to carry him to my houfe.

Senex.

How many will ferve the turne?

Medicus.

Being no madder than he is now, foure will ferve.

Senex.

Ile fetch them. Staie you with him, Maifter Doctor.

Medicus.

No by my faith: Ile goe home to make readie all things needfull. Let your men bring him hither.

Senex.

I go.   *[Exeunt.*

Menechmus.

Are they both gone? Good Gods what meaneth this? Thefe men fay I am mad, who without doubt are mad themfelves. I ftirre not, I fight not, I am not ficke. I fpeake to them, I know them. Well, what were I now beft to do? I would goe home, but my wife fhuttes me foorth a doores. *Erotium* is farre out with me too. Even here I will reft me till the evening: I hope by that time, they will take pittie on me.

Enter Meffenio *the Travellers fervant.*

Meffenio.

* The proofe of a good fervant, is to regard his maifters bufineffe as well in his abfence as in his prefence; and I thinke him a verie foole that is not carefull as well for his ribbes and fhoulders, as for his belly and throate. When I think upon the rewards of a fluggard, I am ever pricked with a careful regard of my backe and fhoulders; for in truth I have no fancie to thefe blowes, as many a one hath. Methinks it is no pleafure to a man to be bafted with a ropes end two or three houres togither. I have provided yonder in the Towne, for all our marriners, and fafely beftowed all my

K 3   mafters

mafters Trunkes and fardels ; and am now comming to fee if
he be yet got forth of this daungerous gulfe, where I feare
me he is overplunged.   Pray God he be not overwhelmed and
paft helpe ere I come.

Enter Senex, *with foure Lorarii, Porters.*

Senex.

Before Gods and men, I charge and commaund you Sirs, to
execute with great care that which I appoint you : if yee love
the fatetie of your owne ribbes and fhoulders, then goe take me
up my fonne in lawe, laie all hands upon him: why ftand ye
ftil ? what do ye doubt ? I faie, care not for his threatnings,
nor for anie of his words.   Take him up, and bring him to
the Phyfitians houfe: I will go thither before.   [*Exit.*

Menechmus.

What newes ? how now mafters ? what will ye do with
me ? why do ye thus befet me ? whither carrie ye me ? Helpe,
helpe, neighbors, friends, citizens !

Meſſenio.

O *Jupiter,* what do I fee ? my maifter abufed by a companie
of varlets.

Menechmus.

Is there no good man will helpe me ?

Meſſenio.

Helpe ye maifter ? yes the villaines fhall have my life
before they fhall thus wrong ye.   'Tis more fit I fhould be kild,
then you thus handled.   Pull out that rafcals eye that holds
ye about the necke there.   Ile clout thefe peafants ; out ye
rogue, let go ye varlet.

Menechmus.

I have hold of this villaines eie.

Meſſenio.

Pull it out, and let the place appear in his head.   Away ye
cutthroat theeves, ye murtherers.

Lo. Omnes.

O, O, ay ; crie pittifullie.

Meſſenio.

Away, get ye hence, ye mongrels, ye dogs.   Will ye be
gone ? Thou rafkal behind there, Ile give thee fomewhat
more,

more, take that. It was time to come maister; you had bene in good cafe, if I had not bene heere now. I tolde you what would come of it.

Menechmus.

Now as the Gods love me, my good friend I thank thee: thou haft done that for me which I fhall never be able to requite.

Meffenio,

I'le tell ye how Sir; give me my freedome.

Menechmus.

Should I give it thee?

Meffenio.

Seeing you cannot requite my good turne.

Menechmus.

Thou art deceived, man.

Meffenio.

Wherein?

Menechmus.

On mine honeftie, I am none of thy maifter; I had never yet anie fervant would do fo much for me.

Meffenio.

Why then bid me be free : will you?

Menechmus.

Yea furelie : be free, for my part.

Meffenio.

O fweetly fpoken; thanks my good maifter.

Servus alius.

Meffenio, we are all glad of your good fortune.

Meffenio.

O maifter, Ile call you maifter ftill. I praie ufe me in anie fervice as ye did before. Ile dwell with you ftill; and when ye go home, Ile wait upon you.

Menechmus.

Nay, nay, it fhall not need.

Meffenio.

Ile go ftrait to the Inne, and deliver up my accounts, and all your ftuffe. Your purfe is lockt up fafely fealed in the cafket, as you gave it mee. I will goe fetch it to you.

Menechmus.

Do, fetch it.

Meffenio.

Meſſenio.

I will.

Menechmus.

I was never thus perplext. Some deny me to be him that I
am, and ſhut me out of their doores. This fellow ſaith he is
my bondman, and of me he begs his freedome: he will fetch
my purſe and monie. Well, if he bring it, I will receive it,
and ſet him free. I would he would ſo go his way. My old
father in lawe and the Doctor, ſaie I am mad: who ever ſawe
ſuch ſtrange demeanors. Well though *Erotium* be never ſo
angrie, yet once againe Ile go ſee if by intreatie I can get the
cloake on her to carrie to my wife.   [*Exit.*

Enter Menechmus *the Traveller,* and Meſſenio.

Menechmus.

Impudent knave, wilt thou ſay that I ever ſaw thee ſince I
ſent thee away to day, and bad thee come for mee after
dinner ?

Meſſenio.

Ye make me ſtarke mad: I tooke ye away, and reſkued ye
from foure great bigboand villaines, that were carrying ye
away even heere in this place. Heere they had ye up; you
cried Helpe, helpe. I came running to you: you and I togither beate them away by maine force. Then for my good
turne and faithfull ſervice, ye gave me my freedome: I tolde
ye I would go fetch your caſket: now in the meane time you
ranne ſome other way to get before me, and ſo you denie it all
againe.

Menechmus.

I gave thee thy freedome ?

Meſſenio.

You did.

Menechmus.

When I give thee thy freedome, Ile be a bondman my ſelfe ;
go thy wayes.

Meſſenio.

Whewe, marry I thanke for nothing.

Enter

Enter Menechmus *the Citizen.*

Menechmus.

Forſworne Queanes, ſweare till your hearts ake, and your eyes fall out, ye ſhall never make me beleeve that I carried hence either cloake or chaine.

Meſſenio.

O heavens, maiſter, what do I ſee?

Menechmus Tra.

What?

Meſſenio.

Your ghoaſt.

Menechmus Tra.

What ghoaſt?

Meſſenio.

Your image, as like you as can be poſſible.

Menechmus Tra.

Surely not much unlike me, as I thinke.

Menechmus Cit.

O my good friend and helper, well met; thanks for thy late good helpe.

Meſſenio.

Sir, may I crave to know your name?

Menechmus Cit.

I were too blame if I ſhould not tell thee anie thing; my name is *Menechmus.*

Menechmus Tra.

Nay my friend, that is my name.

Menechmus Cit.

I am of *Syracuſis* in *Sicilia.*

Menechmus Tra.

So am I.

Meſſenio.

Are you a *Syracuſan?*

Menechmus Cit.

I am.

Meſſenio.

Oho, I know ye; this is my maiſter: I thought hee there had bene my maiſter, and was proffering my ſervice to him. Pray pardon me Sir, if I ſaid any thing I ſhould not.

Menechmus

Menechmus Tra.

Why doating patch, didft thou not come with me this morning from the fhip?

Meffenio.

My faith he faies true. This is my maifter, you may go looke ye a man. God fave ye maifter: you Sir, farewell. This is *Menechmus.*

Menechmus Cit,

I fay, that I am *Menechmus.*

Meffenio.

What a jeft is this? Are you *Menechmus?*

Menechmus Cit.

Even *Menechmus,* the fonne of *Mofchus.*

Menechmus Tra.

My father's fonne?

Menechmus Cit.

Friend, I go about neither to take your father nor your country from you.

Meffenio.

O immortal Gods, let it fall out as I hope; and for my life thefe two are the two Twinnes, all things agree fo jump together. I will fpeake to my maifter. *Menechmus.*

Both.

What wilt thou?

Meffenio.

I call you not both: but which of you came with me from the fhip?

Menechmus Cit.

Not I.

Menechmus Tra.

I did.

Meffenio.

Then I call you. Come hither.

Menechmus Tra.

What's the matter?

Meffenio.

This fame is either fome notable coufening jugler, or elfe it is your brother whom we feeke. I never fawe one man fo like an other: water to water, nor milke to milke, is not liker than he is to you.

Menechmus

Menechmus Tra.

Indeed I thinke thou faieſt true. Finde it that he is my brother, and I here promiſe thee thy freedom.

Meſſenio.

Well, let me about it. Heare ye Sir; you ſay your name is *Menechmus.*

Menechmus Cit.

I do.

Meſſenio.

So is this man's. You are of *Syracuſis?*

Menechmus Cit.

True.

Meſſenio.

So is he. *Moſcus* was your father?

Menechmus Cit.

He was.

Meſſenio.

So was he his. What will you ſay, if I find that ye are brethren and twins?

Menechmus Cit.

I would thinke it happie newes.

Meſſenio.

Nay ſtaie maiſters both : I meane to have the honor of this exploit. Anſwere mee: your name is *Menechmus?*

Menechmus Cit.

Yea.

Meſſenio.

And yours?

Menechmus Tra.

And mine.

Meſſenio.

You are of *Syracuſis?*

Menechmus Cit.

I am.

Menechmus Tra.

And I.

Meſſenio.

Well, this goeth right thus farre. What is the fartheſt thing that you remember there?

I   *Menechmus*

Menechmus Cit.

How I went with my father to *Tarentum,* to a great mart,
and there in the preaſſe I was ſtolne from him.

Menechmus Tra.

O *Jupiter!*

Meſſenio.

Peace, what exclaiming is this? How old were ye then?

Menechmus Cit.

About ſeven yeare old: for even then I ſhedde teeth, and
ſince that time I never heard of anie of my kindred.

Meſſenio.

Had ye never a brother?

Menechmus Cit.

Yes, as I remember, I heard them ſay, we were two Twinnes.

Menechmus Tra.

O Fortune!

Meſſenio.

Tuſh, can ye not be quiet? Were ye both of one name?

Menechmus Cit.

Nay, (as I think) they called my brother, *Soſicles.*

Menechmus Tra.

It is he, what need further proofe? O brother, brother, let
me embrace thee!

Menechmus Cit.

Sir, if this be true, I am wonderfully glad: but how is it
that ye are called *Menechmus?*

Menechmus Tra.

When it was tolde us that you and our father were both
dead, our Graundſire (in memorie of my father's name)
chaungde mine to *Menechmus.*

Menechmus Cit.

'Tis verie like he would do ſo indeed. But let me aſke ye
one queſtion more: what was our mother's name?

Menechmus Tra.

Theuſimarche.

Menechmus Cit.

Brother, the moſt welcome man to mee, that the world
holdeth.

Menechmus Tra.

I joy, and ten thouſand joyes the more, having taken ſo long
travaile and huge paines to ſeeke you.

Meſſenio.

Meſſenio.

See now, how all this matter comes about. This it was that the gentlewoman had ye in to dinner, thinking it had bene he.

Menechmus Cit.

True it is I willed a dinner to be provided for me heere this morning; and I alſo brought hither cloſely, a cloake of my wives, and gave it to this woman.

Menechmus Tra.

Is not this the ſame, brother?

Menechmus Cit.

How came you by this?

Menechmus Tra.

This woman met me; had me in to dinner; enterteined me moſt kindly; and gave me this cloake, and this chaine.

Menechmus Cit.

Indeed ſhe tooke ye for mee: and I believe I have bene as ſtraungely handled by occaſion of your comming.

Meſſenio.

You ſhall have time inough to laugh at all theſe matters hereafter. Do ye remember maiſter, what ye promiſed me?

Menechmus Cit.

Brother, I will intreate you to performe your promiſe to *Meſſenio:* he is worthie of it.

Menechmus Tra.

I am content.

Meſſenio.

Io Tryumphe.

Menechmus Tra.

Brother, will ye now go with me to *Syracuſis?*

Menechmus Cit.

So ſoone as I can ſell away ſuch goods as I poſſeſſe here in *Epidamnum,* I will go with you.

Menechmus Tra.

Thanks, my good brother.

Menechmus Cit.

Meſſenio, plaie thou the Crier for me, and make a proclamation.

Meſſenio.

A fit office. Come on. O yes. What day ſhall your ſale be?

Menechmus

Menechmus Cit.

This day fennight.

Meffenio.

All men, women and children in *Epidamnum*, or elfewhere, that will repaire to *Menechmus* houfe this day fennight, fhall there finde all maner of things to fell ; fervaunts, houfehold ftuffe, houfe, ground and all ; fo they bring readie money. Will ye fell your wife too Sir ?

Menechmus Cit.

Yea, but I think no bodie will bid money for her.

Meffenio.

Thus, Gentlemen, we take our leaves, and if we have pleafde, we require a *Plaudite.*

F I N I S.

A

PLEASAUNT CONCEITED

H I S T O R I E,

C A L L E D

The Taming of a Shrew.

As it hath beene fundry Times acted by the
right Honourable the Earle of PEMBROOKE
his Servants.

Printed at London by V. S. for *Nicholas Ling*, and are to
be fold at his fhop in Saint Dunftons Church-yard
in Fleetftreet. 1607.

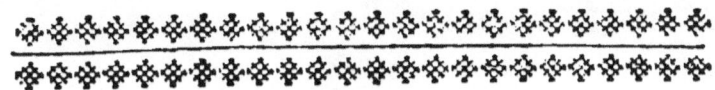

A

PLEASANT CONCEITED

HISTORIE;

CALLED

The Taming of a Shrew.

Enter a Tapster, beating out of his doores Slie *drunken.*

Tapster.

YOU whorefon drunken flave, you had beft be gone,
And empty your drunken panch fomewhere elfe,
For in this houfe thou fhalt not reft to night.   [*Exit Tapfter.*
Slie.
Tilly vally, by crifee Tapfter Ile fefe you anone, ·
Fills the tother pot, and all's paid for: looke you,
I doe drinke it of mine owne inftigation,   [*Omne bene.*
Heere Ile lie awhile: why Tapfter I fay,
Fill's a frefh cufhen heere,
Heigh ho, heere's good warme lying.   [*He falles afleepe.*

Enter a nobleman and his men from hunting.

Lord.
Now that the gloomy fhadow of the night,
Longing to view *Orions* drifling lookes,

L   Leape

Leapes from th' antarticke world unto the fkie,
And dims the welkin with her pitchie breath,
And darkefome night orefhades the criftall heavens,
Heere breake we off our hunting for to night.
Couple uppe the hounds and let us hie us home,
And bid the huntfman fee them meated well,
For they have all deferv'd it well to daie.
But foft, what fleepie fellow is this lies heere?
Or is he dead, fee one what dooeth lacke?

Servingman.

. My Lord, 'tis nothing but a drunken fleepe
His head is too heavie for his bodie,
And he hath drunke fo much that he can go no furder.

Lord.

Fie, how the flavifh villaine ftinkes of drinke.
Ho, firha arife. What fo found afleepe?
Goe take him up, and beare him to my houfe,
And beare him eafily for feare he wake,
And in my faireft chamber make a fire,
And fet a fumptuous banquet on the boord,
And put my richeft garments on his backe,
Then fet him at the Table in a chaire:
When that is done, againft he fhall awake,
Let heavenly muficke play about him ftill,
Go two of you away, and beare him hence,
And then Ile tell you what I have devifde,
But fee in any cafe you wake him not. [*Exeunt two with* Slie.
Now take my cloke, and give me one of yours,
All fellowes now, and fee you take me fo:
For we will waite upon this drunken man,
To fee his countenance when he doth awake,
And find himfelfe clothed in fuch attire,
With heavenly muficke founding in his eares,
And fuch a banquet fet before his eyes,
The fellow fure will thinke he is in heaven,
But we will about him when he wakes,
And fee you call him Lord at every word,
And offer thou him his horfe to ride abroad,
And thou his hawkes and houndes to hunt the deere,
And I will afke what futes he meanes to weare,

And

And what fo ere he faith, fee you doo not laugh,
But ftill perfuade him that he is a Lord.

Enter one.

Meffenger.
And it pleafe your honour your plaiers be come,
And doo attend your honours pleafure here.
Lord.
The fitteft time they could have chofen out,
Bid one or two of them come hither ftraight,
Now will I fit my felfe accordinglie,
For they fhall play to him when he awakes.

Enter two of the Plaiers with packs at their backs, and a boy.

Now firs, what ftore of plaies have you?
Sander.
Mary my lord you may have a Tragicall,
Or a commoditie, or what you will.
The other.
A Comedie thou fhouldft fay, founs thou'lt fhame us all.
Lord.
And whats the name of your Comedie?
Sander.
Marrie my lord tis calde The Taming of a Shrew.
Tis a good leffon for us my L. for us that are maried men.
Lord.
The taming of a Shrew, thats excellent fure,
Go fee that you make you readie ftraight,
For you muft plaie before a lord to night,
Say you are his men and I your fellow,
Hee's fomething foolifh, but what fo ere he faies,
See that you be not dafht out of countenance.
And firha, go you make you readie ftraight,
And dreffe your felfe like to fome lovelie ladie,
And when I cal, fee that you come to me,
For I will fay to him thou art his wife,
Dally with him and hug him in thine armes,
And if he defire to goe to bed with thee

L 2

Then

Then faine fome fcufe, and fay thou wilt anon.
Be gone I fay, and fee thou dooft it well.

Boy.

Feare not mv Lord, Ile handle him well enough
And make him thinke I love him mightilie.   [Ex. Boy.

Lord.

Now firs, go you and make you ready too,
For you muft play affoone as he doth wake.

Sander.

O brave, firha Tom, we muft play before
A foolifh Lord, come lets go make us ready.
Go get a difhclout to make cleane your fhooes,
And Ile fpeake for the properties : My Lord, we muft
Have a fhoulder of mutton for a propertie,
And a little vinegre to make our Divell rore.

Lord.

Very well firha, fee that they want nothing.
                              [Exeunt Omnes.

*Enter two with a table and a banquet on it, and two other, with
Slie, afleepe in a chaire, richlie apparelled and the mufick plaieng.*

One.

So firha, now go call my Lord,
And tell him that all things are ready as he willd it.

Another.

Set thou fome wine upon the boord,
And then Ile go fetch my Lord prefently.   [Exit.

Enter the Lord, and his men.

Lord,

How now, what is all things readie ?

One.

Yea my Lord.

Lord.

Then found the muficke and Ile wake him ftrait,
And fee you dee as earft I gave in charge.
My Lord, my Lord, he fleepes foundly, my Lord.

Slie.

Slie.

Tapfter, gives a little fmal ale : Heigh ho.

Lord.

Heere's wine, my Lord, the pureft of the grape.

Slie.

For which Lord?

Lord.

For your honor, my Lord.

Slie.

Who I, am I a Lord? Jefus! what fine apparell have I got ?

Lord.

More richer far your honour hath to weare,
And if it pleafe you I will fetch them ftraight.

Wil.

And if your honour pleafe to ride abroad,
Ile fetch your luftie fteedes more fwift of pace
Then winged *Pegafus* in all his pride,
That ran fo fwiftlie over *Perfian* plaines.

Tom.

And if your honour pleafe to hunt the deere,
Your hounds ftand readie cuppled at the doore,
Who in running will oretake the Row,
And make the long breathde Tygre broken winded.

Slie.

By the maffe I thinke I am a Lord indeed,
Whats thy name ?

Lord.

Simon and if it pleafe your honour.

Slie.

Sim, that as much to fay *Simion* or *Simon*,
Put forth thy hand and fill the pot.
Give me thy hand, *Sim* ; am I a lord indeed ?

Lord.

I my gracious Lord, and your lovely ladie
Long time hath mourned for your abfence heere.
And now with joy behold where fhe dooth come
To gratulate your honours fafe returne.

Enter the boy in Womans attire,

Slie,

Sim, is this fhe ?

L 3

Lord.

Lord.

I my Lord.

Sle.

Maſſe tis a prettie wench, whats her name ?

Boy.

Oh that my lovelie Lord w.. ild once vouchſafe
To looke on me and leave theſe frantike fits,
Or were I now but halfe ſo eloquent,
To paint in words what he performe in deedes,
I know your honour then would pittie me.

Slie.

Harke you miſtreſſe, will you eate a peece of bread ?
Come fit downe on my knee *Sim* drinke to hir *Sim*,
For ſhe and I will go to bed anon.

Lord.

May it pleaſe you, your honors plaiers be come
To offer your honour a plaie.

Slie.

A plaie *Sim*, O brave, be they my plaiers ?

Lord.

I my Lord.

Slie.

Is there not a foole in the plaie ?

Lord.

Yes my Lord.

Slie.

When will they plaie *Sim* ?

Lord.

Even when it pleaſe your honor, they be readie,

Boy.

My Lord, Ile go bid them begin their plaie.

Slie.

Doo, but looke that you come againe.

Boy.

I warrant you my Lord, I will not leave you thus.

[*Exit* Boy.

Slie.

Come *Sim*, where be the plaiers ? *Sim* ſtand by me,
And weele flowt the plaiers out of their coates.

Lord.

Lord.

Ile cal them my lord.   Ho where are you there?

[*Sound Trumpets.*

Enter two yoong Gentlemen, and a man, and a boy.

Polidor.

Welcome to *Athens* my beloved friend,
To *Platoes* fchoole and *Ariftotles* walks,
Welcome from *Ceftus* famous for the love
Of good *Leander* and his Tragedie,
For whome the *Helefpont* weepes brinifh teares,
The greateft griefe is I cannot as I would
Give entertainment to my deereft friend.

Aurelius.

Thankes nobie *Polidor* my fecond felfe,
The faithful love which I have found in thee
Hath made me leave my fathers princelie court,
The *Duke* of *Ceftus* thrife renowned feate,
To come to *Athens* thus to find thee out.
Which, fince I have fo happily attaind,
My fortune now I do account as great
As earft did *Cæfar* when he conquered moft.
But tel me noble friend, where fhal we lodge,
For I am unacquainted in this place.

Polidor.

My Lord, if you vouchfafe of fchollers fare,
My houfe, my felfe, and al is yours to ufe,
You and your men fhall ftaie and lodge with me.

Aurelius.

With all my heart, I wil requite thy love.

Enter Simon, Alphonfus, *and his three daughters.*

But ftaie, what dames are thefe fo bright of hew
Whofe eies are brighter than the lampes of heaven?
Fairer then rocks of pearle and pretious ftone,
More lovely far then is the morning funne,
When firft fhe opes hir oriental gates.

Alfonfus,

Alfonfus.

Daughters, be gone, and hie you to the church,
And I will hie me downe unto the key
To fee what marchandife is come afhore.   [*Ex. Omnes*

Polidor.

Why how now my Lord, what, in a dumpe,
To fee thefe damfels paffe away fo foone?

Aurelius.

Truft me my friend I muft confefs to thee,
I tooke fo much delight in thefe faire dames
As I do wifh they had not gone fo foone:
But if thou canft, refolve me what they be,
And what old man it was that went with them,
For I do long to fee them once againe.

Polidor.

I cannot blame your honor, good my Lorde,
For they are both lovely, wife, faire, and yong,
And one of them, the yongeft of the three
I long have lov'd (fweet friend) and fhe lov'd me,
But never yet we could not find a meanes
How we might compaffe our defired joyes.

Aurelius.

Why, is not her father willing to the match?

Polidor.

Yes truft me, but he hath folemnly fworne,
His eldeft daughter firft fhall be efpowfde,
Before he grants his yongeft leave to love:
And therefore he that meanes to get their loves,
Muft firft provide for her, if he wil fpeed,
And he that hath her fhall be fretted fo,
As good be wedded to the divell himfelfe,
For fuch a fkould as fhe did never live,
And til that fhe be fped, none elfe can fpeede:
Which makes me thinke, that all my labors loft,
And who fo ere can get hir firme good will,
A large dowrie he fhall be fure to have,
For hir father is a man of mightie wealth,
And an antient Citizen of the towne,
And that was he that went along with them.

Aurelius.

Aurelius.

But he fhall keepe hir ftil by my advife,
And yet I needes muft love his fecond daughter
The image of honor and nobility,
In whofe fweet perfon is compriſde the fumme
Of Natures ſkill and heavenly majefty.

Polidor.

I like your choife, and glad you chofe not mine,
Then if you like to follow on your love,
We muft devife a meanes to find fome one
That will attempt to wed this devilifh ſkould,
And I do know the man. Come hither boy,
• Go your waies firha to *Ferandoes* houfe,
Defire him to take the paines to come to me,
For I muft ſpeake to him immediately.

Boy.

I will fir, and fetch him prefently.

Polidor.

A man I thinke will fit hir humour right,
As blunt in fpeech as ſhe is ſharpe in tongue,
And he I thinke will match hir every way,
And yet he is a man of wealth ſufficient,
And for his perfon worth as good as ſhe:
And if he compaſſe hir to be his wife,
Then may we freely vifit both our loves.

Aurelius.

O might I fee the cenfer of my ſoule
Whofe ſacred beauty hath inchanted me,
More faire then was the Grecian *Helena*
For whofe fweet ſake fo many princes dide;
That came with thoufand ſhips to *Tenedos.*
But when we come unto hir fathers houfe,
Tel him I am a Merchants ſonne of *Ceſtus,*
That comes for trafficke unto *Athens* here,
And here firha, I wil change with you for once,
And now be thou the Duke of *Ceſtus* fonne,
Revel and fpend as if thou wert myfelfe,
For I will court thy love in this diſguife.

Valeria.

My Lord, how if the Duke your father ſhould
By fome meanes come to *Athens* for to fee

How

How you do profit in thefe publike fchooles,
And find me clothed thus in your attire,
How would he take it then thinke you my Lord?
Aurelius.

Tufh feare not *Valeria*, let me alone,
But ftay, here comes fome other company.

Enter Ferando *and his man* Sander *with a blew coate.*

Polidor.

Here comes the man that I did tel you of.
Ferando.

Good morrow gentleman to al at once.
How now *Polidor*, what man ftill in love?
Ever wooing and canft thou never fpeed?
God fend me better lucke when I fhal woo.
Sander.

I warrant you mafter and you take my councel.
Ferando.

Why firha, are you fo cunning?
Sander.

Who I, twere better for you by five marke
And you could tel how to do it as wel os I.
Polidor.

I would thy maifter once were in the vaine,
To trie himfelfe how he could woo a wench.
Ferando.

Faith I am even now a going.
Sander.

I faith fir, my mafter's going to this geare now.
Polidor.

Whither in faith *Ferando?* tel me true.
Ferando.

To bonie *Kate*, the patientft wench alive,
The Divel himfelfe dares fcarce venture to woo her,
Seignior *Alfonfus* eldeft daughter,
And he hath promifde me fix thoufand crownes
If I can win her once to be my wife,
And fhe and I muft woo with fkoulding fure,
And I will hold her too't til fhe be wearie,
Or elfe ile make her yeeld to grant me love.

6

Polidor.

Polidor.

How like you this *Aurelius*, I thinke he knew
Our minds before we fent to him,
But tell me, when do ye meane to fpeake with hir?

Ferando.

Faith prefently, do you but ftand afide,
And I will make hir father bring ir hither:
And fhe, and I, and he, and talke alone.

Polidor.

With all my heart, come *Aurelius*,
Let us be gone and leave him here alone.

Ferando.

Ho Seignior *Alfonfo*, who's within there?

Alfonfo.

Seignior *Ferando* y'are welcome hartily,
You are a ftranger fir unto my houfe.
Harke you fir, looke what I did promife you
Ile perforne, if you get my daughters love.

Ferando.

Then when I have talkt a word or two with hir,
Do you ftep in and give her hand to me,
And tell hir when the mariage day fhall be,
For I do know fhe would be maried faine,
And when our nuptiall rites be once performde
Let me alone to tame hir well inough,
Now call her forth that I may fpeake with hir.

Enter Kate.

Alfonfo.

Ha *Kate*, come hither wench and lift to me,
Ufe this gentleman friendly as thou canft.

Ferando.

Twenty good morrows to my lovely *Kate*.

Kate.

You jeaft I am fure, is fhe yours already?

Ferando.

I tel thee *Kate* I know thou lov'ft me wel.

Kate.

The Divel you do, who told you fo?

Ferando.

Ferando.

My mind fweet *Kate* doth fay I am the man,
Muſt wed, and bed, and marrie bonnie *Kate*.

Kate.

Was ever feene fo groffe an affe as this?

Ferando.

I, to ſtand fo long and never get a kiffe.

Kate.

Hands off I fay, and get you from this place;
Or I will fet my ten commandements in your face.

Ferando.

I prithy do *Kate*, they fay thou art a ſhrew.
And I like thee the better, for I would have thee fo.

Kate.

Let go my hand, for feare it reach your eare.

Ferando.

No *Kate*, this hand is mine, and I thy love.

Kate.

Yfaith fir no, the woodcoke wants his taile.

Ferando.

But yet his bil will ferve, if the other faile.

Alfonſo.

How now *Ferando*, what, my daughter?

Ferando.

Shee's willing fir, and loves me as hir life.

Kate.

Tis for your ſkin then, but not to be your wife.

Alfonſo.

Come hither *Kate*, and let me give thy hand
To him that I have chofen for thy love,
And thou to morrow ſhalt be wed to him.

Kate.

Why father, what do you mean to do with me,
To give me thus unto this brainficke man,
That in his mood cares not to murder me?

                        [She turnes aſide and ſpeaks.

And yet I will confent and marry him,
(For I me thinkes have liv'de too long a maide,)
And match him too, or elfe his manhood's good.

                                     Alfonſo.

Alfonso.

Give me thy hand, *Ferando* loves thee well,
And will with wealth and eafe maintaine thy ftate.
Here *Ferando,* take her for thy wife.
And Sunday next fhall be our wedding day.

Ferando.

Why fo, did I not tel thee I fhould be the man?
Father, I leave my lovely *Kate* with you,
Provide yourfelves againft our marriage day,
For I muft hie me to my country houfe
In hafte, to fee provifion may be made,
To entertaine my *Kate* when fhe doth come.

Alfonso.

Do fo, come *Kate,* why doft thou looke
So fad? be mery wench, thy wedding daie's at hand,
Sonne, fare you wel, and fee you keepe your promife.
[*Exit Alfonso and Kate.*

Ferando.

So, al thus far goes well. Ho *Sander.*

Enter Sander *laughing.*

Sander.

Sander, I faith you are a beaft, I crie God hartilie mercy;
my harts ready to run out of my belly with laughing, I ftood
behinde the doore al this while, and heard what you faid
to hir.

Ferando.

Why, dooft thou thinke that I did not fpeake wel to hir?

Sander.

You fpoke like an affe to hir, ile tell you what,
And I had been there to have woo'd hir, and had this
Cloke that you have, chud have had hir before fhe
Had gone a foot furder, and you talke of Woodcoks
With hir, and I cannot tell you what.

Ferando.

Well firha, and yet thou feelt I have got hir for al this.

Sander.

I mary, twas more by hap then any good cunning.
I hope fheele make you one of the head men of the parifh
fhortly.

Ferando.

Ferando.

Wel firha, leave your jeafting and go to *Polidors* houfe,
The yong gentleman that was here with me,
And tel him the circumftance of al thou knowft,
Tel him on funday next we muft be married,
And if he afke thee whither I am gone,
Tel him into the countrey to my houfe,
And upon Sunday ile be here againe.   [*Exit* Ferando.

Sander.

I warrant you my mafter, feare not me
For doing of my bufineffe.
Now hang him that has not a livery cote
To flafh it out and fwafh it out amongft the prowdeft
On them. Why looke you now, ile fcarce put up
Plaine *Sander* now at any of their hands, for and any
Body have any thing to do with my mafter, ftraight
They come crouching upon me, I befeech you good M.
Sander fpeake a good word for me, and then I am fo
Stowt and take it upon me, and ftand upon my pantofles
To them out of all crie, why I have a life like a giant
Now, but that my mafter hath fuch a peftilent mind
To a woman now of late, and I have a prety wench
To my fifter, and I had thought to have preferred my
Mafter to hir, and that would have bin a good
Deale in my way, but that hees fped already.

Enter Polidors *boy.*

Boy.

Friend, well met.

Sander.

Souns friend, well met. I hold my life he fees not my
     mafters livery coate,
Plaine friend hop of my thum, know you who we are?

Boy.

Truft me fir it is the ufe where I was borne,
To falute men after this manner, yet notwithftanding
If you be angry with me for calling of you friend,
I am the more forry for it, hoping the ftile
Of a foole wil make you amends for all.

                                        Sander.

Sander.

. The flave is forie for his fault, now we cannot be angry,
Well whats the matter that you would do with us ?

Boy.

Marry fir, I heare you pertaine to feignior *Ferando.*

Sander.

I and thou beeft not blind thou maift fee,
Ecce fignum, here.

Boy.

Shall I intreat you to do me a meffage to your Mafter ?

Sander.

I, it may be, and tell you us from whence you come.

Boy.

Marrie fir I ferve yong *Polidor* your maifters friend.

Sander.

Do you ferve him, and whats your name ?

Boy.

My name firha ? I tel the firha is cald *Catapie.*

Sander.

Cake and pie, O my teeth waters to have a peece of thee.

Boy.

Why flave, wouldft thou eate me ?

Sander.

Eate thee, who would not eate Cake and pie ?

Boy.

Why villaine my name is *Catapie,*
But wilt thou tel me where thy maifter is.

Sander.

Nay thou muft firft tel me where thy maifter is,
For I have good newes for him, I can tel thee.

Boy.

Why fee where he comes.

Enter Polidor, Aurelius, *and* Valeria.

Polidor.

Come fweet *Aurelius* my faithfull friend,
Now wil we go to fee thofe lovely dames,
Richer in beauty then the orient pearle,
Whiter than is the Alpine Chriftall mould,

And

And far more lovely than the terrene plant,
That blushing in the aire turnes to a stone.
What *Sander*, what newes with you?

Sander.

Marry sir my maister sends you word
That you must come to his wedding to morrow.

Polidor.

What, shal he be married then?

Sander.

Faith I, you thinke he standes as long about it as you do.

Polidor.

Whither is thy maister gone now?

Sander.

Marry hee's gone to our house in the Countrey
To make al things in a readinesse against my new
Mistrisse comes thither, but heele come againe to morrow.

Polidor.

This is suddainly dispacht belike:
Wel, sirha boy, take *Sander* in with you,
And have him to the buttery presentlie.

Boy.

I will sir: come *Saunder*.   [*Exit* Sander *and the* Boy.

Aurelius.

Valeria, as erst wee did devise,
Take thou thy lute and go to *Alfonsos* house,
And say that *Polidor* sent thee thither.

Polidor.

I *Valeria*, for he spoke to me,
To helpe him to some cunning Musition,
To teach his eldest daughter on the lute,
And thou I know wilt fitte his turne so well,
As thou shalt get great favour at his hands,
Be gone *Valeria*, and say I sent thee to him.

Valeria.

I will Sir, and stay your comming at *Alfonsos* house.

[*Exit* Valeria.

Polidor.

Now sweet *Aurelius*, by this devise
Shal we have leisure for to court our loves,

3   For

For whilſt that ſhe is learning on the lute
Hir ſiſters may take time to ſteale abrode,
For otherwiſe ſheele keepe them both within,
And make them worke whilſt ſhe herſelfe doth play.
But come, lets go unto *Alfonſos* houſe,
And ſee how *Valeria* and *Kate* agrees
I doubt his muſicke ſcarce will pleaſe his ſkoller,
But ſtay, heere comes *Alfonſo*.

Enter Alfonſo.

Alfonſo.
What M. *Polidor!* you are wel met,
I thanke you for the man you ſent to me,
A good Muſition I thinke he is;
I have ſet my daughter and him togither,
But is this gentleman a friend of yours?
Polidor.
He is, I pray you ſir bid him welcome,
He's a wealthy Marchants ſon of *Ceſtus.*
Alfonſo.
Y'are welcome ſir, and if my houſe afforde
You any thing that may content your mind,
I pray you ſir make bold with me.
Aurelius.
I thanke you ſir, and if what I have got
By marchandiſe or travel on the ſeas,
Sattins, or lawnes, or azure coloured ſilke,
Or pretious fiery pointed ſtones of Indy
You ſhall command both them, myſelfe, and all.
Alfonſo.
Thanks gentle ſir, *Polidor* take him in,
And bid him welcome unto my houſe,
For thou I thinke muſt be my ſecond ſonne;
Ferando, Polidor dooſt thou not know
Muſt marry *Kate,* and to morrow is the day.
Polidor.
Such newes I heard, and I came now to know.
Alfonſo.
Polidor tis true, go let me alone,
For I muſt ſee againſt the bridegroome come,

M

That

That al things be according to his mind,
And so ile leave you for an houre or two.　　　　[*Exit.*
　　　　　　　Polidor.
Come then *Aurelius,* come in with me,
And weele go sit a while and chat with them,
And after bring them forth to take the aire.　　　[*Exit.*

　　　　　Then Slie *speaks.*

　　　　　　　Slie.
Sim, when will the foole come againe ?
　　　　　　　Lord.
Heele come againe my Lord anon.
　　　　　　　Slie.
Gis some more drinke here, souns where's
The Tapster, here *Sim* eate some of these things,
　　　　　　　Lord.
So I do my Lord.
　　　　　　　Slie.
Heere *Sim,* I drinke to thee.
　　　　　　　Lord.
My Lord heere comes the Plaiers againe.
　　　　　　　Slie.
O brave, heers two fine gentlewomen.

　　Enter Valeria *with a Lute, and* Kate *with him.*

　　　　　　Valeria.
The senceleſſe trees by musick have bin mov'd,
And at the sound of plesant tuned strings,
Have savage beasts hung downe their listning heads,
As though they had beene cast into a traunce.
Then it may be, that she to whome naught can please,
With Musickes sound, in time may be surprisde.
Come lovely Mistris, will you take your lute,
And play the lesson that I taught you last ?
　　　　　　　Kate.
It is no matter whether I doe, or no,
For trust me, I take no great delight in it.
　　　　　　Valeria.
I would, sweete Mistris, that it lay in me,
To helpe you to that thing that's your delight.

　　　　　　　　　　　　　　　　　Kate.

Kate.

In you with a peftilence, are you fo kind?
Then make a night-cap of your fiddles cafe,
To warme your head, and hide your filthy face.

Valeria.

It that (fweet Miftris) were your harts content,
You fhould commaund a greater thing than that,
Although it were ten times to my difgrace.

Kate.

Y'are fo kind t'were pittie you fhould be hang'd,
And yet me thinkes the foole doth looke afquint.

Valeria.

Why Miftris, doe you mocke me?

Kate.

No, but I meane to moove thee.

Valeria.

Well, will you play a little?

Kate.

Yea, give me the Lute.   [*Shee playet.*

Valeria.

That ftop was falfe, play it againe.

Kate.

Then mend it thou, thou filthy affe.

Valeria.

What, doe you bid me kiffe your arfe?

Kate.

How now jacke fawce? y'are a jolly mate,
Y'are beft be ftill left I croffe your pate,
And make your muficke flie about your eares,
Ile make it and your coxcombe meet.
                    [*She offers to ftrike him with the Lute.*

Valeria.

Hold Miftris, fowns will you breake my Lute?

Kate.

Yea on thy head and if thou fpeake to me.
There, take it up, and fiddle fomewhere elfe,
                    [*She throwes it downe.*
And fee you come no more into this place,
Left that I clap your fiddle on your face.   [*Exit Kate.*

Valeria.

Sowns, teach her to play on the Lute?
The divell fhall teach her firft, I am glad fhee's gone
For I was ne're fo fraid in all my life,
But that my Lute fhould flie about mine eares :
My maifter fhall teach her himfelfe for me,
For Ile keepe me farre enough without her reach,
For he and *Polidor* fent me before,
To be with her, and teach her on the Lute,
Whilft they did court the other gentlewomen,
And heere me thinkes they come together.

Enter Aurelius, Polidor, Emelia, *and* Philena.

Polidor.

How now *Valeria*, where's your Miftris?

Valeria.

At the vengeance, I thinke, and no where elfe.

Aurelius.

Why *Valeria*, will fhe not learne apace?

Valeria.

Yes berladie, fhe haz learn'd too much alreadie,
And that I had felt, had I not fpoke her faire,
But fhe fhall ne're be learnt for me againe.

Aurelius.

Well *Valeria* go to my chamber,
And heare him companie that came to daie
From *Ceftus*, where our aged father dwelles.   [*Exit* Valeria.

Polidor.

Come faire *Emelia*, my lovely love,
Brighter than the burnifht pallace of the Sunne,
The eie-fight of the glorious firmament,
In whofe bright lookes fparkles the radiant fire
Wilie *Prometheus* flily ftole from *Jove*,
Infufing breath, life, motion, foule,
To everie object ftricken by thine eies,
O faire *Emelia*, I pine for thee,
And, either muft enjoy thy love, or die.

Emelia.

Fie man, I know you will not die for love,
Ah *Polidor*, thou need'ft not to complaine,

Eternall

Eternall heaven fooner be diffolv'd,
And all that pierceth *Phœbus* filver eie,
Before fuch hap befall to *Polidor.*

Polidor.

Thankes faire *Emelia* for thefe fweet words :
But what faith *Philena* to her friend ?

Philena.

Why I am buying marchandife of him.

Aurelius.

Miftris, you fhall not neede to buy of me :
For when I crofs'd the bubbling *Canibey,*
And failde along the criftall *Hellifpont,*
I fill'd my coffers of the wealthy mines,
Where I did caufe millions of labouring Moores
To undermine the caverns of the earth,
To feeke for ftrange and new found pretious ftones,
And dive into the fea to gather pearle,
As faire as *Juno* offred *Priams* fonne,
And you fhall take your liberall choice of all.

Philena.

I thanke you fir, and would *Philena* might
In any curtefie requite you fo
As fhe with willing heart could well beftow.

Enter Alfonfo.

Alfonfo.

How now daughters, is *Ferando* come ?

Emelia.

Not yet father, I wonder he ftaies fo long,

Alfonfo.

And where's your fifter that fhe is not here ?

Philena.

She is making of her ready, father,
To goe to church, and if that he were come.

Polidor.

I warrant you hee'l not be long away.

Alfonfo.

Go daughters, get you in, and bid your fifter
Provide herfelfe againft that we do come,

M 3   And

And fee you go to church along with us.

                     [*Exeunt* Philena *and* Emelia,

I marvel that *Ferando* comes not away.

                   Polidor.

His Tailor, it may be, hath bin too flacke
In his apparell which he meanes to weare :
For no queftion but fome fantaftike futes
He is determined to weare to day,
And richly powdered with pretious ftones,
Spotted with liquide golde, thicke fet with pearle,
And fuch he meanes fhall be his wedding futes.

                   Alfonfo.

I car'd not I, what coft he did beftow,
In golde, or filke, fo he himfelfe were here,
For I had rather lofe a thoufand crownes,
Than that he fhould deceive us heere to day :
But foft, I thinke I fee him come.

       Enter Ferando *bafely attired, and a red Cap on his head.*

                   Ferando.

Good morrow father : *Polidor* well met,
You wonder, I know, that I have ftaide fo long.

                   Alfonfo.

Yea mary fonne, we were almoft perfuaded,
That we fhould fcarce have had our Bridegroome heere :
But fay, why art thou thus bafely attired ?

                   Ferando.

Thus richly father you fhould have faide,
For when my wife and I are married once,
Shee's fuch a fhrew, if we fhould once fall out,
Sheele pull my coftly futes over mine eares,
And therefore am I thus attir'd a while :
For many things I tell you's in my head,
And none muft know thereof, but *Kate* and I :
For we fhall live like Lambes and Lions fure,
Nor Lambs to Lions never were fo tame,
If once they be within the Lions pawes,
As *Kate* to me, if we were married once,
And therefore, come, lets to church prefently,

                                 Polidor.

Polidor.

Fie *Ferando*, not thus attired for fhame,
Come to my Chamber, and there fute thy felfe
Of twenty futes that I did never weare.

Ferando.

Tufh *Polidor*, I have as many futes
Fantaftike made to fit my humor fo,
As any in *Athens*, and as richly wrought
As was the Maffie Robe that late adorn'd
The ftately legat of the Perfian King,
And this from them have I made choife to weare.

Alfonfo.

I prethee *Ferando* let me intreat
Before thou go'ft unto the church with us,
To put fome other fute upon thy backe.

Ferando.

Not for the world, if I might gaine it fo,
And therefore take me thus, or not at al.

Enter Kate.

But foft, fee where my *Kate* doth come,
I muft falute hir : how fares my lovely *Kate*,
What, art thou ready ? fhal we go to church ?

Kate.

Not I with one fo mad, fo bafely tir'd,
To marry fuch a filthy flavifh groome,
That as it feemes fometimes is from his wits,
Or elfe he would not thus have come to us.

Ferando.

Tufh *Kate* thefe words adde greater love in me,
And makes me thinke thee fairer then before :
Sweet *Kate*, thou lovelier then Dianas purple robe,
Whiter than are the fnowie Apenis,
Or icie haire that growes on Boreas chin.
Father, I fweare by *Ibis* golden beake,
More faire and radiant is my bony *Kate*,
Then filver Xanthus when he doth imbrace
The ruddie Simies at *Idas* feete,
And care not thou, fweet *Kate*, how I be clad,
Thou fhalt have garments wrought of Median filke,

M 4

Enchac'd

Enchac'd with pretious jewels fetcht from far,
By Italian marchants that with Ruffian ftemes,
Plowes up hu_e furrowes in the *Terrene Maine*,
And better far my lovely *Kate* fhal weare :
Then come fweet love, and let us to the church,
For this I fweare fhal be my wedding fute.   [*Exit.*

Alfonfo.

Come gentlemen go along with us,
For thus, do what we can, he will be wed.   [*Exeunt omnes.*

Enter Polidors *Boy and* Sander.

Boy.

Come hither firha, boy.

Sander.

Boy, oh difgrace to my perfon ! founes, boy
Of your face, you have many boyes with fuch
Pickadenaunts I am fure, founs would you
Not have a bloudy nofe for this?

Boy.

Come, come, I did but jeft, where is that
Same peece of pie that I gave thee to keepe ?

Sander.

The pie ? I, you have more mind of your belly
Then to go fee what your maifter dooes.

Boy.

Tufh, tis no matter man, I prethee give it me,
I am very hungry I promife thee.

Sander.

Why you may take it, and the divel burft
You with it, one cannot fave a bit after fupper,
But you are alwaies ready to munch it up.

Boy.

Why come man, we fhall have good cheere
Anon at the bridehoufe, for your maifters gone to
Church to be married already, and theres
Such cheere as paffeth.

Sander.

O brave, I would I had eate no meate this weeke,
For I have never a corner left in my belly

To

To put a venſon paſtie in, I thinke I ſhall burſt myſelſe
With eating, for ile ſo cram me down the tarts
And the marchpanes out of all crie.

Boy.

I, but how wilt thou do now thy maiſters
Maried, thy miſtres is ſuch a divel, as ſheele make
Thee forget thy eating quickely, ſhee'le beate thee ſo.

Sander.

Let my maſter alone with her for that, for
Heele make hir tame wel inough ere long I warrant thee,
For he's ſuch a churle waxen now of late, that and he be
Never ſo little angry he thums me out of all cry,
But in my mind ſirha, the yongeſt is a very
Prety wench, and if I thought thy maſter would
Not have hir, Ide have a fling at hir
Myſelfe, ile ſee ſoone whether twill be a match
Or no : and it will not, ile ſet the matter
Hard for myſelfe I warrant thee.

Boy

Souns you ſlave, wil you be a Rivall with
My maſter in his love ? Speake but ſuch
Another word and ile cut off one of thy legs.

Sander.

Oh cruel judgment, nay then ſirha,
My tongue ſhal talke no more to you, marry my
Timber ſhal tell the truſty meſſage of his maiſter
Even on the very forehead of thee, thou abuſious
Villaine, therefore prepare thy ſelfe.

Boy.

Come hither thou imperfeÉtious ſlave, in
Regard of thy beggery, hold thee, theres
Two ſhillings for thee, to pay thee for the
Healing of thy left leg which I meane
Furiouſly to invade, or to maime at the leaſt.

Sander.

O ſupernodical foole ! wel, ile take your
Two ſhillings, but ile bar ſtriking at legs.

Boy.

Not I, for ile ſtrike any where.

Sander.

Sander.

Here take your two shillings againe,
Ile see thee hang'd ere ile fight with thee,
I gat a broken shin the other day,
'Tis not whole yet, and therefore ile not fight.
Come, come, why should we fal out?

Boy.

Wel sirha, your faire words have something
Alaied my choler: I am content for this once
To put it up, and be friends with thee,
But soft, see where they are come al from church,
Belike they be married already.

Enter Ferando *and* Kate, *and* Alfonso *and* Polidor *and* Emelia,
and Aurelius, *and* Phylena.

Ferando.

Father farewel, my *Kate* and I must home.
Sirha, go make ready my horse presently.

Alfonso.

Your horse! what son, I hope you do but jest,
I am sure you wil not go so suddainely.

Kate.

Let him go or tarry, I am resolv'd to stay,
And not to travel on my wedding day.

Ferando.

Tut *Kate* I tel thee we must needes go home,
Vilaine, hast thou sadled my horse?

Sander.

Which horse, your curtall?

Ferando.

Souns you slave, stand you prating here?
Saddle the bay gelding for your mistris.

Kate.

Not for me, for I wil not go.

Sander.

The Ostler wil not let me have him, you owe ten pence
For his meate and 6 pence for stuffing my mistris sadale.

Ferando.

Here villaine, goe pay him strait.

Sander.

Sander.

Shal I give them another pecke of lavender?

Ferando.

Out flave, and bring them prefently to the dore.

Alfonfo.

Why fon, I hope at leaft youle dine with us.

Sander.

I pray you mafter lets ftay til dinner be done.

Ferando.

Souns vilaine, art thou here yet?   [*Exit* Sander.

Come *Kate*, our dinner is provided at home.

Kate.

But not for me, for here I mean to dine:

Ile have my wil in this as wel as you,

Though you in madding mood would leave your frinds,

Defpite of you ile tarry with them ftill.

Ferando.

I *Kate* fo thou fhalt, but at fome other time,

Whenas thy fifters here fhall be efpoufd,

Then thou and I wil keepe our wedding day,

In better fort then now we can provide.

For heere I promife thee before them all

We will ere long returne to them againe :

Come *Kate*, ftand not on termes, we will away,

This is my day, to morrow thou fhalt rule,

And I will doe whatever thou commandes.

Gentlemen, farewell, wee'l take our leaves,

It will be late before that we come home.

[*Exeunt* Ferando *and* Kate.

Polidor.

Farewell *Ferando,* fince you will be gone.

Alfonfo.

So mad a couple did I never fee.

Emelia.

Thei're even as wel matcht as I would wifh.

Philena.

And yet I hardly thinke that he can tame her :

For when he haz done, fhe will do what fhe lift.

Aurelius.

Her manhoode then is good I do beleeve.

Polidor.

Polidor.

Aurelius, or elfe I miffe my marke:
Her tongue will walke, if fhe doe holde her hands.
I am in doubt ere halfe a month be paft,
Hee'l curfe the Prieft that married him fo foone,
And yet it may be fhe will be reclaimde,
For fhe is very patient growne of late.

Alfonfo.

God hold it, that it may continue ftill,
I would be loath that they fhould difagree,
But he (I hope) will hold her in a while.

Polidor.

Within thefe two daies I will ride to him,
And fee how lovingly they do agree.

Alfonfo.

Now *Aurelius* what fay you to this?
What, have you fent to *Ceftus* as you faid?
To certifie your father of your love,
For I would gladly he would like of it,
And if he be the man you tell to me,
I gheffe he is a Merchant of great wealth:
And I have feene him oft at *Athens* here,
And for his fake affure thee thou art welcome.

Polidor.

And fo to me whilft *Polidor* doth live.

Aurelius.

I find it fo, right worthy gentlemen,
And of that woorth your friendfhip I efteeme,
I leave cenfure of your feverall thoughts,
But for requitall of your favours paft
Refts yet behinde, which when occafion ferves,
I vow fhal be remembred to the full.
And for my fathers comming to this place,
I do exfpect within this weeke at moft.

Alfonfo.

Enough *Aurelius:* but we forget
Our marriage dinner now the Bride is gone,
Come, let us fee what there they left behind.   [*Exeunt omnes.*

Enter

Enter Sander *with two or three Serving men.*

Sander.

Come firs, provide all things as faft as you can,
For my maifter's hard at hand, and my new miftris
And all, and he fent me before to fee all things ready.

Tom.

Welcome home *Sander:* firrha how lookes our new miftris ? They fay fhee's a plaguy fhrew.

Sander.

Yea and that thou fhalt find, I can tell thee and if thou deft
not pleafe her wel : why my mafter haz fuch ado with, as it
paffeth, and hee's even like a madman.

Wil.

Why *Sander,* what doth he fay ?

Sander.

Why Ile tell you what : when they fhould
Goe to church to be married, he puts on an olde
Jerkin and a paire of canvaffe breeches downe to the
Small of his leg, and a red cap on his head, and he
Lookes as thou wouldft burft thy felfe with laughing
When thou feeft him : hee's ee'n as good as a
Foole for me : and then when they fhould goe to dinner,
He made me faddle the horfe, and away he came,
And ne'er tarried for dinner, and therefore you had beft
Get fupper ready againft they come, for
They be hard at hand I am fure by this time.

Tom.

Sowns, fee where they be already.

Enter Ferando *and* Kate.

Ferando.

Now welcome *Kate.* Where's thefe villaines
Heere ? what, not fupper yet upon the boord ?
Nor table fpread, nor nothing done at all,
Where's that villaine that I fent before ?

Sander.

Now, *adfum,* fir.

Ferando.

Ferando.

Come hither you villaine, Ile cut your nofe,
You rogue, help me off with my bootes : wilt pleafe
You to lay the cloth? Sowns the villaine
Hurts my foote : pull eafily I fay, yet againe ?

           [He beates them all.
    [They cover the boord, and fetch in the meate.

Sowns, burnt and fcorch't, who dreft this meate ?

Wil.

Forfooth *John Cooke.*
    [He throwes downe the table and meate, and all, and
    beates them all.*

Ferando.

Goe you villaines, bring me fuch meate ?
Out of my fight I fay, and beare it hence :
Come *Kate,* wee'll have other meate provided,
Is there a fire in my chamber fir ?

Sander.

I forfooth.   *[Exeunt* Ferando *and* Kate.
    [Manent Serving men, and eate up all the meate.

Tom.

Sownes, I thinke of my confcience my maifter's madde
fince he was married.

Wil.

I laft what a boxe he gave *Sander*
For pulling off his bootes.

Enter Ferando *againe.*

Sander.

I hurt his foote for the nonce man.

Ferando.

Did you fo, you damned villaine?
        [He beates them all out againe.

This humour muft I holde me to a while,
To bridle and holde backe my head-ftrong wife,
With curbes of hunger, eafe, and want of fleepe :
Nor fleepe, nor meate fhall fhe enjoy to night,
Ile mew her up as men doe mew their Hawkes,

                      And

And make her gently come unto the Lewre,
Were fhe as ſtubborne, or as full of ſtrength,
As was the Thracian Horfe *Alcides* tamde,
That king *Egeus* fed with fleſh of men,
Yet would I pull her downe, and make her come,
As hungry Hawkes doe flie unto their Lewre.   [*Exit.*

Enter Aurelius *and* Valeria.

Aurelius.

Valeria attend, I have a lovely love,
As bright as is the heaven criſtalline,
As faire as is the milke white way of *Jove*,
As chaſte as *Phœbe*, in her fummer fports,
As foft and tender as the azure dowlne,
That circles *Citherea's* filver Doves.
Her doe I meane to make my lovely Bride,
And in her bed to breathe the fweete content,
That I, thou know'ſt, long time have aimed at.
Now *Valeria* it reſts in thee to helpe
To compaſſe this, that I might gaine my love,
Which eaſily thou maiſt performe at will,
If that the merchant which thou told'ſt me of,
Will, (as he faide) goe to *Alfonſoes* houfe,
And fay he is my father, and there withall
Paſſe over certaine deedes of land to me,
That I thereby may gaine my hearts defire,
And he is promifed reward of me.
                    Valeria.
Feare not my Lord, Ile fetch him ſtrait to you,
For hee'l doe any thing that you commaund,
But tell me, my Lord, is *Ferando* married then?
                    Aurelius.
He is, and *Polidor* fhortly fhal be wed,
And he meanes to tame his wife ere long.
                    Valeria.
Hee faies fo.
                    Aurelius.
Faith he's gon unto the taming fchoole.

                                   Valeria.

Valeria.

The taming fchoole   why is there fuch a place?

Aurelius.

I: and *Ferando* is the maifter of the fchoole.

Valeria.

That's rare: but what *decorum* doth he ufe?

Aurelius.

Faith I know not: but by fome odde devife
Or other, but come *Valeria* I long to fee the man,
By whom we muft comprife our plotted drift,
That I may tel him what we have to do.

Valeria.

Then come my Lord and I will bring you to him ftraight.

Aurelius.

Agreede then, lets go.   [*Exeunt.*

Enter Sander *and his miftris.*

Sander.

Come miftris.

Kate.

Sander I prethee helpe me to fome meat,
I am fo faint that I can fcarcely ftand.

Sander.

I marry miftris, but you know my maifter
Has given me a charge that you muft eat nothing,
But that which he himfelfe giveth you.

Kate.

Why man, thy mafter needs never know it.

Sander.

You fay true indeed.   Why looke you miftris,
What fay you to a pece of bieffe and muftard now?

Kate.

Why I fay tis excellent meat, canft thou help me to fome?

Sander.

I, I could help you to fome, but that
I doubt the muftard is too chollerick for you.
But what fay you to a fheepes head and garlicke?

Kate.

Why any thing, I care not what it be.

5   *Sander.*

Sander.

I but the garlicke I doubt will make your breath
Stincke, and then my mafter wil courfe me for letting
You eate it.   But what fay you to a fat Capon ?

Kate.

That's meat for a king, fweete *Sander* help me to fome
    of it.

Sander.

Nay berlady then tis too deere for us, we muft
Not meddle with the Kings meate.

Kate.

Out villaine, doft thou mocke me,
Take that for thy fawfineffe.   [*She leates him.*

Sander.

Sounes are you fo light fingred with a murrin,
Ile keepe you fafting for it thefe two daies.

Kate.

I tel thee villaine, ile teare the flefh off
Thy face and eate it, and thou prate to me thus.

Sander.

Here comes my mafter now, heele courfe you.

Enter Ferando *with a peece of meate upon his dagger point and*
    Polidor *with him.*

Ferando.

See heere *Kate*, I have provided meat for thee,
Here take it : what, ift not worthy thanks ?
Go firha, take it away againe, you fhall be
Thankful for the next you have.

Kate.

Why I thanke you for it.

Ferando.

Nay now tis not worth a pin, go firha and take it hence
    I fay.

Sander.

Yes fir ile carrie it hence : Mafter let hir
Have none, for fhe can fight as hungry as fhe is.

Polidor.

I pray you fir let it ftand, for ile eate
Some with her my felfe.

              N   *Ferando.*

Ferando.

Wel firha, fet it downe againe.

Kate.

Nay nay I pray you let him take it hence,
And keepe it for your owne diet, for ile none,
Ile ne're be beholding to you for your meat,
I tel thee flatly here unto thy teeth,
Thou fhalt not keepe me nor feed me as thou lift,
For I will home againe unto my fathers houfe.

Ferando.

I, when y'are meeke and gentle, but not
Before, I know your ftomacke is not yet come downe.
Therefore no marvel thou canft not eat,
And I will go unto your Fathers houfe,
Come *Polidor* let us go in againe,
And *Kate* come in with us, I know ere long,
That thou and I fhall lovingly agree.   *[Exeunt omnes.*

Enter Aurelius, Valeria *and* Phylotus *the Marchant.*

Aurelius.

Now Seignior *Phylotus*, we wil go
Unto *Alfonfos* houfe, and be fure you fay
As I did tel you, concerning the man
That dwels at *Ceftus*, whofe fon I faid I was,
For you do very much refemble him,
And feare not : you may be bold to fpeake your mind.

Phylotus.

I warrant you fir, take you no care,
Ile ufe my felfe fo cunning in the caufe,
As you fhall foone injoy your harts delight.

Aurelius.

Thanks fweet *Phylotus*, then ftay you here,
And I will go and fetch him hither ftrait.
Ho, Seignior *Alfonfo* : a word with you.

Enter Alfonfo.

Alfonfo.

Who's there ? what *Aurelius*, what's the matter
That you ftand fo like a ftranger at the doore ?

Aurelius.

Aurelius.

My father fir is newly come to towne,
And I have brought him here to fpeake with you,
Concerning thefe matters that I told you of,
And he can certifie you of the truth.

Alfonfo.

Is this your father? you are welcome fir.

Phylotus.

'Thanks *Alfonfo*, for thats your name I geffe,
I underftand my fon hath fet his mind
And bent his liking to your daughters love,
And for becaufe he is my only fon,
And I would gladly that he fhould do well,
I tel you fir, I not miflike his choife,
If you agree to give him your confent,
He fhall have living to maintaine his ftate,
Three hundred pounds a yeare, I will affure
To him and to his heyres, and if they do joyne
And knit themfelves in holy wedlecke band,
A thoufand maffie ingots of pure gold
And twife as many bars of filver plate,
I freely give him, and in writing ftraight
I wil confirme what I have faid in words.

Alfonfo.

Truft me, I muft commend your liberal mind,
And loving care you beare unto your fon,
And here I give him freely my confent.
As for my daughter, I thinke he knowes her mind,
And I will inlarge her dowry for your fake,
And folemnife with joy your nuptial rites.
But is this gentleman of *Ceftus* too?

Aurelius.

He is the *Duke* of *Ceftus* thrife renowned fon,
Who for the love his honor beares to me,
Hath thus accompanied mee to this place.

Alfonfo.

You were too blame you tolde me not before,
Pardon me my Lord, for if I had knowne
Your honor had bin here in place with me,
I would have don my duty to your honor.

Valeria.

Valeria.

Thanks good *Alfonso*, but I did come to fee
When thefe marriage rites fhould be performed.
And if in thefe nuptials you vouchfafe,
To honor thus the prince of *Ceftus* friend,
In celebration of his fpoufal rites,
He fhal remaine a lafting friend to you,
What faies *Aurelius* father?

Phylotus.

I humbly thanke your honor, good my Lord,
And ere we part, before your honor here,
Shal articles of fuch content be drawne,
As twixt our houfes and pofterities,
Eternally this league of peace fhall laft
Inviolate and pure on either part.

Alfonfo.

With al my heart, and if your honor pleafe
To walke along with us unto my houfe,
We wil confirme thefe leagues of lafting love.

Valeria.

Come then *Aurelius* I wil go with you. [*Ex. omnes.*

Enter Ferando *and* Kate, *and* Sander.

Sander.

Mafter, the Haberdafher has brought my
Miftris home hir cap here.

Ferando.

Come hither firha: what have you there?

Haberdafher.

A velvet cap fir, and it pleafe you.

Ferando.

Who fpoke for it? didft thou *Kate?*

Kate.

What if I did? come hither firha give me
The cap, ile fee if it wil fit me. [*She fits it on her head.*

Ferando.

O monftrous: why it becomes thee not,
Let me fee it *Kate:* here firha take it hence,
This cap is out of fafhion quite.

Kate.

Kate.

The fashion is good inough : belike you
Meane to make a foole of me.

Ferando.

Why true, he meanes to make a foole of thee,
To have thee put on such a curtald cap :
Sirha be gone with it.

Enter the Taylor *with a gowne.*

Sander.

Here is the *Taylor* too with my mistris gowne.

Ferando.

Let me see it *Taylor :* what, with cuts and jags ?
Sounes thou vilaine, thou hast spoil'd the gowne.

Taylor.

Why sir, I made it as your man gave me direction.
You may read the note here.

Ferando.

Come hither sirha : *Taylor* read the note.

Taylor.

Item a faire round compassd cape.

Sander.

I thats true.

Taylor.

And a large truncke sleeve.

Sander.

Thats a lie master, I said two truncke sleeves.

Ferando.

Wel sir, go forward.

Taylor.

Item a loose bodied gowne.

Sander.

Maister if ever I said loose bodies gowne,
Sew me in a seame, and beat me to death
With a bottome of browne thred.

Taylor.

I made it as the note bade me.

Sander.

I say the note lies in his throate and thou too,
And thou saist it.

N 3   *Tailor*

Tailor.

Nay, nay, ne'r be fo hot firha, for I feare you not.

Sander.

Dooft thou heare *Tailor*, thou haft braved
Many men : brave not me.
Th'aft fac'd many men.

Tailor.

Wel fir.

Sander.

Face not me, ile neither be fac'd nor braved
At thy hands I can tell thee.

Kate.

Come, come, I like the fafhion of it wel inough,
Heere's more adoe than needes, I'le have it, I,
And if you doe not like it hide your eies,
I thinke I fhall have nothing by your will.

Ferando.

Go I fay, and take it up for your maifters ufe.

Sander.

Sounes villaine, not for thy life, touch it not:
Souns, take up my miftris gowne to his
Maifters ufe!

Ferando.

Well fir, what's your conceit of it?

Sander.

I have a deeper conceit of it than you
Thinke for, take up my miftris gowne
To his maifters ufe.

Ferando.

Tailer, come hither, for this time make it :
Hence againe, and Ile content thee for thy paines.

Tailer.

I thanke you fir.   [*Exit Tailer,*

Ferando.

Come *Kate*, wee now will goe fee thy fathers houfe
Even in thefe honeft meane abiliments.
Our purfes fhal be rich, our garments plaine,
To fhrowd our bodies from the winter rage,
And thats inough, what fhould we care for more
Thy fifters *Kate*, to morrow muft be wel,

Aaj

And I have promifed them thou fhould'ft be there,
The morning is well up, lets hafte away,
It wil be nine aclocke ere we come there.

Kate.

Nine aclocke, why tis already paft two
In the afternoone by al the clockes in the towne.

Ferando.

I fay tis but nine aclocke in the morning.

Kate.

I fay tis two aclocke in the afternoone.

Farando.

It fhal be nine then ere you go to your fathers:
Come backe againe, we will not goe to day :
Nothing but croffing me ftil ?
Ile have you fay as I doe ere I goe.   [*Exeunt omne*.

Enter Polidor, Emelia, Aurelius, *and* Philema.

Polidor.

Faire *Emelia,* fummers bright fun Queene,
Brighter of hew than is burning clime,
Where *Phœbus* in his bright æquator fits,
Creating golde and pretious mineralls,
What would *Emelia* doe if I were forc'd
To leave faire Athens, and to range the world ?

Emelia.

Should thou affay to fcale the feate of Jove,
Mounting the futtle airy regions,
Or be fnatcht up as erft was *Ganimede,*
Love fhould give wings unto my fwift defires,
And prune my thoughts that I would follow thee,
Or fall and perifh as did *Icarus.*

Aurelius.

Sweetly refolved, faire *Emelia,*
But would *Philema* fays as much to me,
If I fhould afke a queftion now of thee ?
What if the Duke of *Ceftus* onely fonne,
Which came with me unto your fathers houfe,
Should feeke to get *Philemas* love from me,
And make thee Dutcheffe of that ftately towne,
Wouldft thou not then forfake me for his love ?

N 4   *Philema.*

Philema.

Not for great *Neptune,* no nor *Jove* himfelfe,
Will *Philema* leave *Aurelius* love,
Could he enfta'l me Empreffe of the world,
Or make me Queene and guidreffe of the heaven,
Yet would I not exchange my love for his,
Thy. company is poore *Phylemaes* heaven,
And without thee, heaven were hell to me.

Emelia.

And fhould my love, as earft did *Hercules,*
Attempt the burning vaults of hell,
I would with piteous lookes, and pleafing words,
As once did *Orpheus* with his harmony,
And ravifhing found of his mellodious Harpe,
Intreate grimme *Pluto,* and of him obtaine
That thou might'ft goe, and fafe returne againe.

Philema.

And fhould my love as erft *Leander* did,
Attempt to fwimme the boyling *Hellifpont*
For *Heros* love : no Towers of braffe fhould hold,
But I would follow thee through thofe raging flouds,
With lockes dif-fhevered, and my breaft all bare,
With bended knees upon *Abidaes* fhore,
I would with fmokie fighs and brinifh teares,
Importune *Neptune* and the watry gods,
To fend a guard of filver-fcaled Dolphins,
With founding *Tritons* to be our convoy,
And to tranfport us fafe unto the fhore,
Whilft I would hang about thy lovely necke,
Redoubling kiffe on kiffe upon thy cheekes,
And with our paftime ftill the fwelling waves.

Emelia.

Should *Polidor* as *Achilles* did,
Onely imploy himfelfe to follow armes,
Like to the warlike Amazonian Queene,
Penthefilea, Hectors paramour,
Who toil'd the bloudy *Pirrhus* murd'rous Grecke,
Ile thruft my felfe amongft the thickeft throngs,
And with my utmoft force. affilt my love.

Phylema.

Phylema.

Let *Eole* ftorme: be mild and quiet thou,
Let *Neptune* fwel, be *Aurelius* calme and pleafed,
I care not, I. betide what may betide,
Let fates and fortune do the worft they can,
I recke them not: they not difcord with me,
Whileft that my love and I do well agree.

Aurelius

Sweet *Phylema* bewties minerall,
From whence the fun exhales his glorious fhine,
And clad the heaven in thy reflected raies,
And now my liefeft love, the time drawes nie;
That *Himen* mounted in his faffron robe,
Muft with his torches waite upon thy traine,
As *Hellens* brothers on the horned moone.
Now *Juno* to thy number fhal I adde,
The faireft bride that ever marchant had.

Polidor.

Come faire *Emelia*, the prieft is gon,
And at the church your father and the reft
Do ftay to fee our marriage rites perform'd,
And knit in fight of heaven this *Gordian* kno',
That teeth of fretting Time may ne'r untwift,
Then come faire love and gratulate with me
This daies content and fweet folemnity.   [*Exeunt Omnes.*

Slie.

Sim, muft they be married now?

Lord.

I my Lord.

Enter Ferando *and* Kate *and* Sander.

Slie.

Looke *Sim*, the foole is come againe now.

Ferando.

Sirha, go fetch our horfes forth, and bring
Them to the backe gate prefently.

Sander.

I will fir I warrant you.   [*Exit* Sander.

Ferando.

Ferando.

Come *Kate*, the moone fhines cleere to night me thinkes.

Kate.

The moone? why hufband you are deceiv'd,
It is the fun.

Ferando.

Yet againe, come backe againe, it fhal be
The moone ere we come at your fathers.

Kate.

Why ile fay as you fay, it is the moone.

Ferando.

Jefus, fave the glorious moone.

Kate.

Jefus, fave the glorious moone.

Ferando.

I am glad *Kate* your ftomacke is come downe,
I know it well thou knowft it is the fun,
But I did trie to fee if thou wouldft fpeake,
And croffe me now as thou haft done before,
And truft me *Kate* hadft thou not namde the moone,
We had gone backe again as fure as death.
But foft, who's this thats comming here?

Enter the Duke of Ceftus alone.

Duke.

Thus al alone from *Ceftus* am I come,
And left my princely court and noble traine,
To come to *Athens*, and in this difguife,
To fee what courfe my fon *Aurelius* takes.
But ftay, heres fome it may be travels thither,
Good fir can you direct me the way to *Athens*.

[Ferando *fpeaks to the old man.*

Faire lovely maide, yong and affable,
More cleere of hew and far more beautifull
Then pretious *Sardonix* or purple rockes,
Of *Amitheft* or gliftering *Hiafinth*,
More amiable far then is the plain,
Where gliftering *Cepherus* in filver boures,
Gafeth upon the Giant *Andromede*,
Sweet *Kate* entertaine this lovely woman.

3

Duke.

Duke.

I thinke the man is mad, he cals me a woman.

Kate.

Faire lovely lady, bright and Chriftaline,
Bewteous and ftately as the eie-train'd bird,
As glorious as the morning wafht with dew,
Within whofe eies fhe takes her dawning beames,
And golden fommer fleepes upon thy cheekes,
Wrapt up thy radiations in fome cloud,
Left that thy bewty make this ftately towne
Inhabitable like the burning Zone,
With fweet reflections of thy lovely face.

Duke.

What, is fhe mad too? or is my fhape transformd
That both of them perfuade me I am a woman,
But they are mad fure, and therefore ile be gone,
And leave their companies for feare of harme,
And unto *Athens* hafte to feek my fon.   [*Exit* Duke.

Ferando.

Why fo, *Kate*, this was friendly done of thee,
And kindly too: why thus muft we two live,
One minde, one heart, and one content for both,
This good old man dos thinke that we are mad,
And glad is he I am fure, that he is gone,
But come fwcet *Kate*, for we will after him,
And now perfuade him to his fhape againe.   [*Ex. omnes.*

Enter Alfonfo *and* Phylotus *and* Valeria, Polidor, Emelia,
Aurelius, *and* Phylema.

Alfonfo.

Come lovely fonnes, your marriage rites performed,
Lets hie us home to fee what cheere we have,
I wonder that *Ferando* and his wife
Come not to fee this great folemnity.

Polidor.

No marvel if *Ferando* be away,
His wife I thinke hath troubled fo his wits,
That he remaines at home to keepe them warme,

For

For forward wedlocke as the proverbe fayes,
Hath brought him to his nightcap long ago.

Phylotus,

But *Polidor*, let my fon and you take heed,
That *Ferando* fay not ere long as much of you.
And now *Alfonfo*, more to fhew my love,
If unto *Ceftus* you do fend your fhips,
Myfelfe wil fraught them with *Arabian* filkes,
Rich *Affricke* fpices, Arras counter-pointes,
Mufke, Caffia, fweet fmelling Ambergreece,
Pearle, curtol, Chriftal, jet, and ivory,
To gratulate the favors of my fon,
And friendly love that you have fhewne to him.

Valerea.

And for to honor him and his faire bride,

Enter the Duke *of* Ceftus.

Ile yeerely fend you from your fathers court,
Chefts of refind fugar feverally,
Ten tun of *Tunis* wine, fucket, fweet drugs,
To celebrate and folemnize this day,
And cuftom-free, your marchants fhal commerce
And interchange the profits of your land,
Sending you gold for braffe, filver for lead,
Caffes of filke for packes of wol and cloth,
To bind this friendfhip and confirme this league.

Duke.

I am glad fir that you would be fo franke,
Are you become the *Duke* of *Ceftus* fon,
And revels with my treafure in the towne,
Bafe villaine that thus difhonereft me.

Valeria.

Sownes it is the *Duke*, what fhall I do?
Difhonor thee? why knowft thou what thou faift?

Duke.

Her's no villaine: he will not know me now,
But what fay you? have you forgot me too?

Phylotus.

Why fir, are you acquainted with my fon?

Duke.

Duke.

With thy fon? no truft me, if he be thine,
I pray you fir, who am I?

Aurelius.

Pardon me father, humbly on my knees
I do intreat your grace to heare me fpeake.

Duke.

Peace villaine, lay hands on them,
And fend them to prifon ftraight.

[Phylotus *and* Valeria *runne away.*

Then Slie *fpeakes.*

Slie.

I fay weele have no fending to prifon.

Lord.

My Lord this is but the play, they're but in jeft.

Slie.

I tel thee *Sim* weele have no fending,
To prifon thats flat: why *Sim,* am I not *Don Chrifto Vari?*
Therefore I fay, they fhal not goe to prifon.

Lord.

No more they fhal not my Lord,
They be runne away.

Slie.

Are they run away *Sim?* thats wel.
Then gis fome more drinke, and let them play againe.

Lord.

Here my Lord.   [Slie *drinkes and then fals afleepe.*

Duke.

Ah trecherous boy that durft prefume,
To wed thy felfe without thy fathers leave,
I fweare by faire *Cintheas* burning raies
By *Merops* head, and by feven-mouthed *Nile,*
Had I but known ere thou hadft wedded her,
Were in thy breft the worlds immortal foule,
This angry fworde fhould rip thy hateful cheft,
And hewd thee fmaller then the *Libian* fandes,
Turne hence thy face, oh cruel impious boy.
I did not thinke you would prefume, *Alfonfo,*
To match your daughter with my princely houfe,

And

And ne'r make mee acquainted with the cause.

Alfonso.

My Lord, by heavens I sweare unto your grace
I knew none other but *Valeria* your man,
Had bin the *Duke* of *Cestus* noble son,
Nor did my daughter, I dare sware for her.

Duke.

That damned villaine that hath deluded me,
Whom I did send for guide unto my son,
Oh that my furious force could cleave the earth,
That I might muster bands of hellish feends,
To racke his heart and teare his impious soule.
The ceaslesse turning of celestial orbes,
Kindles not greater flames in flitting aire,
Then passionate anguish of my raging brest.

Aurelius.

Then let my death sweet father end your griefe,
For I it is that thus have wrought your woes,
Then be reveng'd on me, for here I sweare
That they are innocent of what I did,
Oh had I charge to cut off *Hydraes* head,
To make the toplesse *Alpes* a champaine field,
To kil untamed monsters with my sword,
To travel daily in the hottest sun,
And watch in winter when the nights be cold.
I would with gladnes undertake them all,
And thinke the paine but pleasure that I felt,
So that my noble father at my return,
Would but forget and pardon my offence.

Phylema.

Let me intreat your grace upon my knees,
To pardon him and let my death discharge
The heavy wrath your grace hath vow'd against him.

Polidor.

And good my Lord, let us intreat your grace
To purge your stomacke of this Melancoly,
Taint not your princely mind with griefe my Lord,
But pardon and forgive these lovers faults,
That kneeling crave your gratious favor here.

Emelea.

Emelea.

Great prince of *Ceſtus*, let a womans words
Intreat a pardon in your Lordly breſt,
Both for your princely ſon, and us my Lord.

Duke.

Aurelius ſtand up, I pardon thee,
I ſee that vertue wil have enemies.
And fortune wil be thwarting honor ſtil.
And you faire virgin too, I am content
To accept you for my daughter ſince tis don,
And ſee you princely uſde in *Ceſtus* court.

Phylema.

Thanks good my Lord, and I no longer live,
Then I obey and honor you in al.

Alfonſo.

Let me give thanks unto your royall grace,
For this great honor done to mee and mine,
And if your grace wil walke into my houſe,
I wil in humbleſt maner I can, ſhew
The eternall ſervice I do owe your grace.

Duke.

Thankes good *Alfonſo:* but I came alone,
And not as did beſeeme the *Ceſtian* Duke,
Nor would I have it knowne within the towne,
That I was here, and thus, without my traine :
But as I came alone, ſo wil I go,
And leave my ſon to ſolemniſe his feaſt,
And ere't be long Ile come againe to you,
And do him honor as beſeemes the ſon
Of mighty *Jerobel* the *Ceſtian* Duke,
Til when ile leave you, farewel *Aurelius.*

Aurelius.

Not yet my Lord, ile bring you to your ſhip.

[*Exeunt Omnes.*

Slie *ſleepes.*

Lord.

Who's within there ? come hither ſirs, my Lords
Aſleepe againe, go take him eaſily up,
And put him in his own apparel againe,

And

And lay him in the place where we did find him,
Juſt underneath the alehouſe ſide below,
But ſee you wake him not in any caſe.

Boy.

It ſhal be done my Lord, come help to beare him hence.

Enter Ferando, Aurelius, *and* Polidor *and his boy, and* Valeria
and Sander.

Ferando.

Come Gentlemen, nowe that ſupper's done,
How ſhall we ſpend the time til we go to bed?

Aurelius.

Faith if you wil, in trial of our wives
Who wil come ſooneſt at their huſbands cal.

Polidor.

Then then *Ferando* he muſt needes ſit out,
For he may cal I thinke til he be weary,
Before his wife wil come before ſhe liſt.

Ferando.

Tis wel for you that have ſuch gentle wives,
Yet in this trial wil I not ſit out,
It may be *Kate* wil come as ſoone as I do ſend.

Aurelius.

My wife comes ſooneſt for a hundred pound.

Polidor.

I take it. Ile lay as much to yours,
That my wife comes as ſoone as I do ſend.

Aurelius.

How now *Ferando*, you dare not lay belike.

Ferando.

Why true, I dare not lay indeede:
But how, ſo little mony on ſo ſure a thing,
A hundred pound: why I have laid as much
Upon my Dog, in running at a Deere,
She ſhal not come ſo far for ſuch a trifle,
But wil you lay five hundred markes with me,
And whoſe wife ſooneſt comes when he doth cal,
And ſhewes herſelfe moſt loving unto him,

2 Let

Let him injoy the wager I have laid,
Now what fay you? dare you adventure thus?
Polidor.
I, were it a thoufand pounds I durft prefume
On my wives love: and I wil lay with thee.

Enter Alfonfo.

Alfonfo.
How now fons, what in conference fo hard,
May I without offence, know where about?
Aurelius.
Faith father, a waighty caufe about our wives,
Five hundred markes already we have laid,
And he whofe wife doth fhew moft love to him,
He muft injoy the wager to himfelfe.
Alfonfo.
Why then *Ferando* he is fure to lofe it,
I promife thee fon, thy wife wil hardly come,
And therefore I would not wifh thee lay fo much.
Ferando.
Tufh father, were it ten times more
I durft adventure on my lovely *Kate*,
But if I lofe ile pay, and fo fhal you.
Aurelius.
Upon mine honor, if I lofe Ile pay.
Polidor.
And fo wil I upon my faith I vow.
Ferando.
Then fit we downe and let us fend for them.
Alfonfo.
I promife thee *Ferando*, I am afraid thou wilt lofe.
Aurelius.
Ile fend for my wife firft; *Valeria*,
Go bid your miftris come to me.
Valeria.
I will my lord.   [*Exit* Valeria.
Aurelius.
Now for my hundred pound,
Would any lay ten hundred more with me
I know I fhould obtaine it by her love.
                    O   *Ferando.*

Ferando.

I pray God you have not laid too much already.

Aurelius.

Truſt me *Ferando* I am ſure you have,
For you I dare preſume have loſt it al.

Enter Valeria *againe.*

Now ſirha, what ſaies your miſtris?

Valeria.

She is ſomething buſie but ſheele come anone.

Ferando.

Why ſo, did I not tel you this before,
She was buſie and cannot come.

Aurelius.

I pray God your wife ſend you ſo good an anſwere,
She may be buſie, yet ſhe ſaies ſheele come.

Ferando.

Wel, wel; *Polidor*, ſend you for your wife.

Polidor.

Agreed. *Boy* deſire your miſtris to come hither.

Boy.

I wil ſir.   [*Exit Boy.*

Ferando.

I ſo, ſo, he deſires her to come.

Alfonſo.

Polidor, I dare preſume for thee.
I thinke thy wife wil not denie to come,
And I do marvel much *Aurelius*,
That your wife came not when you ſent for her.

Enter the Boy *againe.*

Polidor.

Now, wher's your miſtris?

Boy.

She bade me tell you, that ſhee will not come,
And you have any buſineſſe, you muſt come to hir.

Ferando.

O monſtrous intollerable preſumption,
Worſe than a blaſing ſtar, or ſnow at Midſummer.

Earthquakes,

Earthquakes, or any thing unfeafonable,
She will not come, but he muft come to hir.
Polidor.
Wel fir, I pray you lets heare what
Anfwere your wife will make.
Ferando.
Sirha command your miftris to come
To me prefently.   [*Exit* Sander.
Aurelius.
I thinke my wife for all fhe did not come,
Wil prove more kind, for now I have no feare,
For I am fure *Ferandos* wife, fhe will not come.
Ferando.
The more's the pitty, then I muft lofe.

Enter Kate *and* Sander.

But I have won, for fee where *Kate* doth come.
Kate.
Sweete hufband did you fend for me.
Ferando.
I did my love, I fent for thee to come,
Come hither *Kate*, what's that upon thy head?
Kate.
Nothing hufband but my cap I thinke.
Ferando.
Pul it off and tread it under thy feet,
Tis foolifh, I wil not have thee weare it.
                    [*She takes off her cap and treads on it.*
Polidor.
Oh wonderful metamorphofis.
Aurelius.
This is a wonder almoft paft beleefe.
Ferando.
This is a token of her true love to me,
And yet Ile try her further you fhall fee;
Come hither *Kate*, where are thy fifters?
Kate.
They be fitting in the bridal chamber.
O 2   *Ferando.*

Ferando.

Fetch them hither, and if they wil not come,
Bring them perforce and make them come with thee.

Kate.

I will.

Alfonso.

I promife thee *Ferando*, I would have fworne,
Thy wife would ne'r have done fo much for thee.

Ferando.

But you fhal fee fhe wil do more then this,
For fee where fhe brings her fifters forth by force.

Enter Kate *thrufting* Phylema *and* Emelia *before her, and makes
them come unto their hufbands cal.*

Kate.

See hufband, I have brought them both.

Ferando.

Tis wel done *Kate.*

Emelia.

I fure, and like a loving peece, your worthy
To have great praife for this attempt.

Phylema.

I for making a foole of her felfe and us.

Aurelius.

Befhrew thee *Phylema* thou haft
Loft me a hundred pound to night,
For I did lay that thou wouldft firft have come.

Polidor.

But thou *Emelia* haft loft me a great deale more.

Emelia.

You might have kept it better then,
Who bade you lay?

Ferando.

Now lovely *Kate*, before their hufbands here,
I prethee tel unto thefe head-ftrong women,
What dewty wives do owe unto their Hufbands.

Kate.

Then you that live thus by your pampered wils,
Now lift to me, and marke what I fhal fay,

Th'

Th' eternal power that with his only breath,
Shall caufe this end, and this beginning frame,
Not in time, nor before time, but with time confus'd,
For al the courfe of yeares, of ages, months,
Of feafons temperate, of dayes and houres,
Are tun'd and ſtopt by meafure of his hand,
The firſt world was, a forme without a forme,
A heape confus'd, a mixture al deform'd,
A gulfe of gulfes, a body bodileffe,
Where all the elements were orderleffe,
Before the great Commander of the world,
The King of kings, the glorious God of heaven,
Who in fix daies did frame his heavenly worke,
And made al things to ſtand in perfect courfe,
Then to his image he did make a man
Olde *Adam*, and from his fide afleepe
A rib was taken, of which the Lord did make
The woe of man fo term'd by *Adam* then,
Woman, for that by her came finne to us,
And for her finne was *Adam* doomd to die.
As *Sara* to her hufband fo fhould we,
Obey them, love them, keepe and nourifh them,
If they by any meanes do want our helpes,
Laying our hands under their feet to tread,
If that by that we might procure their eafe,
And for a prefident Ile firſt begin,
And lay my hand under my hufband's feet.

[*She laies her hand under her hufband's feet.*

Ferando.

Inough fweet, the wager thou haſt won,
And they I am fure cannot deny the fame.

Alfonfo.

I *Ferando*, the wager thou haſt won,
And for to fhew thee how I am pleasd in this,
A hundred pounds I freely give thee more.
Another dowry for another daughter,
For fhe is not the fame fhe was before.

Ferando.

Thanks fweet father, gentlemen, good night,
For *Kate* and I will leave you for to night,

O 3   Tis

Tis *Kate* and I am wed, and you are fped :
And fo farewell, for we will to our beds.

        [*Exeunt* Ferando, Kate, *and* Sander.

        Alfonfo.

Now *Aurelius,* what fay you to this ?

        Aurelius.

Beleeve me father, I rejoyce to fee
Ferando and his wife fo lovingly agree.

    [*Exeunt* Aurelius, *and* Philema, *and* Alfonfo, *and* Valeria.

        Emelia.

How now *Polidor ?* in a dumpe ? what faift thou man ?

        Polidor.

I fay thou arte a fhrew.

        Emelia.

That's better than a fheepe.

        Polidor.

Well, fince tis done, come, lets goe.

        [*Exeunt* Polidor *and* Emelia.

[*Then enter two bearing of* Slie *in his owne apparrell againe, and leaves him where they found him, and then goes out : then enters the* Tapfter.

        Tapfter.

Now that the darkefome night is overpaft,
And dawning day appeares in criftall fkie,
Now muft I hafte abroade : but foft, who's this ?
What *Slie,* o wondrous ! hath he laine heere all night ?
Ile wake him, I thinke hee's ftarved by this,
But that his belly was fo ftufft with ale :
What now *Slie,* awake for fhame.

        Slie.

Sim, gives fome more wine, what all the Players gone ? am
not I a Lord ?

        Tapfter.

A Lord with a murrin : come art thou drunken ftill ?

        Slie.

Who's this ? *Tapfter,* O Lord firha, I have had the braveft
dreame to night, that ever thou heardeft in all thy life.

        Tapfter.

Yea mary, but you had beft get you home,
For your wife will courfe you for dreaming heere to night.

    I   *Slie.*

Slie. ⁚

Wil fhe? I know now how to tame a fhrew,
I dreamt upon it all this night till now,
And thou haft wakt me out of the beſt dreame
That ever I had in my life : but Ile to my wife prefently,
And tame her too if fhe anger me.

Tapſter.

Nay tarry *Slie*, for Ile goe home with thee,
And heare the reſt that thou haft dreamt to night.

[*Exeunt omnes.*

F I N I S.

.O 4

The Firſt and Second **P A R T**

OF THE

Troubleſome R.A I G N E of

John King of England.

WITH THE

Diſcoverie of King *RICHARD*

Cordelions baſe Sonne

(Vulgarly named, the Baſtard *Fawconbridge*:)

ALSO

The Death of King JOHN at *Swinſtead Abbey*.

As they were (ſundry times) lately acted by the Queenes
MAJESTIES Players.

Written by *W. Sh.*

Imprinted at *London* by *Valentine Simmes*, for *John Helme*,
and are to be ſold at his Shop in Saint *Dunſtons*
Church-yard in *Fleetſtreet*. 1611.

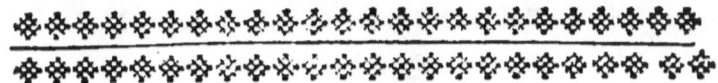

THE

Troublesome R A I G N E of

K I N G   J O H N.

Queen Elianor.

BAR O N S of *England*, and my noble lords;
Though God and fortune have bereft from us
Victorious *Richard* ſcourge of infidells,
And clad this land in ſtole of diſmall hew :
Yet give me leave to joy, and joy you all,
That from this wombe hath ſprung a ſecond hope,
A king that may in rule and vertue both
Succeede his brother in his emperie.

K. John.

My gratious mother queene, and barons all ;
Though farre unworthy of ſo high a place,
As is the throne of mighty *Englands* king :
Yet *John* your lord, contented uncontent,
Will (as he may) ſuſtaine the heavy yoke
Of preſſing cares, that hang upon a crowne.
My lord of *Pembrooke* and lord *Salſbury*,
Admit the lord *Chattilion* to our preſence ;
That we may know what *Philip* king of *Fraunce*
(By his ambaſſadors) requires of us.

Q. Elinor.

Q. Elinor.

Dare lay my hand that *Elinor* can geffe
Whereto this weighty embaffade doth tend :
If of my nephew *Arthur* and his claime,
Then fay, my fonne, I have not miffile my aime.

Enter Chattilion *and the two Earles.*

John.

My lord *Chattilion*, welcome into *England* :
How fares our brother *Philip* king of *France* ?

Chattilion.

His highneffe at my comming was in health,
And will'd me to falute your majeftie,
And fay the meffage he hath given in charge.

John.

And fpare not man, wee are preparde to heare.

Chattilion.

Philip, by the grace of God moft chriftian king of *France*,
having taken into his gardain and protection *Arthur* D. of
Brittaine fonne and heire to *Jeffrey* thine elder brother, re-
quireth in the behalfe of the faide *Arthur*, the kingdome of
England, with the lordfhip of *Ireland, Poiters, Anjow, Toraine,
Maine :* and I attend thine anfwer.

John.

A fmall requeft : belike hee makes account,
That *England, Ireland, Poiters, Anjow, Toraine, Maine,*
Are nothing for a king to give at once :
I wonder what be meanes to leave for me.
Tell *Philip*, he may keepe his lords at home,
With greater honour than to fend them thus
On embaffades that not concerne himfelfe,
Or if they did, would yeeld but fmall returne.

Chattilion.

Is this thine anfwer ?

John.

It is, and too good an anfwer for fo prowd a meffage,

Chattilion.

Then king of *England*, in my mafters name,
And in prince *Arthur* duke of *Brittaines* name,

I doe

I doe defie thee as an enemie,
And wish thee to prepare for bloody warres.

2. Elinor.

My lord (that stands upon defiance thus)
Commend me to my nephew, tell the boy,
That I queene *Elianor* (his grandmother)
Upon my blessing charge him leave his armes
Whereto his head-strong mother prickes him so :
Her pride we know, and know her for a dame
That will not sticke to bring him to his end,
So she may bring her selfe to rule a realme,
Next, wish him to forsake the king of *Fraunce*,
And come to me and to his uncle here,
And he shall want for nothing at our hands.

Chattilion.

This shall I do, and thus I take my leave.

John.

Pembrooke, convey him safely to the sea,
But not in haste : for as we are advisde,
We meane to be in *France* as soone as he,
To fortifie such townes as we possesse
In *Anjow*, *Toraine*, and in *Normandie*.   [*Exit* Chatt.

Enter the Shrive and whispers the Earle of Salisbury *in the eare.*

Salsbury.

Please it your majesty, here is the shrive of *Northhampton-shire*, with certaine persons that of late committed a riot, and have appeald to your majestie, beseeching your highnesse for speciall cause to heare them.

John.

Will them come neere, and while wee heare the cause,
Goe *Salsbury* and make provision,
We meane with speed to passe the sea to *France*.   [*Exit* Salf.
Say shrive, what are these men, what have they done?
Or whereto tends the course of this appeale?

Shrive.

Please it your majesty, these two brethren unnaturally falling at odds about their fathers living, have broken your highnesse
                                                        peace,

peace, in feeking to right their owne wrongs without courfe of lawe, or order of juftice, and unlawfully affembled themfelves in mutinous maner, having committed a riot, appealing from triall in their country to your highnefs : and here I *Thomas Nidigate* fhrive of *Northamptonfhire* do deliver them over to their triall.

John.

My lord of *Effex*, wil thoffenders to ftand forth, and tell the caufe of their quarrell.

Effex.

Gentlemen, it is the kings pleafure that you difcover your griefs, and doubt not but you fhal have juftice.

Philip.

Pleafe it your M. the wrong is mine : yet will I abide all wrongs, before I once open my mouth t'unrip the fhamefull flander of my parents, the difhonor of my felf, and the bad dealing of my brother in this princely affemblie.

Robert.

Then, by my prince his leave, fhall *Robert* fpeake,
And tell your majeftie what right I have
To offer wrong, as he accounteth wrong.
My father (not unknowne unto your grace)
Receiv'd his fpurres of knighthood in the field,
At kingly *Richards* hands in *Palefline*,
When as the walls of *Acon* gave him way :
His name fir *Robert Fauconbridge* of *Mountbery.*
What by fucceffion from his anceftors,
And warlike fervice under *Englands* armes,
His living did amount to at his death
Two thoufand markes revenew every yeare :
And this (my lord) I challenge for my right,
As lawfull heire to *Robert Fauconbridge.*

Philip,

If firft-borne fonne be heire indubitate
By certaine right of *Englands* auntient lawe,
How fhould my felfe make any other doubt,
But I am heire to *Robert Fauconbridge.*

John.

Fond youth, to trouble thefe our princely eares,
Or make a queftion in fo plaine a caufe :
Speake, is this man thine elder brother borne ?

Robert.

Robert.

Pleafe it your grace with patience for to heare,
I not deny but he mine elder is,
Mine elder brother too: yet in fuch fort,
As he can make no title to the land.

John.

A doubtfull tale as ever I did heare,
Thy brother, and thine elder, and no heire;
Explaine this darke Ænigma.

Robert.

I grant (my lord) he is my mothers fonne,
Bafe borne, and bafe begot, no *Fauconbridge.*
Indeede the world reputes him lawfull heire,
My father in his life did count him fo,
And here my mother ftands to proove him fo:
But I (my lord) can proove, and doe averre
Both to my mothers fhame, and his reproach,
He is no heire, nor yet legitimate.
Then (graticus lord) let *Fauconbridge* enjoy
The living that belongs to *Fauconbridge.*
And let not him poffeffe anothers right.

John.

Proove this, the land is thine by *Englands* lawe.

Q. Elinor.

Ungratious youth, to rip thy mothers fhame,
The wombe from whence thou didft thy being take,
All honeft eares abhorre thy wickedneffe,
But gold I fee doth beate downe natures law.

Mother.

My gratious lord, and you thrice reverend dame,
That fee the teares diftilling from mine eies,
And fcalding fighes blowne from a rented heart:
For honour and regard of womanhood,
Let me intreate to be commaunded hence.
Let not thefe eares heere receive the hiffing found
Of fuch a viper, who with poyfoned words
Doth mafferate the bowells of my foule.

John.

Lady, ftand up, be patient for a while:
And fellow, fay, whofe baftard is thy brother?

Philip

Philip.

Not for my felfe, nor for my mother now ;
But for the honour of fo brave a man,
Whom hee accufeth with adulterie :
Heere I befeech your grace upon my knees,
To count him mad, and fo difmiffe us hence.

Robert.

Nor mad, nor mazde, but well advifed, I
.Charge thee before this royall prefence here
To be a baftard to king *Richards* felfe,
Sonne to your grace, and brother to your majeftie.
Thus bluntly, and

Elianor.

Yong man, thou needft not be afhamed of thy kin,
Nor of thy fire. But forward with thy proofe.

Robert.

The proofe fo plaine, the argument fo ftrong,
As that your highneffe and thefe noble lords,
And all (fave thofe that have no eies to fee)
Shall fweare him to be baftard to the king.
Firft, when my father was embaffadour
In *Germaine* unto the Emperour,
The king lay often at my fathers houfe ;
And all the realme fufpected what befell :
And at my fathers backe returne agen
My mother was delivered, as tis fed,
Sixe weeks before the account my father made.
But more than this : looke but on *Philips* face,
His features, actions, and his lineaments,
And all this princely prefence fhall confeffe,
He is no other but king *Richards* fonne.
Then gratious lord, reft he king *Richards* fonne,
And let me reft fafe in my fathers right,
That am his rightfull fonne and only heire.

John.

Is this thy proofe, and all thou haft to fay ?

Robert.

I have no more, nor neede I greater proofe.

John.

Firft, where thou faidft in abfence of thy fire
My brother often lodged in his houfe :

5   And

And what of that ? bafe groome to flaunder him,
That honoured his embaffador fo much,
In abfence of the man to cheere the wife ?
This will not hold, proceed unto the next.

2. Elinor.

Thou faift fhe teemde fixe weekes before her time,
Why good fir fquire, are you fo cunning growen,
To make account of womens reckonings ?
Spit in your hand and to your other proofes :
Many mifchances happen in fuch affaires,
To make a woman come before her time.

John.

And where thou faift, he looketh like the king,
In action, feature and proportion :
Therein I hold with thee, for in my life
I never faw fo lively counterfet
Of *Richard Cordelion*, as in him.

Robert.

Then good my lord, be you indiffrent judge,
And let me have my living and my right.

2. Elinor.

Nay, heare you fir, you runne away too faft :
Know you not, *omne fimile non eft idem?*
Or have read in.   Harke yee good fir,
'Twas thus I warrant, and no otherwife.
Shee lay with fir *Robert* your father, and thought upon king
Richard my fonne, and fo your brother was formed in this
fafhion.

Robert.

Madame, you wrong me thus to jeft it out,
I crave my right : king *John*, as thou art king,
So be thou juft, and let me have my right.

John.

Why (foolifh boy) thy proofes are frivolous,
Nor canft thou chalenge any thing thereby.
But thou fhalt fee how I will helpe thy claime :
This is my doome, and this my doome fhall ftand
Irrevocable, as I am king of *England.*
For thou know'ft not, weele afke of them that know,

P   His

His mother and himfelfe fhall end this ftrife :
And as they fay, fo fhall thy living paffe.

Robert.

My lord, herein I challenge you of wrong,
To give away my right, and put the doome
Unto themfelves.   Can there be likelihood
That fhee will loofe ?
Or he will give the living from himfelfe ?
It may not be my lord.   Why fhould it be ?

John.

Lords, keep him back, and let him heare the doom.
Effex, firft afke the mother thrice who was his fire ?

Effex.

Lady *Margaret*, widow of *Fauconbridge*,
Who was father to thy fonne *Philip* ?

Mother.

Pleafe it your majefty, fir *Rob. Fauconbridge*.

Robert.

This is right, afke my fellow there if I be a thiefe.

John.

Afke *Philip* whofe fonne he is.

Effex.

Philip, who was thy father ?

Philip.

Mas my lord, and that's a queftion : and you had not taken
fome paines with her before, I fhould have defired you to afke
my mother.

John.

Say, who was thy father ?

Philip.

Faith (my lord) to anfwere you, fure hee is my father that
was neereft my mother when I was begotten, and him I thinke
to be fir *Robert Fauconbridge*.

John.

Effex, for fafhions fake demand agen,
And fo an end to this contention.

Robert.

Was ever man thus wrongd as *Robert* is ?

Effex.

Philip fpeake I fay, who was thy father ?

John.

John.

Young man how now, what art thou in a trance?

Elianor.

Philip awake, the man is in a dreame.

Philip.

Philippus atavis ædite Regibus.
What faift thou *Philip,* fprung of auncient kings?
Quo me rapit tempeftas?
What winde of honour blowes this furie forth?
Or whence proceede thefe fumes of majeftie?
Me thinkes I heare a hollow eccho found,
That *Philip* is the fonne unto a king:
The whiftling leaves upon the trembling trees,
Whiftle in confort I am *Richards* fonne:
The bubling murmur of the waters fall,
Records *Philippus Regius filius:*
Birds in their flight make muficke with their wings,
Filling the aire with glorie of my birth:
Birds, bubbles, leaves, and mountaines, eccho, all
Ring in mine eares, that I am *Richards* fonne.
Fond man! ah whither art thou carried?
How are thy thoughts ywrapt in honors heaven?
Forgetfull what thou art, and whence thou camft.
Thy fathers land cannot maintaine thefe thoughts,
Thefe thoughts are farre unfitting *Fauconbridge:*
And well they may; for why this mounting minde
Doth foare too high to ftoupe to *Fauconbridge.*
Why how now? knoweft thou where thou art?
And knoweft thou who expects thine anfwer here?
Wilt thou upon a franticke madding vaine
Goe loofe thy land, and fay thy felfe bafe borne?
No, keepe thy land, though *Richard* were thy fire,
What ere thou thinkft, fay thou art *Fauconbridge.*

John.

Speake man, be fodaine, who thy father was.

Philip.

Pleafe it your majeftie, fir *Robert*
Philip, that *Fauconbridge* cleaves to thy jawes:
It will not out, I cannot for my life
Say I am fonne unto a *Fauconbridge.*

P 2

Let

Let land and living goe, tis honors fire
That makes me fweare king *Richard* was my fire.
Bafe to a king addes title or more ftate,
Than knights begotten, though legitimate.
Pleafe it your grace, I am king *Richards* fonne.

Robert.

Robert revive thy heart, let forrow die,
His faltring tongue not fuffers him to lie.

Mother.

What head-ftrong furie doth enchant my fonne?

Philip.

Philip cannot repent, for he hath done.

John.

Then *Philip* blame not me, thy felfe haft loft
By wilfulneffe, thy living and thy land.
Robert, thou art the heire of *Fauconbridge*,
God give thee joy, greater than thy defert.

Q. Elianor.

Why how now *Philip*, give away thine owne?

Philip.

Madame, I am bold to make my felf your nephew,
The pooreft kinfman that your highneffe hath:
And with this proverb gin the world anew,
Help hands, I have no lands, honor is my defire;
Let *Philip* live to fhew himfelfe worthy fo great a fire.

Elinor.

Philip, I think thou knewft thy grandams minde:
But cheere thee boy, I will not fee thee want
As long as *Elinor* hath foote of land;
Henceforth thou fhalt be taken for my fonne,
And waite on me and on thine uncle heere,
Who fhall give honour to thy noble mind.

John.

Philip kneele downe, that thou maift throughly know
How much thy refolution pleafeth us,
Rife up fir *Richard Plantaginet* king *Richards* fonne.

Philip.

Grant heavens that *Philip* once may fhew himfelfe
Worthy the honour of *Plantaginet*,
Or bafeft glorie of a   s name.

John

John.

Now gentlemen, we will away to *France*,
To checke the pride of *Arthur* and his mates:
Essex, thou shalt be ruler of my realme,
And toward the maine charges of my warres,
Ile ceaze the lafie abbey lubbers lands
Into my hands to pay my men of warre.
The pope and popelings shall not greafe themfelves
With gold and groates, that are the fouldiers due.
Thus forward lords, let our commaund be done,
And march we forward mightily to *France*.   [*Exeunt.*
                              [*Manet* Philip *and his Mother.*

Philip.

Madame, I befeech you deigne me fo much leafure as the
hearing of a matter I long to impart to you.

Mother.

What's the matter *Philip?* I thinke your fuit in fecret, tends
to fome money matter, which you fuppofe burnes in the bottome of my cheft.

Philip.

No madam, it is no fuch fuit as to beg or borrow,
But fuch a fuit, as might fome other grant,
I would not now have troubled you withall.

Mother.

A gods name let us heare it.

Philip.

Then madam thus, your ladifhip fees well,
How that my fcandall growes by meanes of you,
In that report hath rumord up and downe,
I am a baftard, and no *Fauconbridge.*
This groffe attaint fo tilteth in my thoughts,
Maintaining combat to abridge mine eafe,
That field and towne, and company alone,
What fo I doe, or wherefoere I am,
I cannot chafe the flaunder from my thoughts.
If it be true, refolve me of my fire,
For pardon madam, if I thinke amiffe.
Be *Philip Philip*, and no *Fauconbridge*,
His father doubtleffe was as brave a man.
To you on knees, as fometime *Phaeton,*

P 3   Miftrufting

Miſtruſting ſielly *Merop* for his ſire,
Straining a little baſhfull modeſtie,
I beg ſome inſtance whence I am extraught.

Mother.

Yet more adoe to haſte me to my grave,
And wilt thou too become a mothers croſſe?
Muſt I accuſe my ſelfe to cloſe with you?
Slaunder my ſelfe, to quiet your affects?
Thou moov'ſt me *Philip* with this idle talke,
Which I remit, in hope this mood will die.

Philip.

Nay lady mother, heare me further yet,
For ſtrong conceit drives dutie hence awhile:
Your huſband *Fauconbridge* was father to that ſonne,
That carries markes of nature like the ſire,
The ſonne that blotteth you with wedlockes breach,
And holds my right, as lineall in deſcent
From him whoſe forme was figured in his face.
Can nature ſo diſſemble in her frame,
To make the one ſo like as like may be,
And in the other print no character
To challenge any marke of true deſcent?
My brothers mind is baſe, and too too dull,
To mount where *Philip* lodgeth his affects,
And his externall graces that you viewe,
(Though I report it) counterpoiſe not mine:
His conſtitution plaine debilitie,
Requires the chaire, and mine the ſeat of ſteele.
Nay, what is he, or what am I to him?
When any one that knoweth how to carpe,
Will ſcarcely judge us both one countrey borne.
This madam, this, hath drove me from my ſelfe:
And here by heavens eternall lampes I ſweare,
As curſed *Nero* with his mother did,
So I with you, if you reſolve me not.

Mother.

Let mothers teares quench out thy angers fire,
And urge no further what thou doeſt require.

Philip.

Let ſonnes intreatie ſway the mother now,
Or elſe ſhee dies: Ile not infringe my vow,

Mother.

Mother.

Unhappy tafke: muft I recount my fhame,
Blab my mifdeeds, or by concealing die?
Some power ftrike me fpeechleffe for a time,
Or take from him a while his hearings ufe.
Why wifh I fo, unhappy as I am?
The fault is mine, and he the faultie fruit,
I blufh, I faint, oh would I might be mute.

Philip.

Mother be briefe, I long to know my name.

Mother.

And longing die, to fhroud thy mothers fhame.

Philip.

Come madame come, you need not be fo loath,
The fhame is fhared equall twixt us both.
Ift not a flackeneffe in me, worthy blame,
To be fo old, and cannot write my name.
Good mother refolve me.

Mother.

Then *Philip* heare thy fortune, and my griefe,
My honours loffe by purchaffe of thy felfe,
My fhame, thy name, and hufbands fecret wrong,
All maimed and ftaind by youths unruly fway.
And when thou know'ft from whence thou art extraught,
Or if thou knew'ft what fuites, what threats, what feares,
To moove by love, or maffacre by death.
To yeeld with love, or end by loves contempt.
The mightineffe of him that courted me,
Who tempered terror with his wanton talke,
That fomething may extenuate the guilt.
But let it not advantage me fo much:
Upbraid me rather with the *Romane* dame,
That fhed her blood to wafh away her fhame.
Why ftand I to expoftulate the crime
With *pro & contra*, now the deed is done?
When to conclude two words may tell the tale,
That *Philips* father was a princes fonne,
Rich *Englands* rule, worlds onely terror he,
For honours loffe left me with child of thee:

Whofe

Whofe fonne thou art, then pardon me the rather,
For faire king *Richard* was thy noble father.
Philip.
Then *Robin Fauconbridge* I with thee joy,
My fire a king, and I a landleffe boy.
Gods lady mother, the world is in my debt,
There's fomething owing to *Plantaginet.*
I marry fir, let me alone for game,
Ile act fome wonders now I know my name.
By bleffed *Mary* Ile not fell that pride
For *Englands* wealth, and all the world befide,
Sit faft the proudeft of my fathers foes,
Away good mother, there the comfort goes.   [*Exeunt.*

Enter Philip *the* French *king, and* Lewis, Limoges, Conftance,
and her fonne Arthur.

King.
Now gin we broach the title of thy claime,
Young *Arthur* in the *Albion* territories,
Skaring proud *Angiers* with a puiffant fiege:
Brave *Auftria*, caufe of *Cordelions* death,
Is alfo come to aide thee in thy warres;
And all our forces joyne for *Arthurs* right.
And, but for caufes of great confequence,
Pleading delay till newes from *England* come,
Twice fhould not *Titan* hide him in the weft,
To coole the fet-locks of his wearie teame,
Till I had with an unrefifted fhocke
Controld the mannage of prowd *Angiers* walls,
Or made a forfet of my fame to chaunce.
Conftance.
May be that *John* in confcience or in feare
To offer wrong where you impugne the ill,
Will fend fuch calme conditions backe to *Fraunce,*
As fhall rebate the edge of fearefull warres:
If fo, forbearance is a deed well done.
Arthur.
Ah mother, poffeffion of a crowne is much,
And *John* as I have heard reported of,

For

For prefent vantage would adventure farre.
The world can witnefie, in his brothers time,
He tooke upon him rule, and almoft raigne:
Then muft it follow as a doubtfull point,
That hee'l refigne the rule unto his nephew.
I rather thinke the menace of the world
Sounds in his eares, as threats of no efteeme,
And fooner would he fcorne *Europa's* power,
Than loofe the fmalleft title he enjoyes;
For queftionleffe he is an *Englifhman*.

                    Lewis.
Why are the *Englifh* peercleffe in compare?
Brave cavaliers as ere that ifland bred,
Have liv'd and di'd, and dar'd, and done cnough,
Yet never grac'd their countrey for the caufe:
England is *England*, yeelding good and bad,
And *John* of *England* is as other *Johns*.
Truft me yong *Arthur*, if thou like my reed,
Praife thou the *French* that helpe thee in this need.

                    Lymoges.
The *Englifhman* hath little caufe I trowe,
To fpend good fpeaches on fo proud a foe.
Why *Arthur* here's his fpoyle that now is gone,
Who when he liv'd outrov'd his brother *John:*
But haftie curres that lie fo long to catch,
Come halting home, and meete their over-match.
But newes come now, here's the embaffadour.

                Enter Chattilion.

                    K. Philip.
And in good time, welcome my lord *Chattilion:*
What newes? will *John* accord to our command?

                    Chattilion.
Be I not briefe to tell your highneffe all,
He will approach to interrupt my tale:
For one felfe bottome brought us both to *France.*
He on his part will trie the chance of warre,
And if his words inferre affured truth,
Will loofe himfelfe, and all his followers,

                                        Ere

Ere yeeld unto the leaft of your demands.
The mother queene fhee taketh on amaine
Gainft lady *Confiance*, counting her the caufe
That doth effect this claime to *Albion*,
Conjuring *Arthur* with a grandames care,
To leave his mother; willing him fubmit
His ftate to *John*, and her protection,
Who (as fhee faith) are ftudious for his good.
More circumftance the feafon intercepts:
This is the fumme, which briefly I have fhowne.

K. *Philip.*

This bitter winde muft nip fome-bodies fpring:
Sodaine and briefe, who fo, 'tis harveft whether.
But fay *Chattilion*, what perfons of account are with him?

Chattilion.

Of *England*, Earle *Pembrooke* and *Salifburie*,
The onely noted men of any name.
Next them, a baftard of the kings deceaft,
A hardie wild-head, tough and venturous,
With many other men of high refolve.
Then is there with them *Elinor* mother queene,
And *Blanch* her neece, daughter to the king of *Spaine:*
Thefe are the prime birds of this hot adventure.

Enter John *and his followers,* Queene, Baftard, Earles, &c.

K. *Philip.*

Me feemeth *John*, an over-daring fpirit
Effects fome frenfie in thy rafh approach,
Treading my confines with thy armed troupes.
I rather lookt for fome fubmiffe reply
Touching the claime thy nephew *Arthur* makes
To that which thou unjuftly doft ufurpe.

K. *John.*

For that *Chattilion* can difcharge you all,
I lift not pleade my title with my tongue.
Nor came I hither with intent of wrong
To *France* or thee, or any right of thine;
But in defence and purchafe of my right,
The towne of *Angiers:* which thou doft begirt

In

In the behalfe of lady *Conflance* fonne,
Whereto nor he nor fhe can lay juft claime.
Conflance.

Yes (falfe intruder) if that juft be juft,
And head-ftrong ufurpation put apart,
Arthur my fonne, heire to thy elder brother,
Without ambiguous fhadow of difcent,
Is foveraigne to the fubftance thou withholdft.
Q. Elinor.

Mifgoverned goffip, ftaine to this refort,
Occafion of thefe undecided jarres,
I fay (that know) to checke thy vaine fuppofe,
Thy fonne hath naught to do with that he claimes.
For proofe whereof, I can inferre a will,
That barres the way he urgeth by difcent.
Conflance.

A will indeed, a crabbed womans will,
Wherein the divell is an overfeer,
And prowd dame *Elinor* fole executreffe:
More wills than fo, on perill of my foule,
Were never made to hinder *Arthurs* right.
Arthur.

But fay there was, as fure there can be none,
The law intends fuch teftaments as void,
Where right difcent can no way be impeacht.
Q Elinor.

Peace *Arthur* peace, thy mother makes thee wings
To foare with perill after *Icarus,*
And truft me youngling for the fathers fake,
I pity much the hazard of thy youth.
Conflance.

Befhrew you elfe how pitifull you are,
Ready to weepe to heare him afke his owne ;
Sorrow betide fuch grandames and fuch griefe,
That minifter a poyfon for pure love.
But who fo blind, as cannot fee this beame,
That you forfooth would keepe your coufin downe,
For feare his mother fhould be uf'd too well ?
I there's the griefe, confufion catch the braine,
That hammers fhiftes to ftop a princes raigne.
Q. Elinor.

Q. Elianor.

Impatient, franticke, common flaunderer,
Immodeft dame, unnurtur'd quarreller,
I tell thee I, not envie to thy fonne,
But juftice makes me fpeake as I have done.

K. Philip.

But here's no proofe that fhews your fonne a king.

K. John.

What wants, my fword fhal more at large fet down.

Lewis.

But that may breake before the truth be known.

Baftard.

Then this may hold till all his right be fhowne.

Lymoges.

Good words fir fauce, your betters are in place.

Baftard.

Not you fir doughtie, with your lyons cafe.

Blanch.

Ah joy betide his foule, to whom that fpoyle belong'd :
Ah *Richard*, how thy glory here is wrong'd.

Lymoges.

Me thinks that *Richards* pride and *Richards* fall,
Should be a prefident t'afright you all.

Baftard.

What words are thefe ? how do my finews fhake ?
My fathers foe clad in my fathers fpoyle,
A thoufand furies kindle with revenge,
This heart that choller keepes a confiftorie,
Scaring my inwards with a brand of hate :
How doth *Alecto* whifper in mine eares ?
Delay not *Philip*, kill the villaine ftraight,
Difrobe him of the matchleffe monument
Thy fathers triumph ore the favages,
Bafe heardgroom, coward, peafant, worfe than a threfhing flave,
What mak'ft thou with the trophie of a king ?
Sham'ft thou not coyftrell, loathfome dunghill fwad,
To grace thy carkaffe with an ornament
Too pretious for a monarkes coverture ?
Scarce can I temper due obedience
Unto the prefence of my foveraigne,

From

From acting outrage on this trunke of hate :
But arme thee traytor, wronger of renowne,
For by his foule I sweare, my fathers foule,
Twise will I not review the mornings rise,
Till I have torne that trophie from thy backe,
And split thy heart for wearing it so long.
Philip hath sworne, and if it be not done,
Let not the world repute me *Richards* sonne.

Lymoges.

Nay soft sir bastard, hearts are not split so soone,
Let them rejoyce that at the end doe win :
And take this lesson at thy foe-mans hand,
Pawne not thy life to get thy fathers skin.

Blanch.

Wel may the world speake of his knightly valor,
That wins this hide to weare a ladies favour.

Bastard.

Ill may I thrive, and nothing brooke with me,
If shortly I present it not to thee.

K. Philip.

Lordings forbeare, for time is comming fast,
That deeds may trie what words can not determine,
And to the purpose for the cause you come.
Me seemes you set right in chaunce of warre,
Yeelding no other reasons for your claime,
But so and so, because it shall be so.
So wrong shall be subornd by trust of strength :
A tyrants practise to inveit himselfe,
Where weake resistance giveth wrong the way.
To checke the which, in holy lawfull armes,
I, in the right of *Arthur*, *Geffreys* sonne,
Am come before this city of *Angiers*,
To barre all other false supposed claime,
From whence, or howsoere the error springs.
And in his quarrell on my princely word,
Ile fight it out unto the latest man.

John.

Know king of *France*, I will not be commanded
By any power or prince in *Christendome*,
To yeeld an instance how I hold mine owne,

More

More than to anſwere, that mine owne is mine,
But wilt thou ſee me parley with the towne,
And heare them offer me allegeance,
Fealtie and homage, as true liege men ought.

K. Philip.

Summon them, I will not beleeve it till I ſee it,
And when I ſee it, Ile ſoone change it.

[*They ſummon the towne, the citizens appeare upon the walls.*

K. John.

You men of *Angiors*, and as I take it my loiall ſubjects, I
have ſummoned you to the walls: to diſpute on my right,
were to thinke you doubtfull therein, which I am perſwaded
you are not. In few words, our brothers ſonne, backt with
the king of *France*, have beleagred your towne upon a falſe
pretended title to the ſame: in defence wherof I your liege
lord have brought our power to fence you from the uſurper,
to free your intended ſervitude, and utterly to ſupplant the
foemen, to my right and your reſt. Say then, who keepe
you the towne for?

Citizen.

For our lawfull king.

John.

I was no leſſe perſwaded: then in gods name open your
gates, and let me enter.

Citizen.

And it pleaſe your highnes we comptroll not your title,
neither will wee raſhly admit your entrance: if you be lawfull
king, with all obedience we keep it to your uſe, if not king,
our raſhnes to be impeached for yeelding, without more con-
ſiderate triall: wee anſwere not as men lawleſſe, but to the
behoole of him that prooves lawfull.

John.

I ſhall not come in then?

Citizen.

No my lord, till we know more.

K. Philip.

Then heare me ſpeak in the behalfe of *Arthur* ſon of
Geffrey, elder brother to *John*, his title manifeſt, with out con-
tradiction, to the crowne and kingdom of *England*, with
Angiers, and divers townes on this ſide the ſea: wil you ac-

I   knowledge

knowledge him your liege lord, who speaketh in my word,
to entertaine you with all favors, as beseemeth a king to his
subjects, or a friend to his welwillers: or stand to the peril
of your contempt, when his title is proved by the sword.

Citizen.

We answer as before, til you have proved one right, we
acknowledge none right, he that tries himselfe our soveraigne,
to him wil we remaine firme subjects, and for him, and in his
right we hold our towne, as desirous to know the truth, as
loth to subscribe before we know: more than this we cannot
say, and more than this we dare not do.

K. Philip.

Then *John* I defie thee, in the name and behalfe of *Arthur
Plantaginet*, thy king and cousin, whose right and patrimony
thou detainest, as I doubt not, ere the day end, in a set battel
make thee confesse; whereunto, with a zeale to right, I
challenge thee.

K. John.

I accept thy challenge, and turne the defiance to thy
throat.

Excursions. *The bastard chaseth* Lymoges *the Austrich duke,
and maketh him leave the lyons skin.*

Bastard.

And art thou gone! misfortune haunt thy steps,
And chill cold feare assaile thy times of rest.
Morpheus leave here thy silent eban cave,
Besiege his thoughts with dismall fantasies,
And ghastly objects of pale threatning morn.
Affright him every minute with stearne lookes,
Let shadow temper terror in his thoughts,
And let the terror make the coward mad,
And in his madnesse let him feare pursuit,
And so in frensie let the peasant die.
Here is the ransome that allaies his rage,
The first freehold that *Richard* left his sonne:
With which I shall surprize his living foes,
As *Hectors* statue did the fainting *Greekes*.   [*Exit.*

Enter

Enter the Kings Heraulds with trumpets to the wals of Angiers : *they summon the towne.*

Eng. Heraulds.

John by the grace of God king of *England*, lord of *Ireland*, *Anjou*, *Toraine*, &c. demandeth once again of you his subjects of *Angiers*, if you wil quietly furrender up the towne into his hands ?

Fr. Herold.

Philip by the grace of God king of *France*, demaundeth in the behalfe of *Arthur* duke of *Brittaine*, if you will furrender up the towne into his hands, to the use of the said *Arthur*.

Citizens.

Herrolds go tell the two victorious princes, that we the poore inhabitants of *Angiers*, require a parley of their majefties.

Herolds.

We goe.

Enter the Kings, *Queene* Elianor, Blanch, Baftard, Lymoges, Lewis, Caftilean, Pembrooke, Salifbury, Conftance, *and* Arthur *Duke of* Brittaine.

John.

Herold, what anfwer doe the townfmen fend ?

Philip.

Will *Angiers* yeeld to *Philip* king of *France* ?

Eng. Heraulds.

The townfmen on the wals accept your grace.

Fr. Herolds.

And crave a parley of your majefty.

John.

You cittizens of *Angiers*, have your eyes
Beheld the flaughter that our *Englifh* bowes
Have made upon the coward fraudfull *French* ?
And have you wifely pondred therewithall
Your gaine in yeelding to the *Englifh* king ?

Philip.

Their loffe in yeelding to the *Englifh* king.
But *John*, they faw from out their higheft towers

Tho

The chevaliers of *France* and croffe-bow-fhot
Make lanes of flaughterd bodies through thine hoaft,
And are refolv'd to yeeld to *Arthurs* right.
John.
Why *Philip*, though thou bravft it fore the wals,
Thy confcience knowes that *John* hath wonne the field,
Philip.
What ere my confcience knowes, thy army feeles
That *Philip* had the better of the day.
Baftard.
Philip indeed hath got the lions cafe,
Which here he holds to *Lymoges* difgrace.
Bafe duke to flie and leave fuch fpoiles behind :
But this thou knewft of force to make me ftay.
It farde with thee as with the mariner,
Spying the hugie whale, whofe monftrous bulke
Doth beare the waves like mountaines fore the wind,
That throwes out emptie veffels, fo to ftay
His fury, while the fhip doth fayle away.
Philip 'tis thine: and fore this princely prefence,
Madame, I humbly lay it at your feete,
Being the firft adventure I atchiev'd,
And firft exploite your grace did me enjoyne :
Yet many more I long to be enjoyn'd.
Blanch.
Philip I take it, and I thee command
To weare the fame as earft thy father did :
Therewith receive this favour at my hands,
T'incourage thee to follow *Richards* fame.
Arthur.
Ye cittizens of *Angiers* are ye mute ?
Arthur or *John*, fay which fhall be your king?
Cittizen.
We care not which, if once we knew the right;
But till we know, we will not yeeld our right.
Baftard.
Might *Philip* counfell two fo mightie kings,
As are the kings of *England* and of *France*,
He would advife your graces to unite
And knit your forces gainft thefe cittizens,

Q   Pulling

Pulling their battred wals about their eares.
The towne once wonne, then ftrive about the claime,
For they are minded to delude you both.

Cittizen.

Kings, princes, lords, and knights affembled here,
The cittizens of *Angiers* all by me
Entreate your majeftie to heare them fpeake :
And as you like the motion they fhall make,
So to account and follow their advice.

John. Phil.

Speake on, we give thee leave.

Cittizen.

Then thus : whereas the young and lufty knight
Incites you on to knit your kingly ftrengths :
The motion cannot chufe but pleafe the good,
And fuch as love the quiet of the ftate.
But how my lords, how fhold your ftrengths be knit ?
Not to oppreffe your fubjects and your friends,
And fill the world with brawles and mutinies :
But unto peace your forces fhould be knit
To live in princely league and amitie :
Doe this, the gates of *Angiers* fhall give way,
And ftand wide open to your hearts content.
To make this peace a lafting bond of love,
Remaines one onely honourable meanes,
Which by your pardon I fhall here difplay.
Lewis the *Dolphin* and the heire of *France*,
A man of noted valour through the world,
Is yet unmarried : let him take to wife
The beauteous daughter of the king of *Spaine*,
Neece to K. *John*, the lovely lady *Blanch*,
Begotten on his fifter *Elianor*.
With her in marriage will her unkle give
Caftles and towers, as fitteth fuch a match.
The kings thus joynd in league of perfect love,
They may fo deale with *Arthur* duke of *Britaine*,
Who is but young, and yet unmeet to raigne,
As he fhall ftand contented every way.
Thus have I boldly (for the common good)
Delivered what the citie gave in charge.

I

And

And as upon conditions you agree,
So ſhall we ſtand content to yeeld the towne.

Arthur.

A proper peace, if ſuch a motion hold ;
Theſe kings beare armes for me, and for my right,
And they ſhall ſhare my lands to make them friends.

Q. Elianor.

Sonne *John,* follow this motion, as thou loveſt thy mother.
Make league with *Philip,* yeeld to any thing :
Lewis ſhall have my neece, and then be ſure
Arthur ſhall have ſmall ſuccour out of *France.*

John.

Brother of *France,* you heare the citizens :
Then tell me, how you meane to deale herein.

Conſtance.

Why *John,* what canſt thou give unto thy neece,
Thou haſt no foote of land but *Arthurs* right ?

Lewis.

Bir lady citizens, I like your choyce,
A lovely damſel is the lady *Blanch,*
Worthy the heire of *Europe* for her pheere.

Conſtance.

What kings, why ſtand you gazing in a trance ?
Why how now lords ? accurſed citizens
To fill and tickle their ambitious eares,
With hope of gaine, that ſprings from *Arthurs* loſſe.
Some diſmall planet at thy birth-day raign'd,
For now I ſee the fall of all thy hopes.

K. Philip.

Ladie, and duke of *Brittaine,* know you both,
The king of *France* reſpects his honor more,
Than to betray his friends and favourers.
Princeſſe of *Spaine,* could you affect my ſonne,
If we upon conditions could agree ?

Baſtard.

Swounds madam, take an *Engliſh* gentleman ;
Slave as I was, I thought to have moov'd the match.
Grandame you made me halfe a promiſe once,
That lady *Blanch* ſhould bring me wealth inough,
And make me heire of ſtore of *Engliſh* land.

Q 2

Q. Elianor.

Peace *Philip*, I will looke thee out a wife,
We muſt with policie compound this ſtrife.

Baſtard.

If *Lewis* get her, well, I ſay no more:
But let the frolicke *Frenchman* take no ſcorne,
If *Philip* front him with an *Engliſh* horne.

John.

Ladie, what anſwer make you to the K. of *France?*
Can you affect the *Dolphin* for your lord?

Blanch.

I thanke the king that likes of me ſo well,
To make me bride unto ſo great a prince:
But give me leave my lord to pauſe on this,
Leaſt beeing too too forward in the cauſe,
It may be blemiſh to my modeſtie.

Q. Elinor.

Sonne *John*, and worthy *Philip* K. of *France*,
Do you confer a while about the dower,
And I will ſchoole my modeſt neece ſo well,
That ſhe ſhall yeeld as ſoone as you have done.

Conſtance.

I, theres the wretch that brocheth all this il,
Why flie I not upon the bedlams face,
And with my nayles pull forth her hatefull eyes.

Arthur.

Sweet mother ceaſe theſe haſtie madding fits:
For my ſake, let my grandam have her will.
O would ſhe with her hands pull forth my heart,
I could affoord it to appeaſe theſe broyles.
But (mother) let us wiſely winke at all,
Leaſt farther harmes enſue our haſtie ſpeech.

Philip.

Brother of *England*, what dowrie wilt thou give
Unto my ſonne in marriage with thy neece?

John.

Firſt *Philip* knowes her dowrie out of *Spaine*,
To be ſo great as may content a king:
But more to mend and amplifie the ſame,
I give in money thirtie thouſand markes.
For land I leave it to thine owne demand.

Philip.

Philip.

Then I demand *Volqueſſon, Torain, Main,*
Poiters and *Anjou,* theſe five provinces,
Which thou as king of *England* holdſt in *France:*
Then ſhall our peace be ſoone concluded on.

Baſtard.

No leſſe then five ſuch provinces at once?

John.

Mother what ſhal I do? my brother got theſe lands
With much effuſion of our *Engliſh* bloud:
And ſhall I give it all away at once?

Q. Elinor.

John give it him, ſo ſhalt thou live in peace,
And keepe the reſidue ſans jeopardie.

John.

Philip, bring foorth thy ſonne, here is my neece,
And here in marriage I do give with her
From me and my ſucceſſors *Engliſh* kings,
Volqueſſon, Poiters, Anjou, Torain, Main,
And thirtie thouſand markes of ſtipend coyne.
Now cittizens, how like you of this match?

Citizens.

We joy to ſee ſo ſweete a peace begun.

Lewis.

Lewis with *Blanch* ſhall ever live content.
But now king *John,* what ſay you to the duke?
Father, ſpeake as you may in his behalfe.

Philip.

K. *John,* be good unto thy nephew here,
And give him ſomewhat that ſhall pleaſe you beſt.

John.

Arthur, although thou troubleſt *Englands* peace
Yet here I give thee *Brittaine* for thine owne,
Together with the earledome of *Richmont,*
And this rich citie of *Angiers* withall.

Q. Elianor.

And if thou ſeeke to pleaſe thine uncle *John,*
Shalt ſee my ſonne how I will make of thee.

John.

Now every thing is ſorted to this end,
Lets in, and there prepare the marriage rites,

Q 3   Which

Which in S. *Maries* chappell prefently
Shall be performed ere this prefence part.   [*Exeunt.*
                              [*Manent* Conftance *and* Arthur.
                   Arthur.
  Madam good cheere, thefe drouping languifhments
Adde no redreffe to falve our awkward haps,
If heavens have concluded thefe events,
To fmall availe is bitter penfiveneffe :
Seafons will change, and fo our prefent greefe
May change with them, and all to our releefe.
                   Conftance.
  Ah boy, thy yeares I fee are farre too greene
To looke into the bottome of thefe cares.
But I, who fee the poyfe that weigheth downe
Thy weale, my wifh, and all the willing meanes
Wherewith thy fortune and thy fame fhould mount.
What joy, what eafe, what reft can lodge in me,
With whom all hope and hap doe difagree ?
                   Arthur.
  Yet ladies teares, and cares, and folemn fhewes,
Rather then helpes, heape up more worke for woes.
                   Conftance.
  If any power will heare a widowes plaint,
That from a wounded foule implores revenge :
Send fell contagion to infeæt this clime,
This curfed countrey, where the traitors breath,
Whofe perjurie (as proud *Briareus,*)
Beleaguers all the fkie with mif-beleefe.
He promift *Arthur,* and he fware it too,
To fence thy right, and check thy fo-mans pride ;
But now black-fpotted perjure as he is,
He takes a truce with *Elnors* damned brat,
And marries *Lewis* to her lovely neece,
Sharing thy fortune, and thy birth-dayes gift
Betweene thefe lovers : ili betide the match.
And as they fhoulder thee from out thine owne,
And triumph in a widowes tearefull cares :
So heav'ns croffe them with a thriftleffe courfe,
Is all the blood yfpilt on either part,
Clofing the cranies of the thirftie earth,

                                        Growne

Growne to a love-game and a bridall feaft?
And muft thy birth-right bid the wedding banes?
Poore helpeleffe boy, hopeleffe and helpeleffe too,
To whom misfortune feemes no yoake at all.
Thy ftay, thy ftate, thy imminent mifhaps
Woundeth thy mothers thoughts with feeling care,
Why lookft thou pale? the colour flies thy face:
I trouble now the fountaine of thy youth,
And make it muddie with my doles difcourfe,
Goe in with me, reply not lovely boy,
We muft obfcure this mone with melodie,
Leaft worfer wrack enfue our male-content.   [*Exeunt.*

Enter the King of England, *the King of* France, Arthur,
Baftard, Lewis, Lymoges, Conftance, Blanch, Chattillion,
Pembrooke, Salifburie, *and* Elianor.

John.
This is the day, the long-defired day,
Wherein the realmes of *England* and of *France*
Stand highly bleffed in a lafting peace.
Thrice happie is the bridegroome and the bride,
From whofe fweet bridall fuch a concord fprings,
To make of mortall foes immortall friends.
Conftance.
Ungodly peace made by anothers warre.
Philip.
Unhappie peace, that tyes thee from revenge,
Rouze thee *Plantaginet*, live not to fee
The butcher of the great *Plantaginet*.
Kings, princes, and ye peeres of either realmes,
Pardon my rafhnes, and forgive the zeale
That carries me in furie to a deede
Of high defert, of honour, and of armes.
A boone (O kings) a boone doth *Philip* begge
Proftrate upon his knee: which knee fhall cleave
Unto the fuperficies of the earth,
Till *France* and *England* grant this glorious boone.
John.
Speake *Philip*, *England* grants thee thy requeft.

Philip.

Philip,
And *France* confirmes what ere is in his power.

Baſtard.
Then duke ſit faſt, I levell at thy head,
Too baſe a ranſome for my fathers life.
Princes, I crave the combate with the duke
That braves it in diſhonour of my ſire.
Your words are paſt, nor can you now reverſe
The princely promiſe that revives my ſoule,
Whereat me thinkes I ſee his ſinewes ſhake :
This is the boone (dread lords) which granted once
Or life or death are pleaſant to my ſoule ;
Since I ſhall live and die in *Richards* right.

Lymoges.
Baſe baſtard, miſbegotten of a king,
To interrupt theſe holy nuptiall rites
With brawles and tumults to a dukes diſgrace ;
Let it ſuffice, I ſcorne to joyne in fight,
With one ſo farre unequall to my ſelfe.

Baſtard
A fine excuſe, kings if you will be kings,
Then keepe your words, and let us combate it.

John.
Philip, we cannot force the duke to fight,
Being a ſubject unto neither realme :
But tell me *Auſtria,* if an *Engliſh* duke
Should dare thee thus, wouldſt thou accept the challenge ?

Lymoges.
Elſe let the world account the *Auſtrich* duke
The greateſt coward living on the earth.

John.
Then cheere thee *Philip, John* wil keep his word,
Kneele down, in ſight of *Philip* king of *France,*
And all theſe princely lords aſſembled here,
I gird thee with the ſword of *Normandie,*
And of that land I do inveſt thee duke :
So ſhalt thou be in living and in land
Nothing inferiour unto *Auſtria.*

Lymoges.
K. *John,* I tell thee flatly to thy face,
Thou wrong'ſt mine honour : and that thou mai'ſt ſee

How

How much I fcorne thy new made duke and thee,
I flatly fay, I will not be compel'd :
And fo farewell fir duke of lowe degree,
Ile finde a time to match you for this geare.   [*Exit.*

John.
Stay *Philip,* let him goe, the honours thine.
Baſtard.
I cannot live unleſſe his life be mine.
Q. Elianor.
Thy forwardnes this day hath joy'd my foule,
And made me thinke my *Richard* lives in thee.
K. Philip.
Lordings let's in, and fpend the wedding day
In maſkes and triumphs, letting quarrels ceaſe.

Enter a Cardinall from Rome.

Cardinall.
Stay king of *France,* I charge thee joyn not hands
With him that ſtands accurſt of God and men.
Know *John,* that I *Pandulph* cardinall of *Millaine,* and legate from the fea of *Rome,* demand of thee in the name of
our holy father the *Pope Innocent,* why thou do'ſt (contrary to
the lawes of our holy mother the church, and our holy fa her
the Pope) diſturb the quiet of the church, and diſanull the
election of *Stephen Langhton,* whom his holineſſe hath elected
archbiſhop of *Canterburie:* this in his holineſſe name I de-
maund of thee ?

John.
And what haſt thou or the Pope thy maſter to do to demand of me, how I imploy mine own ? know fir prieſt, as
I honor the churca and holy church-men, fo I ſcorne to be
fubject to the greateſt prelate in the world. Tell thy maſter
fo from me, and fay, *John* of *England* faid it, that never an
Italian prieſt of them all, ſhal either have tythe, tole, or pol-
ling peny out of *England;* but as I am king, fo will I raigne
next under God, fupreame head both over ſpiritual and
temporall : and he that contradicts me in this, Ile make him
hop headleſſe.

K. Philip.

K. Philip.

What K. *John*, know you what you fay, thus to blafpheme againft our holy father the Pope?

John.

Philip, though thou and all the princes of *Chriftendome* fuffer themfelves to be abus'd by a prelates flavery, my mind is not of fuch bafe temper. If the Pope will bee king of *England*, let him win it with the fword, I know no other title he can alleadge to mine inheritance.

Cardinall.

John, this is thine anfwer?

John.

What then?

Cardinall.

Then I *Pandulph* of *Padua*, legate from the apoftolike fea, doe in the name of Saint *Peter* and his fucceffor our holy father Pope *Innocent*, pronounce thee accurfed, difcharging every of thy fubjects of all dutie and fealtie that they doe owe to thee, and pardon and forgiveneffe of finne to thofe or them whatfoever, which fhall carrie armes againft thee, or murder thee: this I pronounce, and charge all good men to abhorre thee as an excommunicate perfon.

John.

So fir, the more the foxe is curs'd the better a fares: if God bleffe me and my land, let the pope and his fhavelings curfe and fpare not.

Cardinall.

Furthermore, I charge thee *Philip* K. of *Fraunce*, and all the kings and princes of *Chriftendome*, to make warre upon this mifcreant: and whereas thou haft made a league with him, and confirmed it by oath, I doe in the name of our forefaid father the Pope, acquit thee of that oath, as unlaw-full, beeing made with an hereticke; howe fai'ft thou *Philip*, do'ft thou obey?

John.

Brother of *Fraunce*, what fay you to the cardinall?

Philip.

I fay, I am fory for your majeftie, requefting you to fub-mit your felfe to the church of *Rome*.

John.

John.

And what fay you to our league, if I do not fubmit?

Philip.

What fhould I fay? I muft obey the pope.

John.

Obey the pope, and breake your oath to God?

Philip.

The legate hath abfolved me of mine oath:
Then yeeld to *Rome*, or I defie thee here.

John.

Why *Philip*, I defie the pope and thee,
Falfe as thou art, and perjur'd king of *France*,
Unworthy man to be accounted king.
Giv'ft thou thy fword into a prelates hands?
Pandulph, where I of abbots, monkes, and friers
Have taken fomewhat to maintaine my wars,
Now will I take no more but all they have.
Ile rouze the lazie lubbers from their cels,
And in defpight Ile fend them to the pope.
Mother come you with me, and for the reft
That will not follow *John* in this attempt,
Confufion iight upon their damned foules.
Come lords, fight for your K. that fighteth for your good.

Philip.

And are they gone? *Pandulph* thy felfe fhalt fee
How *France* will fight for *Rome* and *Romifh* rites.
Nobles to armes, let him not paffe the feas,
Let's take him captive, and in triumph lead
The K. of *England* to the gates of *Rome*.
Arthur beftirre thee man, and thou fhalt fee
What *Philip* K. of *France* will doe for thee.

Blanch.

And will your grace upon your wedding day
Forfake your bride, and rollow dreadfull drums?
Nay, good my lord, ftay you at home with me.

Lewis.

Sweet heart content thee, and wee fhall agree.

Philip.

Follow my lords, lord Cardinall lead the way,
Drums fhall be muficke to this wedding day.　　　[*Exeunt.*
Excurfions.

Excurfions. The Baftard purfues Auftria, *and kils him.*

Baftard.

Thus hath K. *Richards* fon performd his vowes.
And offred *Auftria's* blood for his facrifice
Unto his fathers everliving foule.
Brave *Cord.lion,* now my heart doth fay,
I have deferved, though not to be thine heire,
Yet as I am, thy bafe begotten fonne,
A name as pleafing to thy *Philips* heart,
As to be cald the duke of *Normandie.*
Lie there a prey to every rav'ning fowle:
And as my father triumpht in thy fpoyles,
And trode thine enfignes underneath his feet,
So doe I tread upon thy curfed felfe,
And leave thy body to the fowles for food.   *[Exit.*

Excurfions. Arthur, Conftance, Lewis, *having taken* Q.
Elianor *prifoner.*

Conftance.

Thus hath the god of kings with conquering arme
Difpearft the foes to true fucceffion,
Proud, and difturber of thy countries peace,
Conftance doth live to tame thine infolence,
And on thy head will now avenged be
For all the mifchiefs hatched in thy braine.

Q *Elinor.*

Contemptuous dame, unreverent dutches thou,
To brave fo great a queene as *Elianor,*
Bafe fcold, haft thou forgot, that I was wife
And mother to three mightie *Englifh* kings?
I charge thee then, and you forfooth fir boy,
To fet your grandmother at libertie,
And yeeld to *John* your uncle and your king.

Conftance.

'Tis not thy words proud queene fhall carry it.

Elinor.

Nor yet thy threates proud dame fhal daunt my mind.

Arthur.

Sweete grandam, and good mother, leave thefe braules.
5   *Elianor.*

Elianor.

Ile finde a time to triumph in thy fall.

Conſtance.

My time is now to triumph in thy fall,
And thou ſhalt know that *Conſtance* will triumph.

Arthur.

Good mother, weigh it is queene *Elinor*.
Though ſhe be captive, uſe her like her ſelfe.
Sweet grandame, beare with what my mother ſays,
Your highneſſe ſhall be uſed honourably.

Enter a Meſſenger.

Meſſenger.

Lewis my lord, duke *Arthur*, and the reſt,
To armes in haſt, K. *John* relyes his men,
And ginnes the fight afreſh : and ſweares withall
To looſe his life, or ſet his mother free.

Lewis.

Arthur away, 'tis time to looke about.

Elinor.

Why how now dame, what is your courage coold ?

Conſtance.

No *Elinor* my courage gathers ſtrength,
And hopes to leade both *John* and thee as ſlaves :
And in that hope, I hale thee to the field.   [*Exeunt.*
  [*Excurſions.* Elianor *is reſcued by* John, *and* Arthur
  is taken priſoner. Exeunt. Sound *Victory.*

Enter John, Elianor, *and* Arthur *priſoner*, Baſtard, Pembrooke,
  Saliſbury, *and* Hubert de Burgh.

John.

Thus right triumphs, and *John* triumphs in right :
Arthur thou ſeeſt, *Fraunce* cannot bolſter thee :
Thy mothers pride hath brought thee to this fall.
But if at laſt nephew thou yeeld thy ſelfe
Into the gardance of thine uncle *John*,
Thou ſhalt be uſed as becomes a prince.

Arthur.

Arthur.

Uncle, my grandame taught her nephew this,
To beare captivitie with patience.
Might hath prevaild, not right, for I am king
Of *England,* though thou weare the diademe.

Q. Elinor.

Sonne *John,* foone shall wee teach him to forget
Thefe prowd prefumptions, and to know himfelfe.

John.

Mother, he never will forget his claime,
I would he livde not to remember it.
But leaving this, we will to *England* now,
And take fome order with our popelings there,
That fwell with pride and fat of lay mens lands.
Philip, I make thee chiefe in this affaire,
Ranfacke the abbeis, cloyfters, priories,
Convert their coine unto my fouldiers ufe:
And whatfoere he be within my land,
That goes to *Rome* for juftice and for law,
While he may have his right within the realme,
Let him be judgde a traitor to the ftate,
And fuffer as an enemy to *England.*
Mother, wee leave you here beyond the feas,
As regent of our provinces in *France,*
While we to *England* take a fpeedie courfe,
And thanke our God that gave us victorie.
Hubert de Burgh take *Arthur* here to thee,
Be he thy prifoner: *Hubert* keepe him fafe,
For on his life doth hang thy foveraignes crowne.
But in his death confifts thy foveraignes bliffe:
Then *Hubert,* as thou fhortly hearft from me,
So ufe the prifoner I have given in charge.

Hubert.

Frolicke yong prince, thogh I your keeper be,
Yet fhall your keeper live at your command.

Arthur.

As pleafe my God, fo fhall become of me.

Q. Elianor.

My fonne, to *England,* I will fee thee fhipt,
And pray to God to fend thee fafe afhore.

Baftard.

Baſtard.

Now warres are done, I long to be at home,
To dive into the monks and abbots bagges,
To make ſome ſport among the ſmooth ſkind nunnes,
And keepe ſome revell with the ſanzen friers.

John.

To *England* lords, each looke unto your charge,
And arme your ſelves againſt the *Roman* pride.   [*Exeunt.*

Enter the King of France, Lewes *his ſonne, Cardinall* Pandolph
Legate, and Conſtance.

Philip.

What, every man attacht with this miſhap?
Why frowne you ſo, why droope ye lords of *France?*
Me thinkes it differs from a warrelike minde,
To lowre it for a checke or two of chaunce.
Had *Lymoges* eſcapt the baſtards ſpight,
A little ſorrow might have ſervde our loſſe.
Brave *Auſtria,* heaven joyes to have thee there.

Cardinall.

His ſoule is ſafe and free from purgatorie,
Our holy father hath diſpenſt his ſinnes,
The bleſſed ſaints have heard our oriſons,
And all are mediators for his ſoule,
And in the right of theſe moſt holy warres,
His holineſſe free pardon doth pronounce
To all that follow you gainſt *Engliſh* heretikes,
Who ſtand accurſed in our mother church.

Enter Conſtance *alone.*

Philip.

To aggravate the meaſure of our greefe,
All male-content comes *Conſtance* for her ſonne.
Be breefe good madame, for your face imports
A tragicke tale behind thats yet untold.
Her paſſions ſtop the organ of her voyce,
Deepe ſorrow throbbeth miſ-befalne events,
Out with it ladie, that our act may end
A full cataſtrophe of ſad laments.

Conſtance.

Conſtance.

My tongue is tun'd to ſtorie forth miſhap:
When did I breath to tell a pleaſing tale?
Muſt *Conſtance* ſpeake? let teares prevent her talke:
Muſt I diſcourſe? let *Dido* ſigh and ſay,
She weepes againe to heare the wracke of *Troy*:
Two words will ſerve, and then my tale is done:
Elnors proud brat hath rob'd me of my ſonne.

Lewis.

Have patience madame, this is chance of warre:
He may be ranſom'd, we revenge his wrong.

Conſtance.

Be it ne'r ſo ſoone, I ſhall not live ſo long.

Philip.

Deſpaire not yet, come *Conſtance*, go with me,
Theſe clouds will fleet, the day will cleare againe.   [*Exeunt.*

Cardinall.

Now *Lewis*, thy fortune buds with happy ſpring,
Our holy fathers prayers effecteth this.
Arthur is ſafe, let *John* alone with him,
Thy title next is fairſt to *Englands* crowne:
Now ſtirre thy father to begin with *John*,
The Pope ſays I, and ſo is *Albion* thine.

Lewis.

Thanks my lord legat for your good conceit,
'Tis beſt we follow now the game is faire,
My father wants to worke him your good words.

Cardinall.

A few will ſerve to forward him in this,
Thoſe ſhall not want: but let's about it then.   [*Exeunt.*

Enter Philip *leading a friar, charging him ſhew where the Abbots gold lay.*

Philip.

Come on you fat *Franciſcan*, dallie no longer, but ſhew me
where the abbots treaſure lies, or die.

Frier.

Benedicamus Domini, was ever ſuch an injurie?
Sweet S. *Withold* of thy lenitie, defend us from extremitie,

                                                              And

And heare us for S. *Charitie*, oppreffed with aufteritie.
In nomine domini, make I my homily,
Gentle gentilitie grieve not the cleargie.

>> *Philip.*

Gray-gown'd good face, conjure ye,
    Nere truft me for a groat
If this waft girdle hang thee not
    That girdeth in thy coat.
Now bald and barefoot *Bungie* birds,
    When up the gallowes climing,
Say *Philip* he had words enough,
    To put you downe with riming.

>> *Frier.*

O pardon, *O parce*, S. *Francis* for mercie,
Shall fhield thee from night-fpels, and dreaming of divels,
If thou wilt forgive me, and never more grieve me,
With fafting and praying, and Haile *Marie* faying,
From blacke purgatorie, a penance right fory :
Frier *Thomas* will warme you,
It fhall never harme you.

>> *Philip.*

Come leave off your rabble,
Sir, hang up this lozell.

>> 2 *Frier.*

For charitie I beg his life,
    Saint *Francis* chiteft frier,
The beft in all our coventi-,
    To keepe a vintners fire.
O ftrangle not the good old man,
    My hofteffe oldeft gueft,
And I wiil bring you by and by
    Unto the priors cheft.

>> *Philip.*

I, faift thou fo, and if thou wilt the frier is at liberty,
If not, as I am honeft man, I hang you both for company.

>> *Frier.*

Come hither, this is the cheft, thogh fimple to behold,
That wanteth not a thoufand pound in filver and in gold.
My felf wil warrant ful fo much, I know the abbots ftore,
Ile pawn my life there is no leffe, to have what ere is more.

    R   *Philip.*

Philip.

I take thy word, the overplus unto thy ſhare ſhal come,
But if there want of full ſo much, thy necke ſhall pay the
    ſumme.
Breake up the coffer, frier.

Frier.

Oh I am undone, faire *Alice* the nunne
Hath tooke up her reſt in the abbots cheſt.
Sancte benedicite, pardon my ſimplicitie.
Fie *Alice,* confeſſion will not ſalve this tranſgreſſion.

Philip.

What have we here, a holy nunne? ſo keepe me God in
    health,
A ſmooth facde nunne (for aught I know) is al the abbots
    wealth.
Is this the nunries chaſtitie?
Beſhrew me but I thinke
They go as oft to venery as niggards to their drinke.
Why paltry frier and pandar too, yee ſhameleſſe ſhaven crowne,
Is this the cheſt that held a hoord,
    at leaſt a thouſand pound?
And is the hoord a holy whore?
    well, be the hangman nimble,
Hee'l take the paine to pay you home,
    and teach you to diſſemble.

Nunne.

O ſpare the frier *Anthony,*
    a better never was
To ſing a dirige ſolemnely,
    or reade a morning maſſe.
If money be the meanes of this,
    I know an ancient nunne,
That hath a hoord theſe ſeven yeeres,
    did never ſee the ſunne;
And that is yours, and what is ours,
    ſo favour now be ſhowne,
You ſhall commaund as commonly,
    as if it were your owne.

Frier.

Your honour excepted.

Nunne.

Nunne.

I *Thomas*, I meane fo.

Philip.

From all fave from friers.

Nunne.

Good fir, doe not thinke fo.

Philip.

I thinke and fee fo :
Why how camft thou here?

Frier.

To hide her from lay men.

Nunne.

Tis true fir, for feare.

Philip.

For feare of the laitie : a pitiful dred
When a nunne flies for fuccour to a fat friers bed.
But now for your ranfome my cloyfter-bred conney,
To the cheft that you fpoke of where lies fo much mony.

Nunne.

Faire fir, within this preffe, of plate and mony is
The valew of a thoufand marks, and other thing by gis.
Let us alone, and take it all, tis yours fir, now you know it.

Philip.

Come on fir frier, picke the locke, this gere doth cotton
        hanfome,
That covetoufneffe fo cunningly muft pay the lechers ranfome.
What is in the hoord?

Frier.

Frier *Laurence* my lord, now holy water helpe us,
Some witch or fome divell is fent to delude us :
Haud credo Laurentius, that thou fhouldft be pend thus
In the preffe of a nunne we are all undone,
And brought to difcredence if thou be frier *Laurence.*

Frier.

Amor vincit omnia, fo *Cato* affirmeth,
And therefore a frier whofe fancie foon burneth,
Becaufe he is mortall and made of mould,
He omits what he ought, and doth more than he fhould.

Philip.

Philip.

How goes this geere ? the friers cheſt filld with a fauſea
  nunne.
The nunne again lockes frier up,
  to keepe him from the ſunne.
Belike the preſſe is purgatorie,
  or penance paſſing grievous :
The friers cheſt a hell for nunnes !
  how doe theſe dolts deceive us ?
Is this the labour of their lives, to feede and live at eaſe ?
To revell ſo laſciviouſly as often as they pleaſe ?
Ile mend the fault or fault my aime,
  if I doe miſſe amending,
'Tis better burne the cloyiters downe,
  than leave them for offending.
But holy you, to you I ſpeake,
  to you religious divell,
Is this the preſſe that holds the ſumme,
  to quit you for your evill ?

Nunne.

  I crie *peccavi, parce me,*
good ſir I was beguil'd.

Frier.

  Abſolve ſir for charitie,
ſhee would bee reconcil'd.

Philip.

  And ſo I ſhall, ſirs bind them faſt,
This is their abſolution,
  goe hang them up for hurting them,
Haſte them to execution.

Fr. Laurence.

  O *tempus edax rerum,*
Give children bookes they teare them.
O *vanitas vanitatis,* in this wāning *ætatis.*
At threeſcore wel neere, to goe to this geere,
To my conſcience a clog, to die like a dog.
Exaudi me domine, ſi vis me parce
Dabo pecuniam, ſi habeo veniam.
To goe and fetch it, I will diſpatch it,
A hundred pound ſterling, for my lives ſparing.

                                        Enter

Enter Peter *a prophet, with people.*

Peter.

Hoe, who is here? S. *Francis* be your fpeed,
Come in my flocke, and follow me,
    your fortunes I will reed.
Come hither boy, goe get thee home,
    and clime not over hie,
For from aloft thy fortune ftands, in hazard thou fhalt die.

Boy.

God be with you *Peter*, I pray you come to our houfe a
Sunday.

Peter.

My boy fhew me thy hand, bleffe thee my boy,
For in thy palme I fee a many troubles are ybent to dwel,
But thou fhalt fcape them all, and doe full well.

Boy.

I thanke you *Peter*, theres a cheefe for your labor : my fifter
prayes yee to come home, and tell her how many hufbands fhe
fhall have, and fhee'l give you a rib of bacon.

Peter.

My mafters, ftay at the townes end for me. Ile come to
you all anone : I muft difpatch fome bufines with a frier, and
then Ile reade your fortunes.

Philip.

How now, a prophet! fir prophet whence are ye?

Peter.

I am of the world and in the world, but live not as others,
by the world : what I am I know, and what thou wilt be I
know. If thou knoweft me now, be anfwered : if not, enquire no more what I am.

Philip.

Sir, I know you will be a diffembling knave, that deludes
the people with blinde prophecies : you are hee I look for,
you fhal away with me : bring away all the rable, and yon
frier *Laurence*, remember your raunfome a hundred pound, and
a pardon for your felfe, and the reft ; come on fir propher, you
fhall with me, to receive a prophets rewarde,   [*Exeunt.*

Enter

Enter Hubert de Burgh *with three men.*

Hubert.

My mafters, I have fhewed you what warrant I have for this attempt; I perceive by your heavy countenances, you had rather be otherwife imployed, and for my owne part, I would the king had made choice of fome other executioner: only this is my comfort, that a king commaunds, whofe precepts neglected or omitted, threatneth torture for the default: therefore in briefe, leave me, and be ready to attend the adventure: ftay within that entry, and when you heare me crie, God fave the king, iffue fodainely forth, lay hands on *Arthur*, fet him in his chaire, wherein (once faft bound) leave him with me to finifh the reft.

Attendants.

We goe, though loath. [*Exeunt.*

Hubert.

My lord, will it pleafe your honor to take the benefit of the faire evening?

Enter Arthur *to* Hubert de Burgh.

Arthur.

Gramercie *Hubert* for thy care of me,
In or to whom reftraint is newly knowne,
The joy of walking is fmall benefit,
Yet will I take thy offer with fmall thanks,
I would not loofe the pleafure of the eie.
But tell me curteous keeper if thou can,
How long the king will have me tarrie heere.

Hubert.

I know not prince, but as I geffe, not long.
God fend you freedome, and God fave the king.
[*They iffue forth.*

Arthur.

Why how now firs, what may this outrage meane?
O helpe me *Hubert*, gentle keeper help:
God fend this fodaine mutinous approach
Tend not to reave a wretched guiltlefs life.

Hubert.

Hubert.

So firs, depart, and leave the reft for me.

Arthur.

Then *Arthur* yeeld, death frowneth in thy face,
What meaneth this? good *Hubert* pleade the cafe.

Hubert.

Patience yong lord, and liften words of woe,
Harmefull and harfh, hells horror to be heard:
A difmall tale fit for a furies tongue.
I faint to tell, deepe forrow is the found.

Arthur.

What, muft I die?

Hubert.

No newes of death, but tidings of more hate,
A wrathfull doòme, and moft unluckie fate:
Deaths difh were daintie at fo fell a feaft,
Be deafe, heare not, its hell to tell the reft.

Arthur.

Alas, thou wrongft my youth with words of feare,
Tis hell, tis horror, not for one to heare:
What is it man if it muft needes be done,
Act it, and end it, that the paine were gone.

Hubert.

I will not chaunt fuch dolour with my tongue,
Yet muft I act the outrage with my hand.
My heart, my head, and all my powers befide,
To aide the office have at once denide.
Perufe this letter, lines of trebble woe,
Reade ore my charge, and pardon when you know.

> *Hubert*, thefe are to commaund thee, as thou tendreft our
> quiet in minde, and the eftate of our perfon, that pre-
> fently upon the receipt of our commaund, thou put out
> the eies of *Arthur Plantaginet.*

Arthur.

Ah monftrous damned man! his very breath infects the
elements.
Contagious venome dwelleth in his heart,
Effecting meanes to poyfon all the world,

R 4   Unreverent

Unreverent may I be to blame the heavens
Of great injuſtice, that the miſcreant
Lives to oppreſſe the innocents with wrong.
Ah *Hubert!* makes he thee his inſtrument,
To found the trump that cauſeth hell triumph?
Heaven weepes, the faiɴts do ſhed celeſtiall teares,
They feare thy fall, and cite thee with remorſe,
They knocke thy conſcience, moving pitie there,
Willing to fence thee from the rage of hell;
Hell, *Hubert*, truſt me all the plagues of hell
Hangs on performance of this damned deed.
This feale, the warrant of the bodies bliſſe,
Enſureth ſatan chieftaine of thy ſoule:
Subſcribe not *Hubert*, give not Gods part away.
I ſpeake not only for eies priviledge,
The chiefe exterior that I would enjoy:
But for thy perill, farre beyond my paine,
Thy ſweete ſoules lóſſe, more than my eies vaine lacke:
A cauſe internall, and eternall too.
Advife thee *Hubert*, for the caſe is hard,
To looſe ſalvation for a kings reward.

       Hubert.
 My lord, a ſubject dwelling in the land
Is tied to execute the kings commaund.

       Arthur.
 Yet God commaunds whoſe power reacheth further,
That no command ſhould ſtand in force to murther.

       Hubert.
 But that ſame eſſence hath ordaind a law,
A death for guilt, to keepe the world in awe.

       Arthur.
 I pleade, not guilty, treaſonleſſe and free.

       Hubert.
 But that appeale, my lord, concernes not me.

       Arthur.
 Why thou art he that maiſt omit the perill.

       Hubert.
 I, if my ſoveraigne would omit his quarrell.

       Arthur.
 His quarrell is unhallowed falſe and wrong,

           Hubert.

Hubert.
Then be the blame to whom it doth belong.
Arthur.
Why thats to thee if thou as they proceede,
Conclude their judgement with so vile a deede.
Hubert.
Why then no execution can be lawfull,
If judges doomes must be reputed doubtfull.
Arthur.
Yes where in forme of law in place and time,
The offender is convicted of the crime.
Hubert.
My lord, my lord, this long expostulation,
Heapes up more griefe, than promise of redresse ;
For this I know, and so resolvde I end,
That subjects lives on kings commands depend.
I must not reason why he is your foe,
But do his charge since he commaunds it so.
Arthur.
Then do thy charge, and charged be thy soule
With wrongfull persecution done this day.
You rowling eyes, whose superficies yet
I doe behold with eies that nature lent :
Send foorth the terror of your moovers frowne,
To wreake my wrong upon the murtherers
That rob me of your faire reflecting view :
Let hell to them (as earth they wish to me)
Be darke and direfull guerdon for their guilt,
And let the blacke tormenters of deepe *Tartary*
Upbraide them with this damned enterprise,
Inflicting change of tortures on their soules.
Delay not *Hubert*, my orisons are ended,
Begin I pray thee, reave me of my sight :
But to performe a tragedie indeede,
Conclude the period with a mortall stab.
Constance farewell, tormenter come away,
Make my dispatch the tyrants feasting day.
Hubert.
I faint, I feare, my conscience bids desist :
Faint did I say ? feare was it that I named :

My

My king commaunds, that warrant fets me fiee:
But God forbids, and he commaundeth kings,
That great commaunder countercheckes my charge,
He ftayes my hand, he maketh foft my heart.
Goe curfed tooles, your office is exempt,
Cheere thee yong lord, thou fhalt not loofe an eie,
Though I fhould purchafe it with loffe of life.
Ile to the king, and fay his will is done,
And of the langor tell him thou art dead,
Goe in with me, for *Hubert* was not borne
To blinde thofe lampes that nature pollifht fo.

Arthur.

Hubert, if ever *Arthur* be in ftate,
Looke for amends of this received gift,
I took my eiefight by the curtefie,
Thou lentft them me, I will not be ingrate.
But now procraftination may offend
The iffue that thy kindneffe undertakes:
Depart we, *Hubert,* to prevent the worft.   [*Exeunt.*

Enter K. John, Effex, Salifbury, Penbrooke.

John.

    Now warlike followers, refteth aught undone
That may impeach us of fond overfight?
The *French* have felt the temper of our fwords,
Cold terror keepes poffeffion in their foules,
Checking their overdaring arrogance
For buckling with fo great an overmatch,
The arch prowd titled prieft of *Italy,*
That calls himfelfe grand vicar under God,
Is bufied now with trentall obfequies,
Maffe and months mind, dirge and I know not what,
To eafe their foules in painefull purgatorie,
That have miscarried in thefe bloody warres.
Heard you not, lords, when firft his holineffe
Had tidings of our fmall account of him,
How with a taunt vaunting upon his toes,
He urgde a reafon why the *Englifh* affe
Difdaind the bleffed ordinance of *Rome?*

I   The

The title (reverently might I inferre)
Became the kings that earst have borne the load,
The slavish weight of that controlling priest:
Who at his pleasure temperd them like waxe
To carrie armes on danger of his curse,
Banding their soules with warrants of his hand.
I grieve to thinke how kings in ages past
(Simply devoted to the see of *Rome*)
Have run into a thousand acts of shame.
But now for confirmation of our state,
Sith we have proind the more than needfull braunch
That did oppresse the true well-growing stocke,
It resteth we throughout our territories
Be reproclaimed and invested king.

         Pembrooke.

My liege, that were to busie men with doubts,
Once were you crownd, proclaimd, and with applause
Your citie streets have ecchoed to the eare,
God save the king, God save our soveraigne *John*,
Pardon my feare, my censure doth inferre
Your highnesse not depofde from regall state,
Would breed a mutinie in peoples mindes,
What it should meane to have you crownd againe.

          John.

Pembrooke, performe what I have bid thee do,
Thou knowst not what induceth me to this.
Essex goe in, and lordings all be gone
About this taske, I will be crownd anone.

      Enter the Bastard.

Philip what newes, how do the abbots chests?
Are friers fatter than the nunnes are faire?
What cheere with church-men, had they gold or no?
Tell me, how hath thy office took effect?

         Philip.

-My lord, I have performd your highnes charge:
The ease-bred abbots, and the bare-foote friers,
The monks, the priors, and holy cloystred nunnes,
Are all in health, and were my lord in wealth

               Till

Till I had tithde and tolde their holy hoords.
I doubt not when your highneffe fees my prize,
You may proportion all their former pride.

John.

Why fo, now forts it *Philip* as it fhould :
This fmall intrufion into abbey trunkes,
Will make the popelings excommunicate,
Curfe, ban, and breathe out damned orifons,
As thicke as haile-ftones fore the fprings approach :
But yet as harmeleffe and without effect,
As is the eccho of a cannons cracke
Difchargde againft the battlements of heaven.
But what newes elfe befell there *Philip?*

Baftard.

Strange newes my lord : within your territories
Neere *Pomfret* is a prophet new fprung up,
Whofe divination volleis wonders foorth :
To him the commons throng with countrey gifts,
He fets a date unto the beldames death,
Prefcribes how long the virgins ftate fhall laft,
Diftinguifheth the mooving of the heavens,
Gives limits unto holy nuptiall rites,
Foretelleth famine, aboundeth plentie forth :
Of fare, of fortune, life and death he chats,
With fuch affurance, fcruples put apart,
As if he knew the certaine doomes of heaven,
Or kept a regifter of all the deftinies.

John.

Thou tellft me marvels, would thou hadft brought the man,
We might have queftiond him of things to come.

Baftard.

My lord, I tooke a care of had-I-wift,
And brought the prophet with me to the court,
He ftaies my lord but at the prefence doore :
Pleafeth your highneffe, I will call him in.

John.

Nay ftay awhile, wee'l have him here anone,
A thing of weight is firft to be performd.

Enter

Enter the nobles and crowne King John, and then cry God save the king.

John.

Lordings and friends supporters of our state,
Admire not at this unaccustomed course,
Nor in your thoughts blame not this deede of yours.
Once ere this time was I invested king,
Your fealtie sworne as liegemen to our state:
Once since that time ambitious weedes have sprung
To staine the beauty of our garden plot:
But heavens in our conduct rooting thence
The false intruders, breakers of worlds peace,
Have to our joy, made sunne-shine chase the storme.
After the which, to trie your constancie,
That now I see is worthy of your names,
We crav'd once more your helps for to invest us
Into the right that envy sought to wracke.
Once was I not deposde, your former choice;
Now twice beene crowned and applauded king?
Your cheered action to install me so,
Infers assured witnesse of your loves,
And binds me over in a kingly care
To render love with love, rewards of worth
To ballance downe requitall to the full.
But thankes the while, thankes lordings to you all:
Aske me and use me, trie me and finde me yours.

Essex.

A boone my lord, at vantage of your words
We aske to guerdon all our loyalties.

Pembrooke.

We take the time your highnesse bids us aske:
Please it you grant, you make your promise good,
With lesser losse than one superfluous haire
That not remembred falleth from your head.

John.

My word is past, receive your boone my lords,
What may it be? aske it, and it is yours.

Essex.

Essex.

We crave my lord, to pleafe the commons with
The libertie of lady *Conftance* fonne :
Whofe durance darkeneth your highneffe right,
As if you kept him prifoner, to the end
Your felfe were doubtfull of the thing you have.
Difmiffe him thence, your highneffe needs not feare,
Twice by confent you are proclaim'd our king.

Pembrooke.

This if you grant, were all unto your good :
For fimple people mufe you keepe him clofe.

John.

Your words have fearcht the center of my thoghts,
Confirming warrant of your loyalties,
Difmiffe your counfell, fway my ftate,
Let *John* doe nothing, but by your confents.
Why how now *Philip*, what extafie is this ?
Why calls thou up thy eyes to heaven fo ?

                    [*There the five moones appeare.*

Baftard.

See, fee my lord, ftrange apparitions,
Glancing mine eie to fee the diadem
Plac'd by the bifhops on your highneffe head,
From forth a gloomie cloud, which curtaine-like
Difplaid it felfe, I fuddainely efpied
Five moones reflecting, as you fee them now :
Even in the moment that the crowne was plac'd
Gan they appeare, holding the courfe you fee.

               John.

What might portend thefe apparitions,
Unufuall fignes, forerunners of event,
Prefagers of ftrange terrors to the world :
Beleeve me lords, the object feares me much.
Philip thou toldft me of a wizard but of late,
Fetch in the man to defcant of this fhow.

               Pembrooke.

The heavens frowne upon the finfull earth,
When with prodigious unaccuftom'd fignes
They fpot their fuperficies with fuch wonder.

                                            Essex.

Effex.

Before the ruines of *Jerufalem,*
Such meteors were the enfignes of his wrath,
That haft'ned to deftroy the faultfull towne.

Enter the Baftard with the prophet.

John.

Is this the man?

Baftard.   •

It is my lord.

John.

Prophet of *Pomfret,* for fo I heare thou art,
That calculat'ft of many things to come:
Who by a power repleat with heavenly gift,
Canft blab the counfell of thy makers will.
If fame be true, or truth be wrong'd by thee,
Decide in cyphering, what thefe five moones
Portend this clime, if they prefage at all.
Breath out thy gift, and if I live to fee
Thy divination take a true effect,
Ile honour thee above all earthly men.

Peter.

The fkie wherein thefe moones have refidence,
Prefenteth *Rome* the great metropolis,
Where fits the Pope in all his holy pompe.
Foure of the moones prefent foure provinces,
To wit *Spaine, Denmarke, Germaine,* and *France,*
That beare the yoke of proud commanding *Rome,*
And ftand in feare to tempt the prelates curfe.
The fmalleft moone that whirles about the reft,
Impatient of the place he holds with them,
Doth figure forth this ifland *Albion,*
Who gins to fcorne the fee and feat of *Rome,*
And feeks to fhunne the edicts of the pope:
This fhowes the heaven, and this I doe averre
Is figured in the apparitions.

John.

Why then it feemes the heavens fmile on us,
Giving applaufe for leaving of the pope.

B x

But for they chance in our meridian,
Doe they effect no private growing ill
To be inflicted on us in this clime?

Peter.

The moones effect no more than what I faid:
But on fome other knowledge that I have
By my prefcience, ere afcenfion day
Have brought the funne unto his ufuall height,
Of crowne, eftate, and royall dignity,
Thou fhalt be cleane difpoyl'd and difpoffeft.

John.

Falfe dreamer, perifh with thy witched newes,
Villaine thou woundft me with thy fallacies:
If it be true, die for thy tidings price;
If falfe, for fearing me with vain fuppofe:
Hence with the witch, hels damned fecretarie.
Locke him up fure: for by my faith I fweare,
True or not true, the wizard fhall not live.
Before afcenfion day: who fhould be caufe hereof?
Cut off the caufe, and then the effect will die.
Tut, tut, my mercie ferves to maime my felfe,
The roote doth live, from whence thefe thornes fpring up,
I and my promife paft for his deliv'rie:
Frowne friends, faile faith, the divell goe withall,
The brat fhall die, that terrifies me thus.
Pembrooke and Effex, I recall my graunt,
I will not buy your favours with my feare:
Nay murmure not, my will is lawe enough,
I love you well, but if I lov'd you better,
I would not buy it with my difcontent.

Enter Hubert.

How now, what newes with thee?

Hubert.

According to your highneffe ftrict command,
Young Arthurs eies are blinded and extinct.

John.

Why fo, then he may feele the crown, but never fee it.

Hubert.

Hubert.

Nor fee nor feele, for of the extream paine,
Within one houre gave he up the ghoft.

John.

What is he dead?

Hubert.

He is my lord.

John.

Then with him dies my cares.

Effex.

Now joy betide thy foule.

Pembrooke.

And heavens revenge thy death.

Effex.

What have you done my lord? was ever heard
A deed of more inhumane confequence?
Your foes will curfe, your friends will crie revenge.
Unkindly rage, more rough than northern wind,
To clip the beautie of fo fweete a flower.
What hope in us for mercie on a fault,
When kinfman dies without impeach of caufe,
As you have done, fo come to cheere you with,
The guilt fhall never be caft in my teeth.   [*Exeunt.*

John.

And are you gone? the divell be your guide:
Proud rebels as ye are, to brave me fo:
Saucie, uncivill, checkers of my will.
Your tongues give edge unto the fatall knife,
That fhall have paffage through your trayt'rous throats.
But hufht, breath not bugs words too foone abroad,
Left time prevent the iffue of thy reach.
Arthur is dead, I there the corzie growes:
But while he liv'd, the danger was the more;
His death hath freed me from a thoufand feares,
But it hath purchaft me ten times ten thoufand foes.
Why all is one, fuch lucke fhall haunt his game,
To whom the divell owes an open fhame:
His life a foe that leveld at my crowne,
His death a frame to pull my building downe.
My thoughts harpt ftill on quiet by his end,

S   Who

Who living aimed fhrewdly at my roome:
But to prevent that plea, twice was I crown'd,
Twice did my fubjects fweare me fealtie,
And in my confcience lov'd me as their liege,
In whofe defence they would have pawn'd their lives.
But now they fhun me as a ferpents fting,
A tragyke tyrant, fterne and pitileffe,
And not a title followes after *John*,
But butcher, blood-fucker, and murtherer.
What planet govern'd my nativitie,
To bode me foveraigne types of high eftate,
So interlac'd with hellifh difcontent,
Wherein fell furie hath no intereft?
Curft be the crowne, chiefe author of my care,
Nay curft my will, that made the crowne my care:
Curft be my birth-day, curft ten times the wombe
That yeelded me alive into the world.
Art thou there villaine, furies haunt thee ftill,
For killing him whom all the world laments.

Hubert.

Why here's my lord your highnes hand and feale,
Charging on lives regard to do the deed.

John.

Ah dull conceipted pefant, knowft thou not
It was a damned execrable deed?
Shewft me a feale? oh villaine, both our foules
Have folde their freedome to the thrall of hell
Under the warrant of that curfed feale.
Hence villaine, hang thyfelfe, and fay in hell
That I am comming for a kingdome there.

Hubert.

My lord, attend the happy tale I tell,
For heavens health fend Sathan packing hence
That inftigates your highneffe to defpaire.
If *Arthurs* death be difmall to be heard,
Bandie the newes for rumors of untruth :
He lives my lord, the fweeteft youth alive,
In health, with eie fight, not a haire amiffe.
This heart took vigor from this forward hand,
Making it weake to execute your charge.

Joh.

John.

What, lives he! then fweete hope come home agen,
Chafe hence defpaire, the purveyor for hell.
Hye *Hubert* tell thefe tidings to my lords
That throb in paflions for yong *Arthurs* death:
Hence *Hubert*, ftay not till thou haft reveald
The wifhed newes of *Arthurs* happy health.
I goe my felfe, the joyfulleſt man alive
To ftorie out this new fuppofed crime.   [*Exeunt.*

The End of the F I R S T P A R T.

2   THE